D0769103

THE BODY FROM IPANEMA

J.R. Ripley

THE BODY FROM IPANEMA

A Tony Kozol Mystery

Long Wind Publishing
Ft. Pierce, Florida

Also by J.R. Ripley

STIFF IN THE FREEZER
SKULLS OF SEDONA
LOST IN AUSTIN

This is a work of fiction. Any resemblance to actual places, events or persons, living or dead, is purely coincidental.

First Edition 2002

Direct all correspondence for J.R. Ripley to:
Long Wind Publishing
2208 River Branch Drive
Ft. Pierce, FL 34981
LongWindPub@tctg.com
www.LongWindPub.com

ISBN 1-892695-08-1

Library of Congress Cataloging-in-Publication Data

Ripley, J.R. date
The Body from Ipanema / J.R. Ripley.
p.cm.
ISBN 1-892695-08-1 (alk. paper)
1. Kozol, Tony (Fictitious character) — Fiction. 2. Rio de Janeiro (Brazil) — Fiction. 3. Americans — Brazil — Fiction. 4. Guitarists — Fiction. 1. Title.

PS3568.I635 B64 2001
813'.54 — dc21 2001029589
CIP

Printed in Hong Kong 10 9 8 7 6 5 4 3 2 1

I would like to thank the usual cast of characters who shared in making this work possible, in addition to special guest appearances by Dr. Gerald Kennedy and Loretta Giommoni.

Obrigada todo

1

Something odd was going on in the window of Yairi's apartment.

Kozol stared up at the glass. A faint breeze tickled the back of his neck but barely raised a strand of the bushy brown head of hair he sported. How long since he'd had a trim?

Maybe the next time he'd get a buzz cut, the kind his friend, Rock Bottom, the bass player, was fond of. Rock said it was because he was so big and had a lot of heat to exchange with the outside world. He said he had to keep his head clear, like the vents of an air conditioner, for maximum efficiency.

In the heat of the tropics, that might just make sense.

Curtains, the color of weak chicken soup, were closed. Two figures seemed to be struggling behind the drapes, like shadow actors.

Should he knock or move on?

Tony moved on.

But when he got to the corner of the block, where a *capoeira* was being staged by two lanky men the color of his last cup of coffee, Tony turned back around.

Damn.

Alvarez was expecting him.

He'd have to go up.

The *roda de capoeira* had gathered an audience and the sound of their hand clapping and the plucking of a pair of berimbaus, stringed instruments which looked more like fishing rods to Tony than musical instruments, kept the rhythm of the dancers lively. The *berimbau* looked like nothing more than a gourd, a stick and some string; but it did the trick.

The *capoeira* was a form of martial arts, originally developed by African-Brazilian slaves to combat their masters. Sharp, deadly blades were often attached to the combatants ankles. *Capoeira* was prohibited and so the slaves practiced in secrecy. Slowly, the martial art had transformed itself into a kind of hybrid sport and acrobatic dance, requiring far more agility and stamina than Tony could muster.

Tony had seen it practiced impromptu in the streets, or more often in front of the outdoor restaurants and cafes that congested the broad sidewalks along *Avenida Atlantica* in Copacabana, where it was performed for the tourists, in hopes of an elusive tip.

Kozol found himself climbing the dirty concrete stairs to the fading beat. A warm breeze slid under the white linen shirt he'd picked up the day before in a bargain clothes shop off *Rua Visconde de Piraja*. Everything on Piraja, Ipanema's main shopping street, was too rich for his blood.

The moving air crept up his back like the gentle touch of a woman's hand. Tony thought of his new Brazilian girlfriend, Silvia Parra, and her disarming green eyes. His accompanying sigh blended like a chorus with the breeze.

The curtains had stopped moving.

The odor of frying beef and beans, being cooked and served up on broad white plates in the restaurant on the ground floor, rose even to this level, reminding Kozol that he'd missed lunch.

Tony's hand stopped midway between his chest and the battered door. With a slight detour, he wiped a line of sweat from under his nose, listened, then knocked.

There was the abrupt sound of a bounce and a scrape. The tinny, high-strung voice Tony recognized as Yairi's called out, begging for him to wait.

Tony waited.

Moments later, the door spoke. "*Quem e la*?"

"It's me, Yairi. Tony Kozol."

"What do you want?"

Tony's eyebrows shot up. He thought of all the more pleasant things he might be doing in Rio de Janeiro at that time. Especially at that time, considering it was the week of Carnaval, the world's most renowned and wild party and he was lucky enough to be in the middle of it. Lots more exciting than talking to a door that could have used a new coat of paint a couple of decades ago.

A salty rivulet of perspiration caught in his eye. He swiped at it and replied angrily. "What the hell are you talking about? You told me to come!"

Yairi apologized over the rattling of chains and clinking of locks. "That's right. Stupid me. Come on. Come on in!"

Alvarez Yairi pulled Kozol into the apartment and shut the door quickly. He looked like he'd just stepped out of the shower. He also looked like he'd forgotten to take off his clothes before stepping into said shower.

"Is everything alright?"

"Yeah, sure. *Bom.*" Yairi spoke with a thick Portuguese tongue, though his English was quite good—when he wanted it to be. His dark pants and shirt glistened wetly. He wore neither socks nor shoes. He did hold a pair of brightly polished brown loafers in his hand.

As Tony eyed them, Yairi promptly dropped them to the rug and hopped into them. "I am afraid you caught me," said Yairi.

"Yes, I thought I saw something in the window. . ."

A red shadow crossed over Yairi's long, brown face. "In the window?" Yairi shook his head. "No, I was in the shower, Tony."

"In the shower? No, the curtains were moving and I saw you and another man."

"Impossible again, Tony." Yairi waved a wiry hand in the air. "It must have been the wind blowing the curtains and the shadows."

Tony glanced at the sliding glass doors that led out onto the tiny balcony overlooking *Rua Farme de Amoedo*, near the intersection with *Barão da Torre*. Amoedo did run north south, blessing it with the cooler air that swept in off the nearby beaches of Ipanema. But the drapes and the windows were firmly shut. "But— "

"But I'm glad you have come. We will have a good time tonight." Yairi, nearly equal to Tony in height, draped an arm over his shoulder. "First, I require your help with some little thing."

"Oh?"

"Yes." Yairi ran a hand through his dripping hair. "A little muscle is all I need."

Tony laughed. "A little muscle is all I've got. What did you have in mind?"

"I've a package. A bit heavy, I'm afraid." Yairi grinned broadly. "Help me carry it down to the Bugre?"

The Bugre was Yairi's olive green motor vehicle, reminiscent of the dune buggies that were once popular in the States. It sported no top and no doors and its small body was molded fiberglass. The buggy had to be a good twenty years old. Its sole nod to windows was a windshield. The chrome rollbar in back would supposedly offer some measure of safety, but as there were no seatbelts in Yairi's car, this safety was dubious as Tony expected to be thrown from the quirky sport vehicle one day soon, probably to land in front of a bus.

And the name, well, Tony wasn't about to say anything to Yairi about that.

Tony said yes and Yairi excused himself. "I'll just be a moment."

He returned from his bedroom dragging a navy blue duffle bag knotted shut with quarter inch thick rope. The bag was large and bulging. Yairi dragged it across the wood floor to the edge of the rug.

Kozol leaned over to pick up the back-end.

"No, here. Take the rope." Yairi handed Tony the reins.

"I'll lift."

Tony wrapped the rope around his hands and pulled up the slack. The sack had to weight a hundred pounds. "What the heck have you got in here, a body?"

"Yeah, sure. A cop! Ha ha."

"Right. Ha ha."

"No, I joke you, my friend." The thin man kicked the sack. "It's *milho*. Corn," Yairi replied as he pushed a shoulder against the back of the sack and lifted. "I promised my cousin, Joel, I would take it to him. He's a vendor. Joel is taking his stand to Copacabana tonight. All the locals and the tourists will be out, not that the foreigners buy much. But this is a big time of year for him. Money to be made."

Tony nodded in understanding. One of the myriad and somewhat unique sights he'd encountered in his first few days in Ipanema was that of the street vendors, among these, those selling fresh, hot corn.

They wheeled small steel carts with steaming stainless steel bowls filled with ears of fresh corn. The cobs were served on the husks and a rolled up husk stuck in a plastic tub of melted butter was usually present if you wanted to give yours a swipe. A health inspector's nightmare in the United States, but nothing to give his Brazilian counterpart any concern.

Yairi said, "Ready?"

"Yeah, let's go." Tony pulled and lifted. The bulky bag seemed to have a life of its own. Together they made it to the door without unsettling the rug. Kozol leaned his back against the door, catching his breath and searching for the knob. He found it and turned the handle. The door opened inward. He and Yairi struggled around it then dropped the sack on the landing.

"This part will be easy." Yairi gave a grin and a push and the blue duffel bag bounced sluggishly down the hard steps.

Tony heard a snap. "That didn't sound good," he said as the sack of corn came to rest on the sidewalk below. "Can't do the vegetables much good either."

"Vegetables?"

"Yeah, the corn."

"Ah, yes, the corn. It is nothing. Corn is strong. Besides," said Yairi with a smile, "that felt good."

They descended and inspected their work. The navy bag had rolled to the middle of the sidewalk. No one gave it a second notice, just a first. Just long enough to side step around it. The *capoeira* crowd had moved on.

"Look at that." Tony pointed. An ugly oval stain, a good twelve inches in diameter, darkened the already dark sack.

Yairi glanced nervously at the duffel bag. "A little moisture. It's nothing. *Vamos*."

They muscled the heavy bag up into the back of the Bugre parked at the curb and Yairi took the wheel.

A couple of blocks over, Yairi twisted the wheel and aimed the Bugre uphill until they were approaching a rundown section of town that quickly turned into a slum, one of Rio's famous *favelas*. The shanty-towns rose wildly and unplanned into the steep hills above Rio, home to hundreds of thousands of Rio's poor. These regions were still virtually neglected by the government and, often as not, lacked even basic public services like water and sanitation.

A far cry from the five-star hotel where Kozol's new boss, the Latin pop star, Luis Angel, had put them all up on the beaches of Ipanema. Yet not so far at all. . .

Tony shifted nervously in his seat. He'd been warned to stay clear of the *favelas*. While the ordinary folk were not unfriendly, these regions were home to drug lords and all sorts of other sordid and illegal enterprises. Violence was a way of life in the *favelas* and even the police rarely ventured within.

"Your cousin lives here?"

"Yes. Don't worry. We won't have far to go."

"I'm not worried," lied Tony. He felt for his wallet and his passport photocopy and was glad he'd done as he'd been advised and left the original in the safe back in his hotel room. Tony studied the hodgepodge of poorly constructed and often window and roofless buildings with sad interest. How could anyone manage to live here?

Then again, how could they manage to escape?

The Bugre came to a stop on a steep, dirt incline, a narrow street up which rose one dilapidated brown building after another. There was a battered green door on the house on Tony's side.

Yairi hopped out and sauntered over to where a couple of kids, looking no more than eighteen years old, were holding what looked like semi-automatic rifles. They kept the weapons slung over their shoulders carelessly, as if they might have been no more than backpacks like any other eighteen year old college student back in the States might be lugging around campus.

Only these backpacks could kill.

Tony shifted in his seat and wondered where he'd hide when the shooting started. Yairi was pointing at the Bugre. The heavier of the two boys nodded. Money, Brazilian reais, changed hands. How much Tony couldn't tell.

Yairi returned to the Bugre with a smile on his face.

"That's that," he said, wiping his hands together. "Let's unload."

"Okay." Tony hopped out and helped lower the duffel bag to the ground. They maneuvered it up against the shack with the green door. "This is your cousin Joel's house?"

"Yes, but he is not home. I've made other arrangements."

Tony wondered how Yairi knew Joel was not home when he hadn't even rapped on the door. "You sure?" Tony reached for the door with his fist. "Want me to knock?"

Yairi reached for Tony's hand. "No, please." He grinned. "It is not a good idea." He glanced over his shoulders where the two militia boys were watching them. "His wife is ill. She may be resting."

Tony sighed. "Fine. Let's just hurry up, okay?" Despite the sun going down and the creeping coolness, Tony was sweating. Was it the heat or was he just nervous? In any case he wanted to get out of there.

"Don't worry, Tony. We're done."

Tony looked around. He wouldn't have left a sock on the ground in that neighborhood unattended unless he didn't want to see it again, let alone a sack full of corn. "You're just going to leave it here? Like that?" The large sack didn't stand a chance. If Yairi's cousin didn't come soon, it, and its contents, would be gone. The stain on the side of the bag had gotten no bigger.

"Yes, it's okay." Yairi waved to the armed youths. "They will take care of it." Yairi started up the engine and put the Bugre in gear.

"Wait!" Tony jumped in. "This isn't exactly the kind of place I'd like to get stranded."

Yairi twisted the wheel and turned the buggy around on the narrow street. They headed downhill. "Neither would I," he said between narrow lips.

Somehow that didn't make Tony feel any better.

A world away, but not far away, Tony did feel better as

they entered the shaded streets of Ipanema, still a world away from his own home of Ocean Palm, Florida, which he hadn't seen in months, but with its beaches, warm weather, beautiful people and high priced shops, it was near enough. There were even palm trees. And plenty of coconuts.

"So where are we heading? Or is helping you with that duffel bag the only reason you asked me to stop by tonight?"

"No, Tony. There are some friends I want you to meet." Yairi looked away from the road which had just turned into a busy four-way intersection and said to Tony, "No problem?"

"No problem," Tony agreed, nodding for Yairi to at least try and miss that big passenger bus they were about to broadside. Tony could just about picture himself as the next billboard plastered to its side. *Welcome Tourists*, they could write next to his flattened corpse.

Yairi grinned again and twisted the wheel. The Bugre merely sideswiped the bus and both vehicles kept moving. A few cars honked but life went on in paradise.

It was dark now as Yairi squeezed the Bugre between two cars far enough for his front two wheels to rest on the sidewalk. For Brazil, Tony had come to realize, this was par for the course. After all, this was a place where any one parking space was easily large enough for two cars if one had the will. And the locals, like his pal, Yairi, did.

The street sign read *Rua Vinicius de Morais*. Restaurants with outdoor seating were on corners facing each other. Tony heard music coming from a club reachable via a stairs near the car. Tony recognized a Gilberto Gil tune, *Domingo*.

Yairi's friends waved to him from a corner table. Together, Tony and his new Brazilian friend managed to squeeze past the patrons who stood between the tables, drinking their beers, and finally to a large table in the inside corner behind the bar. "My friends," announced Yairi.

Kozol nodded. "*Boa noite*." Tony was sure he'd butchered

the little Brazilian Portuguese he'd managed to pick up but Yairi's friends smiled, so at least he hadn't offended anyone.

"*Esta,*" said Yairi with a slight bow and giving Kozol a tap on the shoulder, "*e meu benquisto amigo, Senhor Tony Kozol, de America.*" Yairi translated. "I told them you are my esteemed friend, Mister Tony Kozol from America."

Hellos went around and back, and Yairi and Tony were invited to sit. Beers were sent for.

The conversation took off in colorful sounding Brazilian Portuguese. It might as well have been gibberish.

Food was brought, unrecognizable dishes with unpronounceable names and unusual flavors.

Tony ate. Voices chattered like parrots gossiping in the rainforest.

Tony's thoughts drifted like the foam atop his glass of Kaiser beer. How had Alvarez Yairi become his friend in three days? The guy, who claimed to be working as a jack-of-all-trades for Luis Angel's management while the artist was in Rio, had just sort of found him and stuck like a fly to one of those bug strips his mom used to hang from the ceiling of their kitchen. The thought of which disgusted him as much now as it did then. He'd had this fear of dead bugs falling into his cereal bowl. Even now, all these years later, he caught himself looking up at the ceiling every once in a while, checking for dropping dead flies.

And then Tony thought of his parents. They both had died when he was fourteen—a boating accident—and he'd been taken in by his Uncle Jonathan and Aunt Louise. Now Uncle Jonathan was doing time and Aunt Louise barely spoke to him. Tony didn't know if it was because she blamed him for her husband's current troubles or if she was too embarrassed to contact him. It had all stemmed from Tony's ugly experience running his uncle's fast food place.

But that was another life.

His life since then had been devoid of close human

contact. Tony was glad that Rock Bottom, whom he'd met on his last gig with Clint Cash and the Cowhands, had gotten them a job working together, even if it was in Rio. There was finally someone to share some history with, even if it was only a history of months. Tony had expected to be on tour with the country star, Clint Cash for the summer, if not permanently, when everything around him blew up.

Par for that course.

Now here he was, sitting with this Brazilian character, Alvarez Yairi, and his somewhat odd looking friends. Three men and a woman.

Two of the men were on the heavy side. Both of these had big cassava heads. One had a mustache and the other a thin goatee. The man on the left had squirrelish brown eyes.

The man on the right only had one eye. It was blue. A black patch over his left eye gave him a sinister look. Though all four of these characters looked quite sinister enough to begin with.

The man with one eye and a mustache and the man with the goatee wore dark shirts and dress slacks. Even their belts matched.

The other man, with his arm draped proprietarily over the woman's shoulders was dressed in a crisp white shirt, open at the collar, exposing more hair than Kozol cared to see. The woman, also in her late thirties, with short hair that looked too red to be natural, was wearing a red sequined top and blue jeans that fit as tightly on her as a snake skin did on a snake. But then, all the women in Ipanema seemed to wear their slacks that way.

Not that Tony was complaining.

And this one, fortunately, had the figure for it. Top to bottom. If anyone at the table was going to expose their cleavage, it should have been her and not her hairy-chested husband.

Tony's eyes were dazzled by the largish, green emerald

earrings she wore. An emerald choker surrounded her neck and a diamond ring— big enough to support Tony for a year —wrapped around her finger, shouted out that she was married. The woman, whose name Tony had caught as Elena was also the lightest skinned of everyone at the table with the exception of Tony himself.

"And how long will you be in our country, *Senhor* Kozol?" It was the man with one eye speaking. Tony couldn't remember his name. Victor something? No, that was his melon headed companion. Hadn't Yairi said they were brothers?

Tony tried not to stare. He shrugged his shoulders. "I'm not sure. It depends on Luis, I suppose. I don't know what the tour plans are beyond our playing the outdoor concert here."

The man nodded as if Tony had passed out some plateful of wisdom. "I see. We must do business soon, no?"

Tony looked sideways.

"Of course," grinned Yairi. "We shall do some business."

"Business?"

"There are many opportunities here in Rio," Yairi answered vaguely.

"Yes, I'm sure," replied Tony, not wanting to offend Yairi or his friends.

The redhead ordered another round of beers. Empty glasses were swept away and fresh ones brought. The dirty dishes had long ago been cleared. Ashes flowed over the tops of the ashtrays. Music flowed down through the ceiling. The streets outside were congested with cars and strolling couples. Tony yearned to be one of them, with his Silvia on his arm.

The conversation had fallen back into Portuguese. The man with the patch kept casting furtive glances at Tony. The man with the woman seemed only interested in her. Obviously the brains of the outfit.

Tony looked at his watch. Silvia would still be at work. She was a dancer at the Club Brasil in the Centro and shows ran into the early morning hours, catering to locals, *Cariocas,* as they were called, and foreigners alike.

Maybe he'd take a taxi over.

Tony's eyelids drooped. Then his head. He and Rock had flown to Rio from Texas little more than three and a half days before. And he'd barely stopped since. Not to mention fallen in love. Still, maybe he'd just go back to the hotel.

"Excuse me," Tony said. "*Com licença.*" He set his beer on the table top and drew some *reais* from his pocket. Though the others protested, he left the money on the table and set his glass on top of it.

"You are leaving?" Yairi asked.

"Yes, I'm sorry." He turned to the others. "I'm very tired."

The one-eyed man rose and extended a heavily ringed hand. "We will do business, no?"

"Yes," said Tony. "Of course."

"Good night, everyone. *Senhora.*"

Yairi rose and shook Tony's hand as well. "You can make it back to the hotel okay from here?"

"Yes, don't worry. I know the way."

"It's merely two blocks over. Head toward the beach and—"

"I know. Then right. I can manage. Goodnight, Yairi." Tony tottered between the tables, thankful that the local beer wasn't any stronger.

"*Tchau*. I'll ring you tomorrow!"

Tony waved without turning back and grabbed a lungful of clear, cool air as he hit the sidewalk. Tobacco was a big habit in Rio and Tony was glad to be out of the smoke induced haze.

Then again, a fine rain had begun to fall, pushed into his face by the ocean breeze. Tony wished he'd worn long pants instead of the flimsy khaki shorts he'd been wearing for two days straight.

He crossed the intersection and followed the uneven sidewalk down the dark sidestreet. Sidestepping to his right to avoid a man in a dark windbreaker, Tony tripped in a hole where a tree had recently been planted and the earth only clumsily, haphazardly restored. He stumbled and righted himself without stopping.

A hand gripped his arm.

"You okay?" The man in the windbreaker spoke heavily accented English. His dark face, was pocked and unshaven. His eyes were crisscrossed with red like the Martian canals. His shoulders were broad as a linebacker's and he looked down at Kozol.

"Yes, I'm fine. Thank you," muttered Tony.

"Too bad," said the stranger. His free hand, clutching something silver and rod-shaped, shot up and then slammed down behind Tony's ear. His words were like a sledgehammer. "Stay away from Silvia."

Tony expected to see stars—like in the books—but saw only pavement as he hit.

If there were any stars, they were gray and unseeable.

2

Someone was kicking him in the ribs.

Tony twisted his head up and away from the sidewalk. It was an old woman with sharp shoes. A small hound on a leash was sniffing his legs.

"*Demente estrangeira. Levantar-se. Ir para casa*!"

Tony heard laughter. Unless it was the dog there was someone else lurking about. His assailant?

Tony made to jump to his feet but only managed to rise to his knees before grabbing his head. A knot the size and shape of Ohio rose from behind his right ear.

A young boy on a bicycle watched him. "She says, 'Crazy foreigner. Get up. Go home!'"

Tony grimaced both from the pain and the old woman's words. "Thanks. *Obrigado*."

The woman, dressed in dangerous shoes, and a gray sweatsuit spat into the street. "*Estes estrangeiros são pior que cães*."

"What she saying now?"

The boy grinned. "She says foreigners are worse than dogs."

Kozol looked at the hound who was peeing against the side of a dress shop opposite. "Well, tell her—"

The boy waited, squeezing his handlebars.

"Never mind." What he wanted to say, he couldn't say to a kid. "*Boa noite.*" Tony nodded to both of them, ignoring the dog, and hobbled back to the Ipanema Palace Hotel, steering far clear of strangers as he went.

He was soaked to the bone.

The security men, dressed in fine suits, gave him the once over, but recognizing him as a paying guest, said nothing.

Tony ignored the further looks of the hotel staff at the registration counter and the startled looks of the two pretty girls manning the concierge desk.

He knew he must look like hell.

The elevator doors opened and he caught his reflection in the mirrored walls.

Yep. No doubt about it.

Avoiding his own image by staring at the changing numbers, Tony had the elevator to himself all the way to the twenty-third floor. One couple had cast a look at him when the elevator car stopped and the doors opened on nineteen but they took the one look at him, another uneasy look at each other, and let the doors close again without getting on.

Tony was too tired to feel offended. Besides, he probably would have done the same.

He limped slowly down the hall, feeling like an old and tired horse smelling the barn after a long day in the fields under a hot sun, turned to the right and reached into his pocket for his keycard. It wasn't in his pocket.

He tried the other.

Nothing.

Tony patted his shorts front and back. His wallet, his room key, his passport copy, all his money and his pocket knife were missing!

"Be home, Rock," Tony muttered, knocking lightly on the door.

Three more tries with the door swimming in and out like

a rectangular, Salvador Dali inspired yo-yo, due to Tony's out of whack vision, and the hotel room door quietly opened.

"Tony!" Rock, wearing black and white vertically striped pajamas which not only made the big guy look taller but gave him the appearance of an escaped convict, pounced into the hall. "What's happened?"

Tony gently pushed him aside and entered the narrow entryway to their room. "I got mugged." He pushed a couple of fingers tentatively against his damp scalp and winced. When he drew back his fingers they were red.

"Shit." Rock popped open the tiny fridge. "I'll get some ice."

"Thanks." Tony turned on the bathroom light and studied his reflection in the mirror. Forget Ohio, this terrain was too mountainous. This was a Wyoming sized lump.

"Here." Rock rolled up some ice cubes in a wash cloth. "So, who did it? Did you get a look at him?"

"Yeah." Tony tentatively drew it towards his wound. "I was walking back to the hotel, tripped and this big guy I've never seen before grabs me. He asked me if I was okay and then slugged me."

"Nice." The bass player rubbed his big hands together. "I'd love to get my hands on him. Maybe I'll go for a walk."

"Forget it, Rock. I'm sure the jerk's long gone by now."

"Yeah, I guess you're right. Still, I'd like to wring his neck."

"You have my permission." Tony gently probed his damp scalp.

Rock began making clicking noises with his tongue.

"Will you cut that out? You sound like a mother hen."

"You really ought to have a doctor look at that. Let's take you to a clinic. I'll bet there's one around here someplace. Or a hospital."

"A hospital?" Tony faced his friend. "Forget it. I'll be fine. All I need is a decent night's sleep."

Rock looked skeptical. Then again, Tony wasn't so sure he believed it himself.

"What if you've got a concussion?"

Tony flapped his arms. "Look. Everything works. I'm fine." A stabbing jolt of pain went from his head to his chest. "I could use an aspirin though," he admitted, clutching the bathroom counter for support, though it seemed to be made of *gelatina*.

"Got some in my toiletry bag," Rock said, digging into his black terrycloth bath kit. "Better take a couple."

He dropped two white pills in Tony's hand. Tony washed them down with a glass of water.

"That's a nasty bump you've got. It needs to be cleaned up."

"I'm going to take a shower, Rock."

"I still say you ought to see a doctor. I could phone the concierge. They could tell us—"

"No, Rock. I don't need a doctor. I would like to find the bastard that hit me. If I do, he's going to need a doctor, or a funeral director. He's got all my cash and a copy of my passport."

Tony applied the melting ice once more to his scalp. "Besides, doctors and hospitals cost money. Look at us, here we are in this swank five-star hotel. It looks good, but the truth is we're all but broke. Luis Angel pays for our room and board. But he doesn't provide medical coverage. And I haven't got any other insurance."

"I've got some money."

"Forget it, Rock."

"But Tony—"

"No, this is Brazil, after all. If I go to the hospital, everyone will be speaking Portuguese, the doctors, the nurses. My luck, some guy will examine my head. I'll smile and nod even when he's saying things I don't understand. And the next thing you know, I've agreed to have a lobotomy!"

Rock laughed. "Yeah, okay. If you can joke around, I guess you're alright. But if you don't wake up tomorrow, don't blame me."

Tony opened the spigots in the tub. "I won't, I promise."

The next morning, Tony wished he'd had that lobotomy. He lifted his head from the bed. His hair stuck to the pillow. Dried blood. And his brain throbbed like an out-of-tune floor tom.

Rock had pulled open the blackout curtains. Near blinding blue light filled the room. "Morning, sorehead" huffed Rock between squats. He did a whole routine of stretching and calisthenics virtually every morning.

And every morning he asked Kozol to join him. Not that Tony ever did.

Tony noted that Rock wasn't asking this morning. A reprieve for the wounded? "Ha-ha. Very funny. You stay up all night thinking up that one? What time is it?"

"Sorry. Eight. Plenty of time for the breakfast buffet. They don't close it down until eleven."

Tony's stomach did a couple of somersaults. "I'm hungry. But I don't know if I can keep anything down."

"How's the wound?"

"Wonderful. I feel like I've got an active volcano growing out the side of my head."

Tony sat up. Their room had a partial view of the beach from Ipanema to Leblon. Vendors were already opening up their kiosks. Runners, walkers and bicyclists were busily running up and down the sidewalk and bike path which followed the gentle curve of the beach.

The phone rang and the jarring horn-like tone was sure to detonate Mount Tony Kozolus.

Rock hurried and picked up the received. "Huh? Policia? Speak English, please." Rock emitted several grunts and uh-huhs before saying they'd be down in fifteen minutes.

"What was that all about?"

"The police want to talk to us."

"What for?"

"I don't know. That was one of the hotel clerks downstairs. A couple of guys from the local police are waiting for us in the lobby."

Tony rolled out of bed. "Great."

They met the men in the front lobby. They weren't hard to find. Two wore uniforms, though not of the same kind. The third stood to their side, gently tickling the keys of the black baby grand piano in the corner opposite the small Holland Jewelers concession next to the entrance. He was wearing a well-fitting but inexpensive brown hounds-tooth coat with a yellow shirt, ginger colored wool tie, and tan trousers. He looked up as Rock and Tony approached. "Mister Kozol and Mister—" he paused, "Bottom?"

Tony said yes for the two of them.

"And you are?" The plainclothesman was so far doing all the talking.

"Tony Kozol. What's this all about?"

The man gestured to the sitting area, three sofas and a large glass table. "Please."

Leading the way, the man in charge spoke, "I am Lieutenant Diego Lobao. My colleagues are Capt. Augusto Almeida of the Policia Militar and Officer Milito of the Municipal Police."

Tony and Rock exchanged looks and flopped down on the nearest couch.

Lt. Diego Lobao was of medium height and build with unwavering blue eyes and twisted brown hair laced with gray. Tony figured the lieutenant was in his fifties or late forties. He was certainly older than his companions. Lobao's squat nose looked Indian. Like most Brazilians, he was probably of mixed blood.

Officer Milito was short and on the plump side. He was definitely the youngest of the three. Tony wondered if cops and donut shops were a stereotype in Rio as well. Milito had a childlike face and Kozol could tell it was a strain for the guy to try and look serious for so long. Tony wanted to tell the poor guy to take a deep breath and relax. Advice he was trying to follow himself.

Capt. Almeida, on the other hand, stood as stiff as the soldier he was and had a crewcut that would have done a GI's barber proud. He had a long sharp nose, almost no lips and white skin. He looked German despite his name.

Lt. Lobao continued. "You are Rock Bottom?"

"That's right." Rock squirmed on the edge of the sofa.

"Is that your real name?"

"It's the name I use."

"May I see your papers?"

Tony and Rock looked at each other. "I didn't bring them. They're up in the room, I'm afraid."

"I've got my wallet." Rock reached into his back pocket.

The police officer studied Rock's driver's license. "Lawrence Rockford Bottom?"

"That's right." There was a touch of defensiveness in Rock's voice.

If the man called Rock *Larry* or even *Lawrence,* there was going to be trouble. He silently handed Rock back his wallet. "You say your papers are upstairs?" His unblinking eyes seemed to be gauging Tony's truthfulness.

"That's right. Well, most of them." Tony touched the side of his head. "Actually, I was robbed last night."

"Is that so?"

Tony nodded. "Somebody stole my wallet, my money, a couple of credit cards and even a copy of my passport."

"This is very serious. Did you report this to the proper authorities?"

Uh-oh. "No, I mean, not yet. He hit me, you see?" Tony turned so the three men could inspect his bump. "It was late. I was going to report it this morning, though." A small lie. And, hopefully, an imperceptible one.

"I see." The man pulled out a cigarette and lit it. A Lucky Strike.

Tony started to speak, then thought better of it.

Half a cigarette later, Lt. Lobao clicked his fingers and Milito produced a color photo from his jacket.

"You know this man?" demanded Lt. Lobao.

Tony looked at the picture. A closeup of a man's face. "No. I mean, yes." Those sagging eyelids, the puffy, pockmarked face. It was impossible to tell if the Martian canals still crisscrossed the man's eyes, because his eyes were shut. "That is, not really."

Lt. Lobao adjudged Tony's comments and reactions as he shuffled another photo to the forefront. It was the same man but this time a full body shot.

Tony pursed his lips. His assailant was lying among a tumble of cardboard boxes up in an alcove. "That's the man who mugged me and stole my wallet. What happened to him?"

Capt. Almeida broke his silence. "Someone seems to have wanted to silence him. For they have sliced his throat like it was a ripe tomato."

Tony gulped.

Rock said, "That's the guy that hit you? Good riddance."

Lt. Lobao cast a sharp gaze at Rock.

"I mean," squirmed Rock, "it's too bad he's been murdered, but after all, he was a crook, wasn't he?"

"Was he?"

Rock looked lost.

"Did you know this man?" demanded the lieutenant.

"No," replied Rock. "I've never even seen him before."

"Lieutenant," interrupted Tony, "what does this have to

do with us? How did you come to find us? Like I said, I hadn't even reported the attack."

Lt. Lobao lit a cigarette and took a slow pull. He set his smoke down in the nearest ashtray atop the glass table and reached into his inside coat pocket.

"My wallet!" Tony reached for his billfold.

Lt. Lobao held the brown leather wallet out of reach. "Not so fast. Evidence, I am afraid."

"Evidence?"

"This is a murder, after all. No?" The lieutenant made a show of inspecting the wallet, rotating it in his slender, nicotine stained hands and letting it drop open. "You admit this is yours?"

"Yes, of course." Tony pointed. "You can see. That's my driver's license. My picture is right on it."

"So it is."

There was awkward silence. Officer Milito lost his concentration as a pretty maid smiled in his direction. The captain scowled at the poor kid and he resumed an air of menace.

"The wallet was found near the body."

"You mean he wasn't carrying it?"

"No," confirmed the lieutenant. "Our men discovered it in a rubbish bin up the street." He opened the money compartment. "There is over one hundred *reais* in here, plus twenty-two dollars American."

"That sounds like just about how much I had on me."

Lt. Lobao said, "Odd, don't you think?"

"That is weird," Rock put in. "Why would he rob you and then toss your wallet away with all the money in it?"

"You ask a good question," the lieutenant commented. "A question I ask myself."

"I don't know," shrugged Tony. "Maybe he was nuts. Maybe he just hit me for no reason?"

"Then why rob you at all?" asked Capt. Almeida.

Kozol looked helplessly from one man to the next. "I don't know."

Lt. Lobao shifted his weight and pulled a pocketknife from his trouser pocket. "Yours?"

"Yes," Tony confessed softly. It was his Swiss Army knife.

"The dead man was carrying it," explained Capt. Almeida. "But the prints on the blade were not his."

"If the knife is yours, I suppose the prints will be too," smiled Lt. Lobao.

"Yes," admitted Tony. "But if you're trying to imply that I slit his throat with my knife and then stuck it in his pocket and—"

"Sit, sit." Lt. Lobao gestured for Tony to relax.

Kozol hadn't even realized he'd risen.

"No one accuses you of anything." Lt. Lobao slapped his hands on his knees. "We have a serious matter here." He set his pack of Lucky Strike on the tabletop.

"So." The lieutenant held up yet another cigarette which Officer Milito lit with a flimsy match. "You will tell us, please, exactly what happened last night." He eyed Rock. "Both of you."

The officer offered the pack to his cohorts who both accepted and to Tony and Rock who both refused. Lt. Lobao then turned back to Tony. "Starting with you, Mr. Kozol."

Tony's stomach growled. Breakfast would have to wait. Second hand smoke would be his appetizer.

Tony recounted his leaving the restaurant.

"About what time was this?" Lt. Lobao held a pencil poised over a small, black notepad.

"Midnight or so."

"The name of the restaurant?"

Tony shut his eyes and tried to concentrate. "Cafe Bossa Nova, I think."

"*Rua Vinicius de Morais* and *Visconde de Piraja,*" blurted Officer Milito.

"Yes, of course." Lt. Lobao made a note.

"Where was the body found?" Tony inquired.

Capt. Almeida placed a hand on Lt. Lobao's shoulder. A look was exchanged and the lieutenant shrugged almost imperceptibly. "The victim was discovered near the *Praça Gen. Osorio*. Do you know this place? Is it where you were attacked?"

"No," answered Tony. "What is it?"

Lt. Lobao explained. "A plaza some few blocks away from the Cafe Bossa Nova."

"Like I said, I was walking to the hotel from the restaurant when he grabbed me. He asked me if I was okay—I'd tripped—I said I was fine and then he hit me."

Tony paused. "He said something else while I was falling." Tony shook his head and instantly regretted the move. Mount Kozolus complained loudly. "I don't remember what though. I mean, he struck me pretty hard and I was on the way down. And out."

"Odd," said Lt. Loboa.

"Extraordinary," Capt. Almeida said thickly.

"Can anyone else vouch for your statements?" the lieutenant asked. His pencil tapped the paper.

"Sure, I suppose so. There were the people I was at the restaurant with. And there was a woman, and a boy, when I woke up on the ground. I don't know their names."

"The names of those you dined with, please?"

Tony searched his memory. "I'm afraid I can't recall any names. Except for Yairi, that is. It was late. And I'm still suffering jet lag. Besides, I never was too good with names."

"Then let's concentrate on the names you do remember. You mentioned a Yairi?" asked the captain.

Tony shook his head. "Alvarez Yairi."

The lieutenant jotted down the name. "And where were you, Mr. Bottoms? You were with your friend?"

"That's Bottom. No," Rock folded and unfolded his hands,

"I was in our room. Hanging out."

"Can anyone vouch for that? Did you have any visitors? The maid perhaps?"

"No, I guess not."

Lt. Lobao's cigarette went up and down in his mouth. "We tracked you through your entry documents, Mr. Kozol. You are here working?"

"That's right. We both are."

"Who is your employer?"

"Luis Angel."

"Luis Angel?" gasped Officer Milito.

"Quiet, Milito."

"Sorry, sir," muttered the policeman. His face reddened.

"Luis Angel the singer?" asked the lieutenant.

"That's right. We're musicians. I play rhythm guitar and Rock is the bass player."

"I see."

Capt. Almeida cut in. "How long will you be in Rio, Mr. Kozol?"

Tony shrugged and watched the lobby doors swing open. A lovely European looking blonde in a thong bikini strode in, smiled in his direction, waved, then headed for the elevators.

Tony smiled back. Rock rolled his eyes. "She wasn't waving at you," he mumbled. Rock pointed with his chin.

Tony turned around. A suave looking gentleman of about sixty, in khaki shorts and a light yellow silk shirt sat in a large red velvet chair in the corner, a newspaper folded on his lap. A confident look on his face. He waved at Tony and grinned.

Tony managed to make his scowl look like a grin. Was the guy laughing at him?

"Mr. Kozol?"

Tony swung around. "Yes?"

"My colleague," said Lt. Lobao, "has asked how long you will be in Rio de Janeiro."

"I'm not sure. That depends on Luis."

"Of course." Lt. Lobao snuffed out his last cigarette, slapped his knees and rose. "I will ask you both two things."

"Yes?"

"Number one, if it should be necessary for you to leave Rio, you will inform me." The lieutenant handed Tony his card.

"What's the other thing?" Rock asked.

"I ask that you stay out of trouble."

"That won't be any problem. Right, Tony?"

"Absolutely. I promise."

"Good. I will have a statement typed up for you to sign regarding this incident. You will read it and sign it."

"Sure. Now?" Tony rose.

"No, you will be telephoned here at the hotel." Lt. Lobao picked up his photos, his pack of Lucky Strike and a morning newspaper that a guest had left on the table. "Gentlemen."

Officer Milito followed the lieutenant out the door. Capt. Almeida studied Tony and Rock a moment longer before he too made his exit.

"Did you see that newspaper on the table?" asked Tony.

"The one that cop took? Yeah, so?"

"I don't understand much Portuguese but I do know some French and some Spanish which are similar. One of the stories on the front page seemed to be about a missing police officer. There was even a photo."

"So?"

Tony hesitated. A dead mugger, a missing cop and a duffel bag that was supposed to contain corn. Tony didn't know much about Brazil's prisons but if they were anything like its *favelas* he didn't need to know anymore. "Nothing. Let's stay out of trouble, that's all."

"Hey, you started it," chirped Rock.

"Yeah," said Tony, lightly rubbing his skull. "How is it that happens?"

"Well—"

"No. Don't answer that."

"Mr. Kozol?"

Tony turned. A man in a valet's uniform stood at his side. "Yes?"

"You have a call, *senhor*." A gloved hand pointed to a courtesy phone on a mirrored tabletop fixed to the wall.

"*Obrigado*." Tony picked up the receiver. "Hello?"

Rock stood with his big arms crossed, leaning against the wall, his eyes shut. When the call ended moments later, he asked, "Who was that?"

"It was Alvarez Yairi."

"Oh, what's up?"

"He wanted to warn me that the police might be coming by."

"That's weird. How come?"

"He wanted to 'advise me' that it is always best to say nothing to the police in Brazil and to 'know nothing', as he put it."

Did you tell him they'd already been here?"

"Yeah."

"What did he say?"

"Nothing. He hung up."

3

Tony skipped breakfast, leaving Rock to ravage the buffet alone. He wasn't feeling so hungry anymore.

At least, not that kind of hungry.

He dressed in a pair of loose cotton shorts, his coolest pale blue polo shirt and his sneakers.

It was early, but Tony was hoping Silvia would be up. Better yet, he was hoping she was still in bed. Silvia Parra's home was a well-kept, white stuccoed two story house, with pale violet shutters, abutting taller apartments on each side on a quiet residential street of Leblon.

To Tony it was all the same but it had been explained to him by his girlfriend that Leblon was separated from Ipanema by the *Jardim de Alah,* a park and aqueduct running from the Atlantic Ocean to the *Lagoa Rodrigo de Freitas e Parque Tom Jobim.*

The salt water lagoon had in distant times been a bay. It had long ago been closed off from the ocean and the aqueduct had been built to keep a fresh replenishment of its waters. The Tom Jobim Park, named for one of Brazil's most famous bossa nova innovators, and circumscribing the lagoon, was a popular locale with outdoor enthusiasts, from bicyclists and joggers to fishermen wading in the shallows with hand-fashioned nets.

Tony reached the house. Though early, it had to be eighty degrees outside and the bright sun followed him like a sizzling yellow shadow. He was perspiring lightly and his head was aching heavily.

Silvia's mother, Ella Parra, and her younger sister, Tzininha, lived on the first floor. The second floor, smaller by half, had been remodeled by the previous owner of the home as an apartment for let. When the Parras moved to Rio de Janeiro from São Paulo some three years past, Silvia moved into the apartment and mother and daughter occupied the first level. They hadn't the funds for reuniting the two floors.

Bad luck for Mrs. Ella Parra but good fortune from Tony's point of view. He avoided the main entrance and pushed the buzzer at the side gate.

Silvia, dressed in a milky nightgown, looked out the window and waved.

Tony signaled back and Silvia buzzed him up.

He climbed the narrow wrought iron stairs to the second floor. Before he could knock, or catch his breath, Silvia was there.

In his arms and on his lips. He kissed her and led her to the bed where they fell side by side, locked in a heady embrace. Silvia's nightgown rode up to her waist. Tony ran his hand up her long tan legs and grabbed her behind. "I missed you."

Silvia's twin basset hounds, Lennon and McCartney, nipped at his heels.

"I thought you would come and see me last night. I thought you would be a gentleman and take me home." She shooed the dogs out the door and they happily bounded down the stairs.

"Sorry," whispered Tony, between bruising kisses. "Something came up. Yairi wanted me to help him and then meet some people."

"Well," said Silvia with a mock pout. She held his chin. "If it was for business, I will forgive you."

He squeezed her fanny and pulled her closer, her hard nipples rubbed through his shirt. "I love you, Silvia."

"I love you, too," she replied softly, her hands reaching under his shirt to stroke his bare skin.

Tony raised her up, pulling the cotton nightgown over her head. Orange-brown freckles fell like a brief sun shower along her upper chest, draping over the edges of her soft shoulders and down her well-toned back.

Tony played connect the dots until he couldn't resist connecting the best two. She gasped as he held her breasts, leaned lower and kissed each one. Her hands reached for his shorts. He didn't fight it.

Their lovemaking was long and hard, the fight of two hungry lovers, ending in a quiet embrace.

Silvia sat up. "I'll go run the bath."

Tony opened his eyes to get a look at her wonderfully naked body. He couldn't believe he'd found someone to love, someone as beautiful and warm as Silvia. Tony wrapped his arms delicately around her slender waist. He rose and softly kissed the nape of her neck.

Silvia turned to face him.

And screamed.

"Oh my god!" Silvia jumped from the sheets and shook.

Tony scrambled to his knees on the mattress. "Jesus, what's wrong?"

Silvia pointed. "Look at all the blood!"

Tony glanced at the white sheets, they were spattered with red. So were the pillows. He touched the side of his head. "Damn."

"What's happened?" cried Silvia.

Tony took her trembling hands. "It's nothing. It's my fault." He turned his head for her inspection. "See? I had a little accident." He scowled at the ruined bedclothes. "Sorry.

I'm afraid I've ruined your sheets. Your mother is going to kill me."

Silvia clutched her bare chest to Tony's face and examined his head. "Never mind the sheets. My god, Tony, what happened to you?"

"It's nothing," he said, taking advantage of his cozy position. A little accident."

"Accident?" Silvia drew back and looked in his eyes. Her fingers softly caressed his open wound.

"Well, some guy hit me. Mugged me."

Silvia gasped and clutched him closer again. "Oh, my poor baby. How could I not see this before? And here we were making love all the while you are wounded!"

"Actually, I found that quite medicinal," Tony said mischievously. "In fact," he licked her belly, "I think I need some more medicine." He reached for her hidden triangle.

She slapped his hand away. "We will do no such thing." Silvia grabbed his hand and pulled him from the bed. "Come on. We must attend to your wounds now."

Tony frowned but allowed himself to be led to the bathroom. The small side window was cranked open, allowing a trickle of air to penetrate.

Silvia grabbed a washcloth, wet it under the tap with cool water and applied it to his head. Tony stiffened. To take his mind off the pain, Tony studied her naked form in the tall vanity mirror. "I'm fine, really, Silvia. I'm fine."

"You are fine when I tell you that you are fine. Hush now."

Tony closed his eyes while she washed blotches of dried blood from his face and hair.

Silvia ran a bath, bubbles and all. They climbed in together.

Tony would have fallen asleep if it hadn't been for the explosion.

Silvia jumped up, slipped, fell down again then rose to her

knees. Tony caught her.

"What the hell was that?" Tony wanted to know. They scrambled out of the tub, Silvia into a long white terry robe and Tony into a far too short terrycloth towel.

Silvia hurried out of the bathroom. Tony was right behind her. The apartment was a large studio with a separate bath and a small dining/kitchen area in the back. A smallish window over the single sink looked out on the apartment buildings on the block behind. Silvia had created a small sitting area by the door to separate her wall-less bedroom using a small sofa and two chairs with a table between them. A partition created a minimal screen.

"Fidel!" she cried, her voice a mixture of fear and dread.

Tony came around the screen clutching the damp towel around his waist. Soap, dripping from his forehead, stung his eyes, blurring his vision.

A large man stood inside the doorway. He looked at Tony and pointed.

If fingers were guns, Kozol had the feeling he'd be dead about now.

"You!" he shouted.

"Fidel, no!" Silvia pressed forward and he shoved her away.

"What?" Tony was temporarily stunned. What was going on? The door had been broken loose from its frame.

The man Silvia called Fidel was yelling at her in Portuguese. Silvia was yelling back. It was no use trying to understand. But it was obvious that she wanted Fidel to leave.

Struggling to keep his towel about his waist with his left hand, Tony confronted the stranger. He was Tony's height but easily twice his age. He wore a heavily decorated uniform of some sort.

"Get out!" the man shouted. "Get out or I will kill you!"

"Fidel! Fidel!" cried Silvia. "Stop, I implore you. *Alto seu loucamente."*

Tony grabbed the uniformed jerk with his right arm. "You get out. The lady doesn't want you here."

Without pause, Fidel lashed out and struck Tony across the side of the head.

Tony cried out. Why the hell was everybody hitting him lately? And why did this guy have to hit the already imposing Mount Kozolus?! Tony swung back. There was a sudden draft and he realized he was no longer decent.

This only seemed to infuriate his attacker all the more because he renewed his blows. Tony raised his arms to defend himself.

A new voice suddenly mingled with the three already screaming ones, not to mention Lennon and McCartney, who had come running back up the stairs barking rapidly in their own singular vocal disharmony.

Fighting off windmills to his head, Tony caught sight of Mrs. Parra in the doorway. A look of pure anger, deep as the bowels of the earth, was carved on her face. The wooden broom in her hand didn't look like it was going to be used at this particular time for any sweeping up.

She came in swinging. "*Vai*! *Vai*!" Mrs. Parra thumped Fidel across the back.

Tony flinched. That had to hurt. Mrs. Parra was not a small woman.

Shouting something incomprehensible at Silvia, Fidel turned for the door. Lennon and McCartney yelped. Mrs. Parra struck the crazed man once more across the spine for good measure. Something cracked. Bone or wood?

"I'm going!" he bellowed. "But this isn't the end of anything."

There was a sudden silence in the apartment as the lunatic's thumping footfalls echoed away down the stairs. Tony realized he was breathing hard.

Mrs. Parra's icy glare had locked in on him now.

Silvia's mother clutched the broomstick across her chest so tightly her knuckles were turning white.

Realizing he was naked, in front of his girlfriend's mother no less, Kozol plucked his towel from the floor, draped it around himself as best he could and fled for the bath.

Only after Tony had closed the bathroom door behind him, congratulating himself on his third successful brush with death in less than twenty-four hours—the mugger, Madman Fidel and the very dangerous Mrs. Ella Parra— did he realize that all his clothes were on the floor beside Silvia's bed.

Great, just great.

He slumped to the cool tile floor and waited. Voices, too soft to make out, carried through the door.

A while later, there was a gentle knock. Tony popped open his eyes and held his breath. "Please let it be Silvia," he prayed.

"Tony?"

"Thank God," he whispered. Tony unlocked the door. He peeped around the corner. "Is your mother gone?"

Silvia nodded. She still looked frightened. "Yes. Mother is gone." Lennon and McCartney were chasing each other around the kitchen, probably waiting for breakfast.

Tony fetched his clothes, picking his shorts off the floor and his shirt from the bed. He laced up his shoes and joined Silvia who was in the kitchen pouring out kibble into a big aluminum dish. She set the bowl on the tile and Lennon pushed out McCartney before grudgingly giving his brother some space.

"So, who was that guy?" Tony leaned against the counter, head throbbing. "You have any aspirin?"

Silvia nodded her head and silently reached into a cabinet over the stove, retrieving a half full bottle of white pills. She handed Tony two, filled a small glass with tap water and handed it to him.

Tony swallowed.

And waited.

Silvia pulled a carton of eggs from the refrigerator and set a cast iron pan on the burner. She lit the flame, turned to Tony and said, "He is my uncle."

"Your uncle?"

"Yes," said Silvia, concentrating on cracking open the eggshells and dropping the eggs into the hot pan where they sizzled in butter.

The aroma brought a pang of hunger to Kozol that he hadn't felt for hours. "Your mother's brother?"

"No." She shoved the eggs around with a wooden spatula. "My father's brother."

"Oh." Tony knew Silvia didn't like to talk about her father. So that effectively shut down that avenue of discussion. He tried another. "What's his problem? Why did he come busting in here like that and knocking down the door?"

Silvia added salt, pepper and chives. "He does not approve."

"Of what? Me?"

"Yes." She poured coffee into two small cups and set one on the counter beside her lover. Her damp hair spilled over the back of her white robe and smelled of mango scented shampoo.

"What's his name? Fidel?"

"*Sim.*" Her reply was soft, almost missing.

"Is it because I'm a foreigner?"

Silvia sighed and fingered the handle of her cup. "It is because we are not man and wife. My uncle is very old fashioned."

Tony frowned. "Your mother doesn't seem to mind—" he thought of her holding that broom across her chest like she was preparing to battle Little John himself, " — much."

Silvia managed a small smile. "Perhaps she only expresses it differently." She pulled the pan from the fire and served the eggs on small dishes with chunks of bread and slices of pineapple. "Sit."

Tony sat.

Silvia took her seat, picked up a fork and picked at her eggs.

Tony ignored his food and his protesting stomach. "You know," he said tenderly, "I'd like to marry you."

Silvia's hand stopped moving. The only sign of life was the tear that had begun to well up in her eye. She looked up and deeply into Tony's eyes. "Would you?"

"Yes." He took her hand, gently removing the fork. "I would."

Silvia pressed her lips together and fought back her tears. "That would be so wonderful," she sobbed.

"Will you marry me, Silvia?"

Silvia jumped from her chair and paced across the kitchen to the balcony. Twisting around to face him, she said, "But it is impossible. There are so many problems." She wrung her hands.

"Like what?"

Silvia was silent for a moment, and looking lost. Finally, she spoke."It would be too hard for you here, Tony. There are so many things you do not understand."

Tony stood. "Maybe." He hadn't given that much thought. Hell, he hadn't given it any thought.

Silvia cast a look at the broken door. "What would you do?"

He shrugged. "I don't know. You could come to America with me." He took a step in Silvia's direction.

"America?"

Tony grinned. "Yeah, even Lennon and McCartney can come. It'll be the next British Invasion of America—via Brazil."

She wiped the tears from her face then started crying all over again. Tony took her in his arms and squeezed. "Marry me, Silvia."

"Yes," she promised.

4

"*Senhor* Kozol!"

Tony looked up from the sidewalk. Waves of heat shimmered up off the hood of an olive green Mercedes, a rare enough car in a country where such vehicles, he was told, sold for twice what they would in the United States. And this one looked new.

Tony squinted and promised himself that he'd pick up a pair of sunglasses. "Yes?" He stepped to the curb.

The driver of the car, which had been parked opposite, crossed to his side and stopped. "How are you? Okay?"

Tony's brain went into a stall then perked up. "Oh, you." It was one of Alvarez Yairi's friends. The one with the looker wife and the hairy chest.

The man, dressed now in a white silk shirt and gray trousers, stuck his hand out the window. There was a large diamond ring on his pinkie. Tony had noticed it the night before. He wore his thick black hair brushed sharply back, kept there no doubt with gel or hair spray. He had cunning green eyes and a big white smile that he used to his advantage. "Rodriguez, remember?"

Tony nodded his head. "Yes, of course."

"Can I give you a lift?"

"Thanks, but I'm only going back to the hotel."

"Hop in." Teeth flashed.

Tony hopped in. "How did you find me?"

The sharp-dressed man shrugged. "Ipanema is not so very big."

Tony furrowed his brow. Ipanema was not so small either.

"So," said Rodriguez, "you are okay now?"

"Huh?"

One hand left the steering wheel and Rodriguez pointed at Tony's head.

Tony's hand went instinctively to his wound. "Oh, yes. I'm fine."

"Nothing serious?"

"No, nothing serious."

"There is so much crime in Rio," lamented Rodriguez. "I must apologize for all of us that you have been attacked."

"That's okay, it's not your fault. There's plenty of crime in Florida, too."

"Ah yes, Florida." Rodriguez guided the highly polished, leather appointed Mercedes towards the beach. The sunroof was open and the air conditioner was set for seventy degrees.

Tony's head was getting a sunburn and his arms and legs were raising goose bumps.

"I should like to see America one day." A young woman in an orange thong slid past the driver's side and Rodriguez whistled appreciatively.

"How did you hear about my getting mugged anyway? I didn't even report it to the police until this morning."

Rodriguez's hands gripped the wheel ever tighter as he rounded a difficult curve and swung back towards the Ipanema Palace Hotel. He stopped in front, ignoring the valets, and spoke. "You reported this to the police?"

"Yes. They came looking for me this morning. It turns out the man who attacked me was attacked himself. Killed actually."

"That is unfortunate," Rodriguez said, taking a silver toothpick from the ashtray and picking imaginary bits from his too-white teeth. "We must all be very careful."

"Yes." Tony put his hand on the door handle. "You never did say how you knew about the attack."

"Ipanema is—"

"—not so very big. I know," said Tony, though he didn't. He opened the passenger side door and slipped out.

"Little Armando will be relieved to hear that you are well."

Little Armando, that was the name of the guy with the patch over his eye. "Tell him hello for me," Tony said.

"Is there anything else I can tell him?"

"Anything else?"

"Do you anticipate any problems?"

Tony thought about what he'd told the police. Whoever mugged him was dead. He had a paying job and a girlfriend. Not just a girlfriend, a future wife. They could return to America. Tony could find some kind of work there, as a musician or maybe even as a lawyer, if he had to, and the State allowed. Silvia wouldn't have to work if she didn't want to. He'd see to that. She talked about opening up a dance studio. "No, no problems at all."

Rodriguez was visibly pleased. "Little Armando is interested in the Four-Star-STA fully automated mixing board."

Tony's eyebrows shot up. "Really?"

"It's for a friend of his."

"Well, you can't do any better. It's state of the art. I wouldn't mind having one of those babies myself. Luis Angel has one in his setup. I've had my eye on it."

"Good." Rodriguez twisted his ring round and round his finger. "So, you know how it works?"

"Yeah, sure."

"*Bom*. Soon then, eh? I'll be in touch."

"Sure. See you soon. *Até logo*." Tony tapped the roof of the car, gave the door a shove and waved Rodriguez on his way.

"No problems at all," Tony said with a smile to the doorman who returned his smile with a baffled look of his own.

"We've got a problem," Rock said, as Tony stepped into the room.

"What kind of a problem? You can't figure out what to order for lunch?"

Rock shook his head no.

"You've been mugged? You can't find your shoes?" Kozol looked pointedly at Rock's bare feet. He was lying on the unmade bed, clothed but shoeless.

"None of the above," said Rock, munching on a bag of potato chips.

Tony hoped he hadn't gotten those from the minibar where they were six dollars U.S. per bag. It was unclear if Luis Angel's management was footing that part of their expenses.

"Luis wants to see us. And, according to his assistant, Miss Prissy Pants, he's none too happy."

Tony bit his cheek. So much for no problems. Miss Prissy Pants was Rock's name for Luis' personal assistant, a young Brazilian woman named Alba Zica. She was very protective of her charge and looked down on nearly everyone in the band. "Meaning what? He's not happy with us for some reason? Hell, we haven't even had a chance to play!"

Rock Bottom and Tony Kozol had been last minute replacements for the two fired musicians before them, joining an eight piece band, not counting the four backup singers, two male and two female who accompanied the young heartthrob on stage.

A friend of Rock's had gotten them the gig. So far, it had meant no work and plenty of play time in Rio de Janeiro at

Carnaval season. Though they had a free show in the park coming up soon, Luis Angel didn't seem all that interested in rehearsing. There had been one lackluster rehearsal the first day in town. Luis had been drunk or high, or both, coming in off a flight from Buenos Aires and the rehearsal had been short and not too sweet.

Tony and Rock hadn't laid eyes on their boss since then. Luis Angel was a lot different than the last hat act Tony had worked for. His previous employer had been a strict businessman and showman who believed in well-disciplined rehearsals.

The big guy shrugged, crumpled up the empty bag of chips and tossed it into the nearest bin. He wiped bits of salt from his face with the back of his hand, which was tattooed with the numbers one through five. So was his other hand. Rock had explained to Tony that it helped him learn to play the bass guitar.

A guy in a bar one night had suggested that Rock had done it to learn to count his fingers. After he said it, the guy was counting his teeth where'd they'd fallen in the sawdust on the floor.

"All I know is she called an hour ago wanting us to come up to the penthouse. I told her you were out and she started yammering away at me wanting to know where you'd gone. I told her I wasn't your damn babysitter. Then Prissy settled down long enough to order me to stay put until you returned. Then we're to go up." Rock punched his pillow. "Here I am, Carnaval time in Rio, stuck in a lousy hotel room."

Though he wasn't hungry, Tony pulled open the little refrigerator door, grabbed a four dollar soda and an eight dollar can of macadamia nuts and started munching.

"What are you doing? Haven't you eaten yet?"

Tony stuffed nuts into his cheeks and took a sip of his *Guaraná* soda. "You kidding? I'm so full, I think I'm gonna be sick. But if we're about to be unemployed, Luis Angel can pay our bill in full."

Rock grinned. "Toss me another bag of chips."

Tony and Rock stood inside the double doors of the Presidential Suite, their fifty-four dollar eating binge complete.

Floor to ceiling sliding glass doors gave out onto the patio overlooking the Atlantic. Elegant furniture was scattered tastefully about the living room. Expensive looking paintings hung on the walls.

"Kind of puts our room to shame, don't it?" Rock remarked.

Tony acceded.

"Think either of us will ever be able to afford a place like this?"

The scuttlebutt was that the Presidential Suite ran about eight thousand *reais* a night. That was about four thousand dollars American. "No."

Rock grudgingly agreed.

A personal doorman, no doubt an employee of the hotel, had shown them in. It was Alba Zica, wearing a shamrock green dress that held her voluptuous hips at bay, who greeted them. Her shoulder length brown hair was tied sharply behind in a Princess Anne braid. She wore gold-rimmed eye glasses that did nothing to hide the natural beauty she'd been blessed with. Tony was certain Brazil was hoarding more than its fair share of beautiful women. And though Miss Zica was a bit on the pudgy side it did nothing to detract from her sexual appeal.

Alba Zica had big brown eyes.

And no sense of humor.

She tapped her gold watch. "You're late."

"For what?" Rock couldn't help saying.

She pursed her purplish lips and, though far shorter,

seemed to look down over the rims of her glasses at the bass player.

Rock dropped his gaze.

Round One had gone to the delightful Miss Alba Zica. Prissy Pants. This was the first time either of them had seen the young woman in anything other than dress slacks. Maybe she had an Irish funeral to attend later.

"Where have you been, Tony?"

"I was out—" Tony didn't feel like bringing up Silvia with Miss Prissy Pants. It was none of her business after all. "I went shopping."

Alba Zica took this news as a personal affront, crossed her slender arms over her small chest and said, "You must inform me of your location and activities at all times. Mister Angel is your employer and he works on his own schedule. Not yours," the assistant said, pointing a finger first at Kozol and then Rock.

Rock saluted. Tony declined to do the same.

Miss Zica curled the index finger of her right hand. A sharp polished nail, painted sea green, danced in the air. "Come with me."

"You're in trouble," Rock said teasingly under his breath.

"Shut up, Rock," mouthed Tony.

Prissy Pants swung around. "You said something, Tony?"

Tony reddened like a ripening beet. "Me? No, nothing."

The young woman continued her march down the long hall that led finally to the kitchen and an informal dining area which also opened onto the balcony that ran half the length of the building.

Luis Angel, eyes closed, a slice of cucumber balanced delicately atop each eyelid, lay atop a lounger in a pair of navy blue swim trunks of the Speedo variety.

With his oiled skin, the young star looked like a salad baking in the sun. His curly black locks stirred gently in the light breeze. His well muscled stomach rose up and down slowly and evenly.

Luis Angel's father had been a star before the younger Angel had even been born. Ricardo Angel was a famous Latin crooner and film actor. Even Kozol had heard of him.

Luis Angel was going for a comfortable ride on his daddy's coattails.

And Tony hated him for it.

"Luis?"

Miss Zica lightly touched the young singer's arm. He grunted. "Those *musicians*," she said the word as if it were a disease, "you wanted to see are here."

Luis grunted once more. He opened his bloodshot eyes. The cucumber slices rolled down his belly and rested on his crotch. His toast-colored irises seemed unsure of themselves and trembled as if suffering an internal brainquake.

Miss Zica wasted no time picking off the cucumber slices and placing them on a dirty plate on the nearby table which was itself shaded by a large pink umbrella.

Luis propped himself up and began speaking. Tony and Rock looked at the young man and then at each other. Fearing to speak back.

The problem was, the kid was speaking in Portuguese!

Miss Zica came and whispered in the young heartthrob's ear.

He grinned. "How stupid of me. Sometimes I forget who I'm talking to." Luis rose and bounced catlike to the kitchen where he pulled a bottle of cold beer from the fridge. "Boys?"

Tony knew better than to refuse. "*Obrigado*."

Rock wasted no time popping the top and taking a healthy swig. "Yeah, thanks."

"So," said Luis, leaning against the counter, his flat belly annoying the hell out of Tony who always seemed to carry a little extra flesh around his middle no matter how much he tried to watch his diet. "Everything okay with you men? Room is okay? Rio is fun?"

"What I've seen of it," Rock said, none too vaguely, while giving Miss Prissy Pants, who'd followed them indoors, the eye.

"That's good." The younger Angel chugged his *Antarctica* and reached for another. He popped the lid and flipped it on the counter where it careened off the blender, bounced into the sink and came to rest in the drain. "Here's the problem."

Tony waited.

"My old man got a call from the governor today. That's Alexandre Pires, governor of the state, saying that I was getting in trouble!" He wiped his beer bottle against his stomach. "Turn the air up, will you?"

Alba Zica hurried down the hall in the direction of the thermostat.

"Then my dad calls me from Madrid. I'm thinking, what the hell is my old man talking about? I'm drinking a little, fucking a little. . .So what? That's what we Angels do. I mean, the old man himself taught me!"

Tony smiled and nodded lightly. How wonderful. A family tradition.

"Sounds good to me," Rock chimed in.

"Yeah. So then he tells me that somebody in my group is getting his chops busted by the police." Luis aimed his beer bottle at Tony. "You."

Tony squirmed. "It's not what you think. I got mugged last night." Tony twisted his head for the young star's benefit. "See?" It had become his badge of honor like a war vet's scars.

"Yeah, yeah, I know all about that," Luis said, brushing him off. Beer in hand, he wrapped his arms around Tony and Rock's shoulders. "I told the old man to relax, that I'd handle it. Everybody just needs to mellow a little." He hummed a familiar tune. "Like *Mellow Yellow*, get it?"

"Got it." Sweat and oil accosted Tony's nostrils and, because of Luis' effusiveness, soiled his clothes and bare arms. Not a pleasant blend of sensations.

"So, let's have some fun. We'll get drunk. We'll get high. We'll get laid." Luis released them and snapped his fingers.

His personal assistant hurried into the kitchen. She handed the young star an envelope. He ripped it open and pulled out two big cards. "I got you guys tickets to the Sambadrome. Tomorrow," he said mischievously, "we party!"

"Thanks," said Rock profusely. He grabbed the tickets from the younger man's hand before they could disappear.

"Yeah, that's really nice of you, Mister Angel."

"Call me Luis, guys." He cocked his thick dark brow. "If you've never been to the samba parade," Tony and Rock shook their heads no, "you're in for a treat. And I'm one of the judges."

Miss Zica pulled Rock's arm. They'd been dismissed. She led them out.

"The car will pick us up downstairs at five tomorrow!" called Luis. "Tony, hold back."

Tony told Rock to go on ahead and stopped in the hall. "Yes?"

Luis draped his arm over Tony's back. Tony wished Luis would learn some new conversation techniques. "Let's keep out of trouble, okay."

"I'm not looking for trouble."

Luis looked at Tony, his head bouncing lightly up and down. His white teeth flashed like spotlights. "Rio can be a lot of fun, a hell of a lot of fun."

Tony waited.

"But you've got to watch out who you hang out with, know what I mean?"

Tony shrugged. "Not really. I haven't been hanging out with anyone."

Luis rubbed his chin with the side of his Antarctica. "I mean there are a lot of unsavory guys around here—"

Tony figured he was looking at one just then but refrained from voicing his opinion.

"—Even women. I mean, Brazil is loaded with hot women, young and old. You like young girls or do you prefer them older, maybe?"

"Uh—"

"Tomorrow I'll introduce you to some hot, hot babes. No need tying yourself down with just one!"

"Thanks, but—"

Luis clapped Tony across the back. "Don't mention it. We're friends and what are friends for if not that?"

Tony opened his mouth to retort, then decided it was easier to play along. "*Obrigado.*" He changed the subject to something more palatable. "By the way, when's the next rehearsal."

"I don't know," said Luis somewhat indifferently. He scratched the stubble on his chin.

"The show's Monday."

"Yeah," grinned the young star, "plenty of time. Now get out of here and if you see Yairi tell him I need him!"

"What did he say?" Rock asked as the door shut behind Tony and the two men found themselves alone in the anteroom leading to the penthouse.

"I have no idea."

"Still," Rock waved the Sambadrome tickets in the air, "he can't be too mad."

"Are you kidding? I'd say he's about as pissed as a guy like that can get. We've got to be careful, Rock," Tony said. "Kids like that are impulsive and our jobs are on the line. I mean, where do we go from here if we lose this job?"

Rock shrugged. "So what are we going to do?"

"First off, we're going to find Alvarez Yairi."

"What for?"

"To get back in Luis' good graces, that's what for. He said he was looking for Yairi. We're going to make sure he finds him."

"Okay, if you think that's more fun than hitting the beach—"

"I know, I know. I'm not blind. I've seen the girls down there."

Rock grinned like a high schooler. "Yeah, man. Of course, I was thinking of inviting Miss Prissy Pants to join me for a picnic."

Tony laughed. "She'd have *you* for lunch." He punched the elevator call button. "Come on, let's ring Yairi."

Tony fished Yairi's number out of his pocket and dialed. After several rings a woman's voice started speaking in Portuguese.

"Hello? *Alô*? Speak English?"

"Yes."

"I'd like to speak to Yairi, please."

"This is the operator. Can I help you?"

"Operator? No, I dialed my friend's number." Tony repeated the digits. "I'd like to speak with him."

"I'm sorry that number has been deserviced."

"Deserviced? What does that mean exactly?"

"What's going on?" said Rock.

"Wait," said Tony. "There must be some mistake." He repeated the phone number.

"Deserviced," the machine-like voice repeated.

Tony started to protest when by the dial tone he realized he'd been *de-connected*.

Rock's face was a question mark.

"Stupid operator says Yairi's phone has been disconnected. It's worse than in the States."

It was a ten minute walk to Yairi's apartment. Tony rapped on the door. No answer. "Yairi? Hey, it's me, Tony Kozol!"

Rock pushed Tony out of the way. He'd always thought Tony's knocking inadequate. "Let me try." He pummeled the door. It shook on its hinges yet held. A lesser door would have gone down for the count.

A pale face, blotched with brown spots, holding up a head of thin gray hair, poked out of the door on the landing below and glared at them. A twisted nose flared. The man spoke with a voice that gave a long history of tobacco and alcohol. "*Quem é você? O que quer?*"

"*Ola, senhor.*" Tony pulled Rock's hand from the door handle which he'd been jiggling. Tony smiled and spread his hands. A universal gesture of 'Don't shoot me, I'm unarmed.'

He hoped.

"*Sao fazendo*?" The old man looked angry.

Tony descended slowly and Rock followed after him. Tony didn't want to spook the old guy. All he needed was for the man to telephone the police and he and Rock would be hauled in on an attempted burglary! "Do you speak English?"

The man's brow furrowed deeply. He said nothing.

"English." Tony sighed. "Alvarez Yairi?" He pointed to the upstairs door. "*Senhor* Yairi. I look for *Senhor* Yairi."

"Forget it. This isn't getting us anywhere." Rock pulled Tony away from the elderly man. "He doesn't speak English."

"Yeah." Tony turned towards the street.

"I do."

Rock and Tony turned back around. A woman, small in height, wide in girth, her black and gray hair pulled up tightly atop her head, stood next to the old man in the doorway. She wiped her hands on a red and white apron that wasn't about to notice one more stain.

"*Senhora*? You speak English?"

"Yes. My husband and I manage this building. What can I help you? You gentleman would like an apartment?"

"No, actually we've come to see our friend, Alvarez Yairi."

The woman grunted. Her face contorted as if she'd just

swallowed a peeled lime.

"Is something wrong, *senhora*?"

"*Senhor* Yairi is gone."

"Gone? Gone where, *senhora*?"

In one quick movement, she slapped her hands together, then her right hand shot into the air, like a bird taking flight. "Gone. Moved out."

"But that can't be. I was here only yesterday evening."

"Well, he is gone now."

"Are you certain?"

"Maybe he just went out for a little—" suggested Rock.

The old woman bit her tongue, shook her head in obvious disgust and said, "Wait here."

The woman disappeared inside her apartment. The elderly gentleman glowered at Tony and Rock the entire time and they were relieved when his wife reappeared. "Come," she said.

She pounded slowly up the stairs on stout but firm legs. There was a scent of cooked codfish and leeks twisted in her hair as tightly as any plait. Pulling a keyring from her apron pocket, she opened the door to Yairi's apartment. "Come, come," she beckoned.

Tony and Rock followed her inside.

"It's empty!"

5

The woman pulled open the draperies, flooding the room with white light. "What did I tell you?"

Rock returned from the bedroom. "Yeah, man. This is weird. There's nothing left."

Tony scratched his head, reopening his wound and cursing. "How could he just disappear?"

The big guy shrugged. It was one of the things he did best.

"You find Alvarez, you tell him he still owes me two months rent!" She went to the kitchen and closed an open cabinet. "At least he left things neat and clean. That's better than most renters do."

Tony agreed. The place was spotless. "And you have no idea where Yairi's gone?"

She shook a substantial fist. "If I did. . ."

A horn, sounding like the beeping of that clever *Road Runner* in those *Wile E. Coyote* cartoons, chirruped repeatedly on the street below.

The landlady opened the sliding glass door and shouted. No doubt telling the driver to shut up and move along.

Tony looked down. A vintage open-backed produce truck, covered with grime and loaded with a variety of vegetables, was double parked in front of the restaurant downstairs. There was okra, manioc, broccoli, carrots and some sort of little tomatoes. The old truck's wooden slats bulged from the weight of the foodstuffs pressing against them. If they burst. . .

A man, heavyset, with a segment missing from his thick nose, like a puzzle missing a piece, was waving up. He had a gold crown on one of his upper teeth.

"Who's that?" Rock asked.

"Never seen him before."

A hand popped up on the driver's side and a man lifted his head out the window. "Tony! Tony Kozol!"

It was Rodriguez.

Rodriguez hopped out into the road and waved for Tony to come down.

"Oh, it's that Rodriguez character." Tony would never have recognized him from the neck down. Rodriguez was wearing worn and filthy blue overalls. Even from a distance, Tony could imagine the smell. His elegant black loafers looked out of place.

"Who's Rodriguez?"

"A friend of Yairi's."

"Good, then maybe he'll be able to tell us where to find him and we can get on with our lives."

"Yeah, come on. Let's go talk to him." Tony thanked the landlady for her time and he and Rock hurried downstairs, past the still glowering husband and out into the street.

Rodriguez offered Tony a grubby hand and Tony felt obliged to shake it. He introduced Rock. "You are looking for Yairi, no?"

"That's right. How did you know?"

Rodriguez pushed a hand through his hair. "Ipanema is not so very—"

"—Big. I know. So where is he? Luis Angel is looking for him."

"Ahh, yes. No problem."

Tony groaned. Even though he'd only been in Brazil a couple of days he'd learned two things at least. One, 'No Problem,' was usually best translated as 'Big Problem.' Number two, no one and nothing was ever on time.

The street was slowly being plugged up as cars and drivers fought to pass the big truck. "Hop in!" Rodriguez called, pulling open the passenger side door. "Move over, Oswaldo."

The passenger with the missing piece and matching blue overalls slid into the middle of the benchseat.

Tony only wanted to find Yairi, send him to Luis and then go have dinner with Silvia before she went to work. Tons of brownie points in his plan. "No, I can't. We don't have time. If you can tell us how to get a hold of Yairi—"

Cars honked and protested.

"No time. I must move the truck before I get a ticket." He held the door. "Come on. I'll explain on the way. Take you to him."

Tony hesitated then jumped inside.

Rock took one look at the cramped truck and frowned.

"I am afraid your friend will have to ride in the back," apologized Rodriguez.

Rock huffed. "In the—"

"Come on, Rock. I want to get this over with. I promised Silvia I'd take her to a nice restaurant this evening."

"Oh, all right. But you owe me."

"It is not so very far. Don't worry." Rodriguez lowered the tailgate and Rock squeezed in amongst some broccoli and carrots. Flies attacked his eyes as if they were overripe cherry tomatoes.

Tony rolled up his window so he wouldn't have to listen to the big guy grumble. The truck rolled through town, through Leblon and on.

"So," Tony said, trying to maintain some civil distance between himself and the taciturn Oswaldo, "what's happened to Yairi?"

"Alvarez has moved to a new apartment. He'd been looking for some time and the place he wanted came available suddenly. Didn't he mention it to you?"

"No," replied Tony. "In fact, last time I spoke to him this morning he hung up."

"The telephone service here is notoriously bad," explained Rodriguez. "Must have been a disconnection."

They passed up the coast, away from Leblon. "Yairi moved out here?"

Rodriguez said something in Portuguese to Oswaldo who laughed. Tony wondered what the big joke was. He hoped Rock was okay in the back. The roads out this way were none too smooth. Big potholes in the broad street hinted at a brontosaurus having used the surface as a practice samba stomping grounds sometime in the past epoch.

At the base of a hill, up which rose a huge brown slum, Rodriguez turned. He pushed the produce truck up two streets and parked in front of a grocery shop. There was no glass in the front window, only wooden bars so closely spaced a child couldn't have stuck a stunted hand through.

Rodriguez hopped out.

Oswaldo gave Tony a nudge. Tony got the hint. He unlatched his door and stepped out.

Rock had helped himself out of the back and was pressing his vertebrae. "I call shotgun on the way home. You can sit in the rear with the lousy veggies next time."

The truck groaned woefully as its brakes settled against its drums.

Rock looked at Tony. "Where are we anyway?"

Tony shrugged. "I don't know. Let's just find Yairi and get out of here." He paused. Shabbily dressed strangers gave them the eye. "Before dark."

Rock nodded.

"We must make our leave of the truck here," Rodriguez

explained. Oswaldo was now backing the truck up and turning away.

"Hey! Wait!" cried Tony. "How will we get back to town?"

Rodriguez patted him on the back. "No problem, Tony. Come on, follow me."

Their guide, Rodriguez, led them uphill, threading through a jungle of despair, past dilapidated buildings which looked incapable of supporting life more evolved than the cockroach. Tony wondered what would happen if there were a fire up here. Would the fire department even respond? Did they have earthquakes? He'd heard that floods often came, loosening the earth from the steep hills and sending mud and homes careening down the mountain, taking unaccounted lives with them.

Tony and Rock tried to keep from staring at the people they passed. Children, if not naked, were dressed in threads and tatters. Young men stood idly by with apparently nowhere to go.

Finally, midway up, the mountain leveled off. They had reached a plateau of sorts. A long, concrete block building stood to the left of a small square. Few lingered. Armed men and boys seemed to be keeping away the riffraff.

Rodriguez led them straight to the three story high, unpainted edifice.

The shock on Tony's face was unmistakable as a guard pulled open the big, solid wooden doors and exposed the building's innards.

"There must be a thousand people in here!" cried Rock.

"What is this?" Tony's eyes flitted about the room. Dazzling colors abounded. Feathers, sequins, bold, shiny fabrics. Sweaty men and women, boys and girls raced about or danced in place.

Rodriguez beamed proudly. "This is our samba school. It is our last chance to perfect our costumes and get ready for the competitions starting tomorrow."

"It's incredible," said Rock.

"Yeah," answered Tony. "I've never seen anything like it."

Suddenly a rumble of thunder set the gigantic hall to shaking and Tony feared the whole place would collapse.

"Not to worry, Tony," shouted Rodriguez. "It is only the *bateria* warming up." He pointed to the far corner. Through the maze of dark skin and bright colors, Tony and Rock could just barely make out a drum corps in a far pocket of the room.

"Yeah, man," Rock said. "I've read about that. They keep the beat throughout the parade for their samba school; playing tambourines and those drums—"

"The *recoreco* and *cuica*," explained Rodriguez. "Ah, here is my wife, Elena. You remember, Tony?"

Elena appeared from out of the crowd like an earthly angel on highheels. Her red hair sparkled with silver sprinkles. A handful, a rather small handful, of brown and white feathers covered her crotch.

And, except for the emerald choker about her neck, that was it.

"Yes, of course," she leaned against Tony and gave him a kiss on the cheek. "How are you, Tony?"

"Good," Tony managed to say.

She turned pertly to Rock. "And you are?"

Rock grinned, red-faced. "Rock Bottom, *senhora*."

"My pleasure."

Rock mumbled and looked shyly at his feet.

Rodriguez asked his wife how the rehearsals were going.

"Fine," she replied. "Except for João and Leon."

Rodriguez nodded sympathetically.

"Those two have been at each other's throats all day. I swear, it's only a matter of time before one man kills the other."

"João stole Leon's wife," explained Rodriguez.

"Even though Leon had left her a year ago!" added Elena.

"Still Leon has not forgiven João the humiliation. You're right, Elena. I fear there will be trouble. João should have stayed away. To return to Rio with Leon's wife was foolish. But," he added on a note of hope, "once one kills the other, things will return to normal."

"Not soon enough for me," commented Elena.

Tony looked at Rock in disbelief. Life didn't seem to be worth much here on the mountain. Not a pleasant thought.

Rodriguez muttered something to his wife and she pointed up a narrow flight of concrete steps. Rodriguez nodded, patted his wife's bare rump, and beckoned Tony and Rock to follow him.

From above, the samba school was a magnificent sight and it was with regret that Tony tore his eyes from it as Rodriguez beckoned yet again.

They entered a small office with a light fixture, a silver dish with a single bulb, hanging from a rough ceiling. Another door stood opposite. The room was cluttered and otherwise uninhabited. The anomaly was the fancy, polished cherry wood table. It was a good two meters long with three matching chairs to a side. The whole set looked like it could have been picked out of an Ethan Allen catalog.

As Tony tried to make sense of their situation, the far door opened. Little Armando and his brother, Victor, came striding into the room. Tony might have been glad to see the two men if they hadn't been flanked by yet two more men carrying overlarge pistols stuffed into the belts of their overlarge bellies.

Little Armando smiled and looked Tony and Rock over with his one blue eye. "Sit, my friends."

Without any clear options, Tony sat. Rock submitted as well. The muffled, unending sounds of samba continued from below; unwavering, unrelenting, background music.

"Who is your friend, Tony?" Little Armando and his

brother took chairs side by side across from Tony and Rock.

"This is Rock," Rodriguez answered for him. "He is a good friend of Tony's. And in the band as well."

"Ah, a cohort." Little Armando rubbed his fat hands together. "I understand."

Tony was glad somebody did.

"Drinks, Rodriguez." Little Armando introduced himself and his younger brother, Victor, to Rock.

Rodriguez went to the sidebar and began mixing a pitcher of chemicals.

"Have you had our *caipirinha,* gentlemen?" Little Armando inquired.

They said no.

"A shame. Make sure they are excellent, Rodriguez."

Rodriguez nodded and continued mixing. He poured from a bottle labeled *São Francisco.* He cut some limes with an ugly curved knife. Tony wished Rodriguez might have washed his hands first. Now he was plucking ice out of a grungy cooler.

"It is our national drink," Victor said. "*Cachaça,* lime, sugar and crushed ice."

"*Cachaça*?" Tony repeated.

"*Cachaça,* or *pinga* as we also call it, is cane spirits, alcohol. Forty proof or better."

"Ouch," said Rock.

Little Armando continued his lesson. "*Cachaça* is as old as Brazil itself from the time of the great sugar plantations. Now there are over hundred varieties. The cheapest of which are quite lethal."

"Rot gut," said Rock appropriately.

Little Armando's brow creased in thought and then he laughed. "Yes, precisely!"

Rodriguez brought the drinks round to the table on a small platter.

Little Armando held his glass up to the light. "But a well

made *caipirinha* is a work of art. To your health and success, my friends."

Tony drank and stifled a violent cough. Rock quickly dismissed half his glass without so much as a blink. Even the armed bodyguards were drinking. Booze and guns, what could be wrong with that?

Two drinks and fifteen minutes of small talk later, Little Armando raised a question. "Your show with Luis Angel in the park is scheduled for Monday afternoon. When will your next rehearsal be, Tony?"

"I'm not certain. I was asking Luis that question myself earlier today. Why?" Tony couldn't imagine what the dangerous looking man's interest might be.

Little Armando swirled his drink. "I wouldn't want Luis' show to be put—how should I say—to any trouble."

"Why should there be any trouble?"

Rock waved for another drink and Rodriguez obliged. He'd unzipped his overalls to reveal a pair of grey wool slacks and a black polo shirt.

"Precisely," agreed Little Armando, though to what Tony couldn't imagine. "Why should there be any trouble? Luis is one of our own."

"What do you mean?"

"He is Brazilian and a *carioca,* like his father. It would be disgraceful if they were not treated with the respect they deserve. . .they've earned."

"Of course," said Tony. "Believe me, I am very respectful—"

"I know this, Tony. So," his fingers drummed the cherry wood, "this is what we must do." He glanced from Rock to Tony.

Tony interrupted. "About Yairi, shouldn't he be here?"

Little Armando said several sharp words to Rodriguez who gestured with his hands and spoke in placating tones. "I'm afraid Yairi has been detained."

"Don't worry," Victor said with a liquor induced slur, "everything is under control."

Tony gave Rock a look. Rock's look was glazed. What was going on?

"As I said, here is what we must do." Little Armando leaned across the table as he spoke. "The concert in the park is at three o'clock. Over at five. In time for Luis to attend the Sambadrome, no doubt."

Tony nodded. He expected his boss would probably be at the event both nights, after all, he said he was a judge.

"He will be done with the equipment then." He snapped his fingers and Victor produced a small vial which he handed to his brother. Little Armando handed the tiny glass bottle to Tony.

Tony shook it.

Little Armando grabbed his hand. "Be careful. That's acid."

"Acid?" Tony dropped the vial on the table top. Gasps were heard around the room. "Sorry." Tony gingerly picked up the vial and rubbed the polished wood. "No harm done."

Rock was looking at the bottle in Tony's hand. He set down his third empty glass. "What are we supposed to do with that shit?"

"Pour just a little on the console."

"Huh?" Rock scratched his head.

Tony felt like mimicking him but refrained.

"The Four-Star-STA," Victor said.

"What for?" Tony said, his voice constricted.

"Don't worry," explained Little Armando. "It is not so strong. It's just good enough to make it look bad." He laughed at his own little joke. "Like a short circuit. Then we will take it for repairs, no?"

Tony looked at Rodriguez who was grinning. He turned to Little Armando. A trail of sweat had formed down the back of his neck. "You're joking?"

Victor tossed a stack of bills on the table. "Ten thousand dollars American."

"On delivery. All you have to do is make sure your crew loads the mixing board onto our truck for service. It won't be any trouble. Everyone is getting paid something for his trouble and Luis can have a replacement board sent in by plane in time for his next show in Brasilia."

"I don't know. . ." began Tony. They were asking him to help rip off his new boss. That mixing board was worth over a half million dollars! And, with the heady import duties that the Brazilian government imposed, that was one expensive board. No doubt Little Armando and Victor were fences and probably already had a buyer lined up for the big ticket item. It wasn't like they had any use for it themselves.

Little Armando's face turned ugly. Not that it was pretty to begin with. His lone eye grew large and pulsed like a star about to go nova. "You are not going back on our arrangement, are you, *Senhor* Kozol?"

Rock gripped Tony's arm and whispered. "What the hell is going on? What have you gotten us into?"

The two guards, though they might not have understood the words, understood their boss's emotions and stood nearer the table.

"Tony, Tony." Rodriguez rose and picked up the money. Little Armando nodded. Rodriguez cut the pile in two and pushed half in Tony and Rock's direction. "Half up front. You see? We are honest business men."

"With all due respect," Rock put in, "we can't take your money, Mr. Armando, sir."

Little Armando leaned back in his chair. The wooden back creaked and threatened to break. He banged his glass on the table. "I'm afraid I must insist."

Tony felt his tongue go dry. His heart pounded in his chest. This was not good.

There was a shout from below, a woman's scream. The

pounding music came to a halt. More screams, this time it sounded like men shouting.

Rodriguez ran out the door to the balcony.

Shots were fired and more women's screamed filled the hall. Little Armando and Victor began shouting as one and the two guards raced out and down the stairs, pistols drawn. Little Armando and his brother were right behind them, but not so close as to be in any danger themselves.

"Those idiots, João and Leon!" Rodriguez exclaimed. "They've finally done it. Leon has shot the cuckold bastard!"

Tony whispered, "Let's go, Rock."

"What?"

Tony gestured to the far door. "That way. Out the door."

"Are you insane? You don't even know where it leads—"

"Maybe not," said Tony, "but it sure as hell beats staying here because here isn't going to lead anyplace good. I'm for taking our chances."

"I don't know," drawled Rock, skeptically.

"Come on," urged Tony. "We don't have much time. They'll all be back any minute." Tony rose on cane spirits weakened legs. "Come on."

Rock pushed himself up from the table and nodded. They raced to the door, flung it open and bolted down the steep, nearly vertical stairway. Rock had shut the door behind them and they stumbled downwards in darkness.

"Fuck!" cursed Rock as he tripped and banged his forehead against the wall.

"Quiet!" warned Tony. Then he cursed himself as he crashed into another wall.

Rock slammed into his backside. "What did you stop for?"

"End of the line." Tony's hand explored the wall. "No, it's a door! Help me find the handle."

"Got it," exclaimed Rock. He twisted and pulled.

"Slowly," cautioned Tony. "We don't know who's out there."

Rock cracked open the door and Tony stuck his head out. Kozol whispered, "I'll take a peek."

A face, the color of a dark chocolate bar left overnight in the fridge, peeked back.

Tony howled in surprise and slammed the door shut with his back. Breathing heavily, he said, "There's somebody out there."

There were shouts from above. Rodriguez was calling their names and now he was calling for Little Armando.

"We have to make a choice and quick," Tony said.

"Your call."

Tony nodded. He opened the door. The face was still there. Only now he realized it was attached to a young girl in a thin, red dress. Her feet were bare and her long black hair hung loosely across her slender shoulders. Sharp bangs fell from her forehead. She looked at them in puzzlement then smiled.

Tony held a finger to his lips and hoped the gesture meant the same thing in Brazil as it did back home. "Come on, Rock."

They stepped out into the dying light. The sun was setting over the mountain that still rose above them. The horizon reflected the zenith of the *favela*.

The young girl, probably no more than ten, skipped ahead, turned and beckoned Tony and Rock.

"Which way?" Rock said softly.

Tony looked up and down. They were in a narrow dirt surfaced alley. Raw sewage wormed its way down the mountain, clinging to the edges of the makeshift buildings. Children were playing, splashing through the waste as though unmindful of it.

Several people hurried up and down. The tiny roads went in every direction, an unplanned maze of confusion.

And danger.

The girl had gone further down a slender path that led

sideways along the mountain.

Pounding on the stairs behind meant only one thing. . .

"Run!" Tony ran after the girl, who was skipping away, turning her head in their direction every couple of moments as if to be sure they were following.

Tony leaned against the building and huffed. He was winded and scared. By his reckoning, they'd been running for ten minutes or so. The girl had stopped to pet a skinny gray mongrel with patchy fur. "We've got to get away from here, Rock."

Rock, crouching and out of breath himself, concurred. "But how? Do you even know where we are? For all I know, we could have been running in circles. All these houses look the same!"

Tony nodded nervously. The sun was over the mountain now, on its way toward the Andes, to brighten someone else's day. While he and Rock were trapped in the *favela*.

At night.

"Can't you ask that kid for directions?"

The sour look Tony gave his companion was barely visible yet clear. "Call me a pessimist, but something tells me that girl doesn't speak English."

"Oh, yeah," said Rock, scratching his head. "I almost forgot."

An unshod boy, no more than five years old, passed by, said something to the girl then turned off. Tony was stunned that a young child would be left alone on the streets of the *favela* at night. Where were his parents?

The young girl shooed the dog away and motioned for the two men to follow. She turned to the left as the boy had moments before.

Tony and Rock groaned in unison and slowly went after her.

"Uh-oh," said Rock.

Tony's hair stood on end. Motionless, he studied the band of desperate looking boys facing them. They varied in age from five to twenty, he'd guess. Several had knives. The younger boys had sticks. Some were sandaled. Half were shirtless.

A disquieting number had automatic weapons.

Tony counted at least fifteen faces, including that of the little boy he'd felt sorry for only a minute ago.

And not one smile.

Except for the girl who'd led them there and she was saying something now to the tallest.

This boy had a sloping forehead and deep-set, cunning eyes. He wore a yellow and green striped t-shirt and loose black shorts. He was barefoot and appeared to carry no weapon. His muscles were long and sinewy. He listened, nodded and stepped forward.

Tony risked a look back. The band had formed an arc sharp as a scythe. If they tried to run, no doubt they'd be cut off.

The girl had set them up.

6

"*Quem é você*?" The boy was looking at Rock.

"What's he saying?" Rock muttered in confusion.

"He wants to know who you are."

"Oh, why didn't he just say so?" Rock smiled. "I'm Rock."

The boy's eyes narrowed.

Rock said, "Who are you?"

The boy chewed his lip. "You are American."

"That's right," Tony answered. "I'm Tony." Thank god the kid spoke English.

"What are you doing at Fat Armando's?"

Fat Armando? It seemed the boy was no fan of the one-eyed man. And now that Tony knew the guy better as a one-eyed bandit, he wasn't so fond of the man himself. He struggled to find the right answer. The answer that would please this boy and not get him a knife in the stomach. "Rodriguez brought us there."

"Why?"

"We thought we were going to see a friend of mine. Instead, Little Armando—Fat Armando—asked us to do something and we left." Tony and Rock stood side to side, watching the boys who circled them like half-starved vultures.

"You ran?"

Tony shrugged. "We needed to get away."

The youth seemed to consider this. "Who was this friend you thought you would see?"

"Alvarez Yairi."

"This name means nothing to me." He shouted some words in Portuguese and the boys headed up the street. "Come."

The little girl who'd led them there smiled at Tony and skipped away with the boys.

The house they were taken to could only be described as a fortress. The walls were thick and barred with heavy iron. The door was nearly as dense as the walls themselves. And the room was crammed with cocaine.

In plain sight.

"Sit." The youth flopped down on a dirty mattress against the far wall. Several of his cohorts came into the room while many more of the them stood guard outside.

Rock and Tony sat on the floor. There was a big screen television set on the opposite wall. They were watching *Baywatch* without the sound. Tony wondered what these impoverished youths made of such a world when even to him such a life, especially now, seemed impossible.

A preteen, with a pistol twice the size of his hand, shouted to two young women in the small kitchen in the rear. One of the girls hollered back and gripped a cast iron pan. She dropped it onto a stovetop burner. Seconds later, a cloud of burning lard spread from the kitchen, dancing into the low ceilinged room. Kozol's stomach turned upside down and inside out.

"You will be my guests for the night."

Tony started to protest then thought better of it. A rack of weapons attached to the wall above the mattress, including ugly looking machine guns seemed to argue against this.

"I am Candino. Tell me what you saw at Fat Armando's."

The youth lit a hand-rolled cigarette and inhaled deeply.

Tony and Rock repeated their steps. There wasn't much to tell and Candino appeared bored. "In the morning, one of my boys will lead you down to the highway. You will not come here again."

Tony nodded. You couldn't have dragged him back up that mountain. Young girls brought food and drink. None too tasty, but all filling. They slept on the bare floor.

Tony dreamed he was being chased by Silvia's uncle. The crazy old brute was shooting at him. Tony tossed and awoke with a start. It was hot in the room though the small flame that had been flickering in the corner fireplace was out.

He heard shots and shouting.

The fortress was under attack. Candino and his men burst out the door guns ablaze with flashes of tiny fire.

Rock and Tony clung to the floor. Bullets ricocheted off the concrete walls. The door off the kitchen flew open and a man decked out in olive drab, military style clothing jumped in waving a machine gun. He was masked.

He grabbed Tony and pulled him up. "*Vamos*!"

Tony struggled. Rock grabbed for the gun.

"Stop!" The man pointed his weapon at Tony's chest. "Look." He pulled off his ski cap.

"Yairi!"

A boy leapt into the open doorway. Yairi fired. The boy cried and fell back into the street. Yairi ran through the kitchen. "Follow me!"

Tony and Rock wasted no time.

They wound round and round like tiny figures on a giant surreal clock face. The sounds of fighting grew distant then faded altogether.

Tony wondered whether even Yairi knew what he was doing or where he was going. The streets were deserted. There were no lights in the houses. But then, these houses often had no electricity except that which had been illegally hooked up, stolen from the power companies.

Yairi grabbed Tony by the shoulder. "In here." He pulled open a broad metal door. It was a garage and Yairi's Bugre was inside.

Tony jumped in on the passenger's side. Yairi laid his machine gun across the dash and stuck his key in the ignition.

"Oh, no you don't." Rock refused to get in.

"What's wrong?"

"Yes, we must go, my friend," urged Yairi.

"I called shotgun, remember?"

"Rock—"

His friend's face was unmoving. "Oh, all right." Tony climbed over and sat on the rear end. There was no backseat. "Let's get out of here."

They literally hurled through the slum and down the steep mountain. The streets, such as they were, were empty. Some were so narrow it looked to Tony as if they'd have to turn the Bugre on its side to squeeze through, but Yairi never slowed down to even consider this eventuality.

It was a good thing there were no pedestrians, Tony figured, because Yairi didn't seem to be in a slowing, let alone stopping, mood. It was all Tony could do to hold onto the vehicle by his fingertips to keep from being thrown clear himself.

The Bugre bounced over a downed chain link fence and into the highway. The vehicle only came to a stop as Yairi jumped the curb at an outdoor cafe across the street from the beaches of Leblon.

Before Tony could open his mouth, Yairi had jumped out and started screaming. First in Brazilian Portuguese, then in English.

A waiter, pretending not to notice the machine gun on the dashboard, gestured to a nearby table protected from the rising sun by a sturdy red umbrella. They were the first customers of the morning.

"What the fuck were you guys thinking going in there like that?" Yairi yanked out a chair and set his foot atop it, nearly kicking out its wicker bottom. "You trying to get killed?"

Rock sank into his chair.

Tony rubbed his neck. "We were trying to find you. Luis was looking for you. Said he needed you."

"Bah, that spoiled little brat needs a good spanking. And that's all he needs."

Tony couldn't disagree with Yairi there. "Rock and I went to your apartment and you were gone. And your phone disconnected."

"So the fuck what? I moved. Big deal." Yairi ordered three coffees, *café com leite*. "You smart boys decided to go looking for me in a slum! You think I moved to a stinking slum?!" Yairi grinned madly, exposing his uneven, butter colored teeth.

"No. Rodriguez thought— "

"Rodriguez thought," scoffed Yairi. "Rodriguez can't think. You guys better stay in town if you know what's good for you. You let me deal with Little Armando and his *malandros*."

"*Malandros*?" Rock said, dropping clumps of hard sugar into his coffee.

"Layabouts, crooks," Yairi said.

"Are you one of Little Armando's *malandros*?"

The expression on Yairi's face turned ugly. He leaned into Tony's face. "I am Alvarez Yairi. I am my own boss." He thumped his chest with his finger. "But I do what I have to do to survive. This is Brazil, not fucking America. It's not easy to eat always. You saw those slums."

"Come on, you two, relax. You're drawing attention." Rock looked pointedly towards the interior of the cafe/restaurant where a small group of waiters was staring out at them.

The two men eyed one another then sat.

Tony tested his own coffee. "Little Armando wants us to help him steal some equipment from Luis Angel."

Yairi said unblinkingly, "Then I suggest you do it."

"No way," Tony replied.

"Little Armando will be disappointed."

"How disappointed?" Tony asked.

Rodriguez made a sad clown's face. "Very disappointed."

"Just exactly who is this Little Armando?" Rock asked.

Rodriguez finished his coffee and demanded a second. He ordered a plate of sweet rolls. "Little Armando and his brother Victor are animal bankers."

"Animal bankers?" Tony had visions of seedy *favela* banks where people came to deposit goats and withdraw sheep.

"I will explain." Yairi masticated his pastry as he spoke. "At the end of Empire, in 1889 or so, the Baron Joao Batista Drummond lost his royal subsidy for the private zoo he'd built near the Emperor's Palace. Though private, the Baron was quite proud of his zoo and it was open to all. But, maintaining a zoo is quite expensive. What was the Baron to do?"

Yairi looked to Rock and Tony for the answer. They had none and Yairi continued. "As good fortune would have it, the Baron met a Mexican adventurer. This man sold him the rights to a lottery game he had invented, or so he claimed. In this game, individual types of flowers were assigned specific numerical values.

"The Baron, a quite intelligent man, realized that by substituting pictures of animals for flowers he might raise money for his zoo. The game became wildly successful as a form of lottery. The animals themselves fit into the typical Brazilian's belief system. After all, the animals represent Gods and belief in numerology is also quite strong. The Baron had hit upon a winning formula—the *jogo do bicho*."

"I still don't get it," Rock complained, stuffing a sweet roll in his mouth.

"The lottery grew, particularly in the slums. It is cheap and proliferated among the masses. The strong and quick-witted grew rich. The animal bankers became the first elite of the *favelas*. It is similar to numbers running in the United States, no?"

"I suppose," agreed Tony. "And these guys also run the other rackets then, like heisting expensive PA equipment?"

"Yes, exactly."

"Isn't all this illegal?"

"The government declared the animal lottery illegal in 1946 but it is as popular as ever. Besides, the animal bankers were the first to contribute large amounts of capital and resources to the samba schools. So you see, the animal bankers were also quite generous social benefactors."

"And you approve?" Tony asked his friend.

"It is a way of life. I need not approve nor disapprove."

Rock asked, "And where does Candino fit into all this?"

"Who?"

"The kid running the gang that you rescued us from."

"Oh," Yairi said. He waved to the waiter, said something in Portuguese and was presented with a bill. "So that was his name. This boy is a drug dealer. Quite a small gang really. The largest gang on the hill is Celso Frota's group. They've controlled most of the drug action in the *favela* for the past five years. Candino must be making a play for his territory. He won't have long to live."

The unsympathetic words sent a chill up Kozol's back. "Why do you say that?"

"The drug dealer's life is a good one, but a short one," grinned Yairi. "Between wars with other opportunistic drug dealers and wars with the animal bankers for control, one cannot survive long."

"Little Armando seems to be surviving," Tony noted.

"Yes," Yairi agreed somberly. "That is why it is best not to cross him. He is very stern and very resourceful. It is with his help that we found you last night."

"I was wondering about that," Rock said.

Yairi's laugh carried through the cafe which had been slowly filling; groups of businessmen mingled with half awake, brightly dressed tourists and energetic joggers in tight fitting shorts. "Two white men in the *favela* at night? Anyone could have found you! My two year old niece could have found you!"

Yairi lowered his voice. "When Little Armando explained to me what had happened, we went looking for you at once. Everyone in the *favela* was talking about you and so you were easy to uncover."

"And here I thought nobody was paying attention," Tony said.

"Even when no one appears to be paying attention, the eyes are watching." Yairi tapped his eyelids. "Little Armando's men were only too happy to shoot up Candino's little place—he and his brother despise the drug dealers—and so help rescue you. All the more reason that you owe him."

"Even after we ran out on him?"

Yairi waved a hand in the air. "Don't worry. I heard about the shooting in the samba hall. I explained to Little Armando that you must have been spooked and ran."

"And he bought it?"

"I admit, he was skeptical at first. But I reminded him that you were not born to the *favela* and that you are merely musicians from America. Then he understood."

Tony glowered at the obvious insult, true though it was. "There is still no way I can help him steal that console. It's illegal and immoral. I don't know about Rock, but I don't feel like doing time in a Brazilian penitentiary. And what would Luis think if he knew?"

Yairi smiled. "Ask him if you like. He is no fool. Luis will not mind. Why should he? Insurance buys him a new board and he makes Little Armando happy."

"This is crazy."

"For your own safety, it would be unwise to refuse."

Frustrated at finding no clear way out of this definitely illegal and potentially lethal mess, Tony asked, "But why us?"

"Little Armando had made an arrangement with Luis Angel's previous guitar player. He assumes you will abide by this arrangement."

"Why, just because I was hired to replace him?"

Yairi shrugged. "It seems so."

Rock cleared his throat. "There is one other problem, Tony."

Tony glowered at his companion. "What's that?"

Rock reached into his pocket and carefully laid a stack of bills on the table.

"That's Little Armando's money!" Tony cried hoarsely.

"Yeah," Rock said apologetically.

"But what are you doing with it? And cover it up for chrissakes!" Tony picked up his dirty napkin and dropped it over the wad.

"I don't know. I mean, Rodriguez had laid it there on the table in front of us. . . and then there were the gunshots. And they ran off and you said to hurry up and—I don't know—I just grabbed the money and ran!"

Tony held his head in his hands and groaned.

7

Yairi squeezed his old Bugre up to the front entrance of the Ipanema Palace Hotel gaining sour looks from the doormen.

Rock climbed out the passenger's side.

Tony hopped off the back. Before Yairi could back up, Kozol laid a hand on his shoulder. "Get out."

"What?"

"I said get out."

"What for?"

"Because I'm taking the Bugre and I'm going to the beach."

"What?" Yairi looked confused. "The beach is only steps away." He pointed across the street.

Tony shook his head no. "I'm going to get my girlfriend. I'm going to have a real breakfast. Maybe take a real bath and I'm going to the beach and I'm too damn tired to walk and way beyond too tired to talk about it." He jerked his thumb. "Out."

Yairi looked at Rock for help but Rock was laughing.

Yairi grumbled. "You don't even have license to drive in Brazil."

"I don't have a license to commit grand theft either—that

doesn't seem to present anybody here with a problem."

"Oh, alright." Yairi climbed over the side. "But be careful. This car is a classic!"

Tony waved. "Later, Rock!" He handed Yairi his machine gun which was conveniently wrapped in the tablecloth Yairi had ripped off from the cafe.

Rock saluted. Yairi crossed his arms, cradling his loaded firearm, and fumed.

For what it was worth, the little vehicle handled well. Though it could have used new springs. Assuming it had any springs at all. Tony glanced at the gauges. At least there was enough fuel.

Tony whizzed up the streets to Silvia's house, his hair flying in the breeze.

For once it felt good to be alive.

Tony found a free spot just big enough for the Bugre in the shade of a tree right near Silvia's home. He didn't have his watch and hoped he wasn't waking her. A young woman, shopping bag in hand, smiled. He smiled back and rang the buzzer. A moment later the lock released and Tony pushed open the gate.

He took the stairs two at a time and knocked thrice.

Silvia opened the door. She was wearing loose pajamas the color of a robin's egg. "Tony, it's you!"

"Yes, of course it's me." He kissed her smooth cheek. "Who were you expecting?"

Silvia ran a hand vainly through her tussled hair. "No one." She held the door open and glanced down the steps. Lennon and McCartney sniffed his shoes.

"I smell, don't I?" Tony suddenly realized. His clothes were filthy as well. Dodging bullets and sleeping in the dirt could do that to a body.

Silvia smiled and waved her hand in front of her nose. "Really? I hadn't noticed."

"Very funny."

Silvia shut the door.

"Glad to see you got your door fixed. Though you shouldn't let up just anybody that rings at the gate."

"You're right. It's early. I wasn't thinking. Mother got one of the neighbors to repair the door. He is a handyman."

Tony ran a hand along the doorframe. "He did a nice job." He ran his hand along Silvia's side. "Your mother did a nice job on you, too."

Silvia leaned forward to kiss him. Tony pulled his head away. "I haven't brushed my teeth either. If you think my clothes stink—"

"I'll take my chances." She kissed him. When their mouth wrestling ended and they came up for air, Silvia said, "So, you are like a magician, no?"

"What do you mean?"

"Always appearing and disappearing." She put her hands on her hips. "You didn't call me all yesterday afternoon."

Tony's shoulders sunk.

"You stood me up for dinner."

His back curved. "Sorry, Silvia." Tony took her hands. "Something came up. I couldn't get away." Literally.

Silvia looked skeptical.

"Come on. It's a beautiful day. I'm going to make it up to you!"

She glanced at the clock by her bedside. "I don't know, baby, I had plans. . ."

"What plans? Come on."

"But I promised mother I would go shopping. She's expecting me—"

"So? You can go shopping some other time."

"But what will we do?"

"We're going to the beach," Tony explained. "But first, we are going ring shopping."

"Ring shopping? I don't understand. . ."

"For your engagement ring."

"Oh, Tony," Silvia laid her hands around Tony's neck and sobbed.

He patted her behind. "Get dressed and I'll take a quick rinse."

She nodded, kissed his swollen lips and went to the wardrobe. Tony bathed quickly, brushed his teeth and shook as much dirt out of his shoes and clothes as he could manage.

"Here." Silvia handed Tony a large white t-shirt. "I sleep in it sometimes. It will fit you?" Silvia herself had put on a pink floral dress, through which Tony could make out a bright yellow bikini, and slipped into a pair of open-toed white sandals. Her hair smelled of strawberries and watermelon.

Tony tossed his dirty shirt in the corner and pulled the fresh one over his head. "Perfect. Let's go."

She ran a hairbrush through her tresses, tossed it on the counter, checked his wound, pronounced it clean and healing well. "Okay, I'm ready."

Tony squeezed her hand.

Silvia opened the apartment door, holding Lennon and McCartney at bay with her foot.

"Wait," said Tony, "shouldn't you tell your mother you're coming with me?"

Silvia bit her lip. "I know. I'll leave her a note. That way she will not be able to argue." The young woman drew a small sheet of white paper from a pad near the telephone and wrote a short note at the kitchen table. She folded it carefully in four pieces and tucked it into the edge of the door as they left.

"My car is in the garage." Silvia drove a green Fiat.

"Forget it," Tony said, dangling Yairi's key. He pointed at the curb.

"Not that?" Silvia laughed.

"Why not? Climb in." He helped her over the side. "I thought we could hit the R. Holland store to pick out your ring," Tony said above the whining of the engine and blowing of the wind.

"R. Holland? Oh no, Tony. That's really quite expensive. They cater to the tourists."

The jewelry business, Tony quickly learned as Silvia tutored him, was huge in Brazil, most notably its gem industry and R. Holland was one of the leading firms with a large building in downtown Ipanema and smaller stores throughout the city, the country and even the world. They even had small branches in the major hotels like the Ipanema Palace Hotel where he was being put up by Luis Angel.

Brightly polished, precious stones filled the windows of countless stores. Rio de Janeiro was an earthly paradise of gems—emeralds, opals, aquamarine, topaz, tourmaline and rubies, and that wasn't all.

"So what do you suggest?"

"Well, if you are serious?" She looked up at him with loving eyes.

"Of course, I'm serious." He leaned over and kissed her nose.

"Watch out!" she cried, hanging onto the side of the buggy as Tony avoided a faster taxi cutting in his path. "I have a cousin in the Centro district. I'm certain she would give us a discount."

Tony beamed. "Then lead on."

Tony followed his lover's directions up through Copacabana to the central business district of Rio. "I don't know," exclaimed Tony as he drove up a wide street notable for closed up shops. "Are you sure she'll be open?"

"Many proprietors close for Carnaval but Giselle will be open. She never closes."

Sure enough, the Galeria Giselle was open for business.

Silvia was greeted by a slender young woman in her early thirties dressed fashionably in a solid green silk dress and matching high heel shoes who was just seeing off a customer.

She wore a dazzling ruby necklace. But then, Tony figured she could afford to, after all it was her store. The two women hugged, exchanged giggles in Portuguese then broke into English.

"So, I am pleased to meet you, Tony."

"You, too. You must be Giselle." He held out his hand and the jeweler shook it warmly.

"Yes, I am."

"I'm glad you speak English."

"In my business it is necessary to speak at least a little of many languages."

Tony nodded his understanding.

Giselle, with a slender face, large pale green eyes and skin the color of cinnamon bark, smiled and took her cousin's hands. "You are to be married. How wonderful."

Silvia trembled and beamed, a tiny tear aching to form at the corner of her eye.

"Come," said Giselle, "I'll show you some quite nice rings." She turned to Tony who followed at a distance, as he slowly wandered towards the back of the narrow jeweler's; admiring glass case after glass case filled with exquisite pieces. "Do you have a particular budget in mind?"

This was the hard part. "Money is no object," Tony declared, pulling his last credit card from the pocket of his grungy shorts—the one he'd kept in his safe at the hotel and that the mugger hadn't gotten hold of. "The sky is the limit. The sky being the three thousand dollar limit on my MasterCard."

Giselle grinned.

Silvia watched her cousin expectantly.

"Don't worry, Silvia," she said calmly, "we will find just the ring for you."

Tony drifted off on a red velvet stool as the two women drifted into Portuguese, no doubt discussing the finer points of what appeared to be an endless supply of diamond rings.

Every so often Silvia would nudge him to ask him what he thought.

As his lover held out her hand, displaying a smallish diamond on a slender band, Tony said, "That one." He pointed to a glass display case containing a number of diamond rings, earrings and bracelets; part of some designer's collection. One ring toward the center kept drawing his eye. Even to his untrained and probably untrainable eye, it looked great.

"What, baby?" She handed the little ring back to her cousin.

"That one." He pressed his finger down on the glass.

Giselle's lips puckered awkwardly. "Yes, it is quite lovely, but—"

"Let's take a look at it."

"Okay," Silvia agreed.

Giselle unlocked the glass cabinet and placed the ring on her cousin's finger. It is a little loose." She twisted the ring in place. The big diamond glowed like a magic stone.

"It is beautiful. . ." Silvia said wistfully.

"Yes," began Giselle, "but it is a bit more expensive than the others we have been looking at."

"How much?"

"About twelve thousand. It's one of my best stones."

Silvia gasped.

"*Reais*?" Tony asked hopefully.

Giselle shook her head no. "Dollars." She pulled a book from behind the counter and her finger ran down a page to a figure. "You see? Normally, it is twenty thousand. I've given as generous a discount as I can manage. I'm afraid I can't go any lower. This is my cost." She looked as disappointed as Silvia.

"It is lovely," Silvia said, pulling off the ring, "but I'm afraid it's out of the question."

Tony said, "We'll take it."

"What?" cried Silvia. "What are you saying, baby? We haven't enough. Let me look at that one again. The—"

Tony leapt from his stool and turned to Giselle. "I'll give you all I've got left on my credit card. And. . .I don't know. Somehow I will get the rest!"

Giselle twisted the ring in her fingers, mimicking the wheels of her brain, as the gears turned inside her head. "I will charge fifteen hundred dollars to your credit card, Tony. After all, you mustn't be left with nothing."

"But what about the rest?" Silvia wanted to know.

"We will arrange a payment plan." She smiled in Tony's direction. "This is acceptable, no?"

Tony signed the papers.

Lunch was spread across a green blanket on the hot sands of Copacabana Beach across from the Copacabana Palace Hotel, a majestic inn built in the Nineteen Thirties for the visiting King of Belgium. A half dozen energetic soccer matches went on around them. Men in too-small bathing suits did pull-ups on the free chin-up bars, as intent on showing off their muscles as the girls were in showing off their own unique assets. Orange suited street cleaners kept the beach sidewalk reasonably clean.

Tony savored Silvia's bikini clad form more than he did the food. He joined her in the ocean only to feel the sting of salt water in his head wound, forcing him to retreat. Silvia gently washed away the salt with a bottle of water purchased from one of the ubiquitous vendors.

They watched a slender young man with long straggly black hair sculpt life-size nude figures, male and female, out of golden brown sand. A tiny cardboard box solicited contributions from 'lovers of beauty' as Silvia translated. Tony dropped in a *real*.

Dark clouds threatening to cast an afternoon shower upon the young lovers drove them to the Bugre and the safety of

Silvia's house. Lennon and McCartney were in the yard. Mrs. Parra was cooking in the downstairs kitchen and could be seen and smelled from the steps leading to Silvia's upstairs apartment.

Silvia led Tony to bed but they didn't sleep. And finally, Tony was forced to leave.

He groaned as he rose from the bed and pulled on his clothes. "Sorry," he said again. "But Luis is expecting Rock and I. He invited us, after all. I can't afford to refuse."

"Yes, you poor boys. A night in the Sambadromo watching the schools parade and the naked women. I should feel sorry for you."

Tony kissed her lips for the thousandth time that afternoon. "I'd rather be with you."

Silvia smiled. "I know that. Otherwise I'd never let you go. My sister, Tzininha, will be there also. Though I doubt you will spot her among the crowd. Wave if you do." She pouted. "I wish I did not have to work." Silvia rubbed her ring finger; the spot where her new ring would soon rest.

As if reading her mind, Tony said, "Giselle promised your engagement ring would be sized tomorrow and delivered by the day after tomorrow."

"I know." She stood on tiptoes and kissed Tony on the forehead. "It is so expensive. You are a crazy American!"

"Crazy in love." He turned to go. "And remember, we keep our engagement a secret until Tuesday."

She nodded.

"We'll have a big dinner at the finest restaurant in town. You pick the place. And we'll invite everyone—Rock, Yairi, Luis, your mother, your uncle—"

"My. . .uncle?"

Tony beamed from ear to ear. "Yeah, what the heck, everybody! We have a saying in America, 'Let bygones be bygones.'" He lifted her off her feet, kissed her deeply and let her go. "I'll see you in the morning."

Rock was sitting in the lobby reading the International Miami Herald, the only English language newspaper around. He tossed it down on the sofa as Tony swung through the door. Rock was wearing a pair of blue jean shorts with one of the complimentary Carnaval t-shirts that the hotel had given to the guests. It bore the name of the hotel, within the green borders of Brazil. There was a likeness of Vasco da Gama, the Portuguese explorer and navigator, an old sailing ship, presumably Vasco's, a rendition of a purple sequined woman with her golden hair tied up over her head and spouting down like a fountain, dancing atop a float decorated with animal images. "Where the hell have you been?"

The lobby was crowded with fancy folk in their evening wear dressed for a night on the town at the height of Carnaval. Many wore exotic costumes. The pianist was playing *Garota de Ipanema— The Girl From Ipanema.* It was only about the hundredth time he'd heard her cover the Tom Jobim and Vinicius de Moraes penned tune since he'd been staying at the Ipanema Palace Hotel.

Tony felt sorry for the woman. It reminded him of all those piano players stuck in piano bars in the United States forced to play Billy Joel's *Piano Man* ad infinitum. Not that it was a bad song but how many times a night could a person stand to perform the same song? A friend of his had once quit the business, having gone berserk in a nightclub in Key West one night when the fourteenth drunken patron of the night stumbled in off Duval Street, tossed a buck in his snifter and demanded to hear Piano Man.

His friend, Mike, lifted the glass snifter smashed it against the keys several times in succession and said, with fragments flying everywhere, "That's the chorus. If you want to hear more give me a twenty and I'll play a verse on your goddam ass."

The frightened patron left through the front door and Mike soon left through the back never to be seen again. Last

Tony heard, he was a struggling songwriter giving music lessons out of his house trailer.

"I was with Silvia. Relax. We've got plenty of time."

Rock shook his head in the negative. "Luis and his entourage left in their limo an hour ago. You're late."

"What do you mean?" He grabbed Rock's wrist and looked at his watch. "It's just quarter till six now."

"Yeah, and we were supposed to leave at five."

"Damn. Was he mad?"

Rock made his 'have you got to ask?' face. "Oh, and Yairi has been looking for you."

"Speak of the devil. Yairi!" Tony waved in the direction of the reception desk.

Yairi said something to the clerk and hurried over. "There you are! I've been asking for you. Did you bring back the Bugre?"

"No, I sold it on the black market."

Yairi scowled. "Not even funny." He looked at both men. "So, Rock says you are off to the *Sambadromo*."

"We were. It seems we've missed our ride. You should've gone on, Rock."

"What? Without my *compadre*?"

"Not to worry, gentlemen. Yairi to the rescue. I am going to the *Sambadromo* myself. We will go all together."

"I call shotgun!" Tony and Rock shouted in unison.

Rock squeezed his feet between Tony and Yairi. "Avenida Atlantica is blocked off," noticed Tony. "We'll never get to the *Sambadromo*."

"Yes, the police have shut it down for the night."

A huge crowd was gathering along the beach and spilling out into the road. A wide truck with a railing along the top blared samba from huge speakers. Near naked girls danced on top.

"Don't worry," said Yairi, driving up the sidewalk and

cursing at slow moving pedestrians. He nudged several of the slowest moving, or more obstinate, along with his front bumper. "We'll take the back streets."

"I'd just be happy if you took the streets," complained Rock, struggling to maintain hold.

Soon enough, Yairi did. He swept past cars and buses and even, to Tony's chagrin, police cars. They drove through a long tunnel and came out in a part of town Tony didn't recognize.

Ignoring the shouts of security men and women, Yairi drove up to a covered entrance, pressed the Bugre between a couple of dumpsters, pocketed the key and hopped out. "We'll go in here."

Tony paused and listened to the loud music coming from within. "Sounds like it's already started."

Rock handed Tony his pass and they approached the security checkpoint. A red carpeted trail led from the street to the entrance of the stadium. The thirty-eight meter tall statue of Christ the Redeemer rose in the distance atop mighty *Morro do Corcovado*, one of Rio's most famous hills.

A harried looking woman with a turned up nose and a horse shaped head looked at their passes, then Yairi's. She started complaining in Portuguese. Yairi pulled her to the side. A moment later, Yairi led them through.

"This is called the tourist section," he explained heading up a short flight of stairs. "Lots of tables and a pretty good view." He pointed overhead and then across the way. "Later, we'll check out the boxes. That's where many of the local rich watch. The bleachers," he added, disparagingly, "are for the masses."

"I'm ready to check out the boxes now," Rock said.

"Why?" Tony asked.

"I can think of at least a dozen reasons. Look." Rock pointed up to the first booth to the right. A row of topless young Brazilian beauties were swaying to the beat. Cameras flashed furiously in their direction. The girls smiled and waved. Rock waved too.

Yairi slapped Rock on the back. "Welcome to *Carnaval*, my friends!"

Yairi led them to a table and ordered a round of Kaiser beers from a passing hostess.

Tony watched in awe as hundreds of dancers, in a swirl of green and pink, swept along the parade track, caught between two huge floats which were themselves nearly three stories tall. Dancers were perched up and down on the floats as well, in various stages of dress and undress.

"That's *Mangueira,*" Yairi said. "One of the biggest schools."

The parade track was 700 meters in length and every inch of it was full. Each samba school boasted thousands of members, including up to four hundred drummers and as many as half a dozen elaborate floats.

Rio's sixteen top samba schools took two nights to pass through the Oscar Niemeyer designed *Sambadromo* before an audience of over sixty thousand, chanting, dancing fans. The schools were so long and the stories they told so elaborate that it took about an hour and a half for each school to march from one end of the otherwise austere stadium to the other.

The rest of the year, so Tony had been told, the *Sambadromo* served as a public school. It had been constructed in 1984. Before that, the samba schools paraded along the wide avenues of downtown Rio, creating awe and excitement, as much as havoc and congestion. The *Sambadromo,* built on *Rua Marqués de Sepucái* was supposed to be the solution.

Perhaps it was.

The best samba school would be chosen by a small jury, which this year included Luis Angel. The scoring was based on multiple factors including the floats and decorations, the storyline, dancing and choreography, percussion and harmony, the leading commission and, of course, the samba song itself. It was a competition as hotly contested and as highly prized in Brazil as the World Soccer Cup.

Not everyone was impressed. Tony noticed a sixty-something year-old Japanese tourist in dark trousers and a short sleeve white shirt two tables over sitting with three companions. He was fast asleep. A high tech camera hung useless around his neck.

Anybody who could sleep through all that music needed his rest. Badly. It was just about the most sustained level of strident music that Tony had ever encountered. And he loved it.

"I'm going to check out the Bob's Food Stand," announced Rock. "Want anything?"

"Another Kaiser," Yairi suggested.

"You got it. How about you, Tony?"

Tony turned his head away from the dance. "Surprise me." He tugged at the collar of his t-shirt. It was hot. Bodies pressed close, blocking the faint breeze struggling to get through.

Yairi jumped out. "Let's get nearer the street."

"But all those seats are reserved—"

"Don't worry. No problem." He pushed Tony ahead and went for a street level box jammed with jostling men and women. Several wore costumes of some exotic Amazonian yellow parrots.

The *bateria*—drum corps— was passing now. Fireworks shot up at the front of the *Sambadromo*.

The man standing beside Tony slumped. Yairi caught him. He grinned. "Poor guy's drunk."

Tony saw a bright red patch on the man's shirt. Yairi pulled the man's nylon jacket shut and zipped it up.

"He's been hurt!"

"Nonsense." Yairi pulled the man to his feet. Tony assisted him. It was like trying to hold up a marionette. The man's eyes didn't open, but his mouth gaped. The crowd around them paid no attention, intent on the frenzied parade.

"I'm telling you," Tony said loudly in his friend's ear, "this guy's been stabbed—or shot or something." He felt the man's wrist. "I don't feel a pulse."

Yairi slapped the man's cheeks. His brown skin had lightened two shades. "Hey, buddy. Wake up."

"I'm getting the police."

"Tony, Tony. It's no problem. Let him sleep. Besides, where are you going to find a cop?"

Tony looked around the thousands of heads and saw a man in uniform. He pointed. "Right there." He squeezed past drunken revelers and made his way to the uniform which had now begun moving in the opposite direction.

He caught up with the officer some minutes later. "Excuse me." Tony tapped the figure on the shoulder. "Do you speak English?"

The surly young man shook his head no. His hand rested on his pistol. He wore a bright yellow t-shirt. Large black letters on the back spelled out *Defesa Civil RJ*. He had a wide red belt with a thin gray stripe, khaki trousers with a matching cap and high, sturdy black boots.

"A man has been hurt." Tony struggled for words and found none. "Hurt? Understand?"

This man could have been a statue.

Tony motioned for the official to follow him but the guy didn't move.

Tony tried again.

When he and the cop finally returned to Section 9 where Tony had left Yairi and the fallen stranger, he found his friend not at the rail, but back at their table, clapping his hands, moving to the infectious beat, and holding an animated conversation with a pleasant looking fellow the next table over, who had an Australian accent. Yairi was discoursing on the chances of the school *Imperatriz*

Leopoldinense besting *Beija-Flor*.

Tony looked around for the injured man. "Where is he?"

"Who? Rock? He is not back yet." Yairi tipped his chin and smiled at the officer.

"No, the guy who'd been hurt. Where did he go? What did you do with him?"

Yairi laughed and sipped his Kaiser. "I told you, Tony. The man was only—how do you say?— overindulged. His friends woke him up and took him away."

Yairi said something in Portuguese to the officer who looked at Tony, said some unfathomable words in his direction and left.

Rock returned to the table carrying a tray laden with french fried potatoes, beer and ice cream sandwiches. "Dinner is served."

By the time they'd finished the tray, *Estação Primeira de Mangueira* had finished its march and funneled into the open space before Niemeyer's Arch, a futuristic looking concrete bowl over which a graceful arch balanced delicately as a bird frozen in mid-flight. The *Praça da Apotéose*, Apotheosis Square, filled with thousands of dancing *cariocas* coming to a heady climax; kings and queens for the night.

No more had been said about the mysterious 'dead' stranger. Yairi kept the subject of conversation fixed on parade and samba history, explaining the story being told in song and dance as it had been told before their eyes.

The orange suited sanitation workers took over the parade route now, pushing brooms and driving big yellow sweepers, picking up errant feathers, sequins and unidentifiable trash. A tall, dark skinned man, nearly as thin as his broomstick, got into the act, dancing wildly with the broom. The crowd applauded appreciatively.

"Come on," Yairi said, finishing his cup of beer. "Now's our chance!"

He moved through the tables.

"Chance for what?" called Tony, glancing back to make sure Rock was following.

Yairi hopped the low green railing protecting the parade street from the throngs. The road itself was wide as a four lane highway.

Tony and Rock hesitated at the fence then jumped over, racing to catch up with Yairi. Security men began shouting. So did the crowd. And Tony wasn't sure if they were rooting for them or against them.

Tony ran faster and made it to the opposite fence first.

A phalanx of security guards in bright yellow t-shirts was waiting for him.

"No problem," Yairi said pushing his way through an open gate. Bored, frazzled looking press photographers grabbed sodas and waters from a trough of ice, awaiting the next samba school to take to the parade street.

From his body language, Yairi looked like he was apologizing to the security men. The only thing Tony caught for sure was the mention of Luis Angel's name, twice.

Begrudgingly, the three men were allowed to stay.

"Luis is upstairs." Yairi charged up the rough concrete steps.

Tony was sweating, as much from the run across the parade street as from the sweltering heat of Section 2.

They found Luis and his famous cohorts in a private enclosed box being served by a waiter in a trim red jacket. A sliding refrigerated case held an endless variety of beers, sodas, juices and water. An ice-filled cooler on the floor floated bottles of chilled champagne.

Luis was being propped up by two young women in red hotpants and sequined silver halter tops. He held an empty champagne glass in one hand. Tony recognized a couple of band members as well as all four of Luis' backup singers.

When Luis caught sight of the three men, he cried out. "Yairi! There you are! I've been looking for you all afternoon.

You too, Tony, Rock. Come on in."

Tony and Rock, lingering in the doorway, entered.

"Grab a beer." Luis hollered instructions to the waiter.

The waiter handed the two musicians plastic cups of beer.

A crackling of fireworks in the distance meant the next school was about to begin. There were a couple of dozen people in the low ceilinged box. Several sat on the cement rail. It couldn't have been more than six inches wide. Tony wondered how many fell to their death.

Not to mention what he'd seen of the floats. Dancers clung to flimsy poles thirty feet off the ground astride moving vehicles that often contained smoke, water, fire and more moving parts than his Saab. And none of those floats looked like they'd pass any sort of safety inspection back in the States. And the Fire Marshall would have shut the whole shabang down before it had even gotten started.

But hey, this was Brazil!

And maybe they'd never heard of lawyers. . .

Luis pulled Yairi off to the corner away from the street and appeared to be browbeating him. Tony couldn't help but smile. As much as he liked Yairi, he was nothing but trouble.

He told Rock what had occurred in his absence.

"Maybe he really was only drunk?" Rock said.

"Could be," Tony agreed. "But Yairi just seems to attract trouble. I mean, every time I'm near the guy somebody seems to end up dead."

"That's funny," commented Rock.

"What's funny?"

"That's the same way I feel about you. . ."

"You're lucky you're bigger than me," quipped Tony.

"Aren't I though."

The crowd let out a cheer. The next school was coming forward. The swell of pounding drums led the way. Those in the box leaned forward to get a better view.

Luis pressed between Rock and Tony. "So you two finally

showed up. It's about time."

"Sorry, my fault," Tony said.

"Yeah, I know. Forget it." He held out a joint.

"No, thanks," Tony said.

"I'll just have another beer," Rock said heading for the waiter.

"I like him," Luis said. He wore a black silk shirt, unbuttoned to the waist with tight black trousers. A gold chain hung from his neck.

"Him who?"

"Rock." He put his arm around Tony.

Here were go again, Kozol groaned.

"I like you, too."

"Well," Luis definitely couldn't be gay, "thanks." Not with his record with the opposite sex.

The two blondes in halter tops made their presence known. They were small breasted by American standards. But here in Brazil, larger wasn't necessarily better. Tony had heard that many women in Brazil had breast reductions, believing that smaller was sexier.

Go figure.

"Marisa and Zizi," explained Luis. "I've been keeping them warm for you."

Tony stepped back. "For me?"

"Yeah," said Luis, casually inhaling his joint and handing it to Marisa. "You and Rock."

"But-but I thought they were with you."

"Nah, I've got a date." He pointed to a stunning woman with long dark hair sidling up to a swarthy looking, silver haired gentleman. His arm was around her slender waist—when it wasn't drifting lower.

She wore a clinging white dress. "Astrud Pinto. Stars in one of those *novelas*. Like a soap opera, you know?" Luis waved to Astrud. She looked like a young Sonia Braga.

The actress extricated herself from her gentleman admirer

and kissed Luis long and slow on the lips.

Zizi had insinuated herself up against Tony and handed him a glass of champagne from which she helped herself. Her eyes were as blue as cobalt. She squeezed in on the railing and motioned for Tony to join her.

He did.

Tony clung on for dear life. The ground looked awfully far away. He saw Luis introduce Marisa to Rock. The two new friends sat on a bench and chatted. Tony had always admired Rock's ability to talk to anyone—when he chose to—apparently even language was no barrier.

Dinner was served around one o'clock in the morning. Rice with pineapple and chicken in some kind of sauce. Tony ate.

Yairi spat, "Bah. This stuff is okay, but give me some good Brazilian *feijoada* anytime."

If Brazil had an official dish, *feijoada* would be it. Made of black beans, white rice, shredded kale, fried manioc flour, slowly cooked with large quantities of meat, including pork offcuts—a remnant of colonial times when only the worst parts of the animals were given to the slaves. The dish, of Portuguese origin, had taken on African influences, like the use of strong spices, and become distinctly Brazilian.

Several drinks later, yet another samba school was midway along, stretched out like a living, breathing organism as bright as any tropical bird, stretching hundreds of yards in both directions. Zizi grabbed Tony's arms and placed them around her bare midriff. She shouted as a large float passed before their eyes. "This is my *escola*!"

Faces from the boxes on either side grinned and shouted. Some waved flags bearing the names of their schools. A beauty wearing nothing but yellow and green body paint waved at the jury box.

Tony waved back, clutching Zizi with one hand. She pushed his hand up to her breasts and rubbed. She turned her neck and kissed him on the lips, her tongue exploring his mouth. Tony fell back against a man seated on the ledge behind him.

What was she doing?!

He had to tell Zizi he had a girlfriend.

The man behind laughed and pushed him back up. That was when Tony saw a face peering at him from the box to his left.

"Tony!" There was shock and disappointment in that voice.

Those green eyes, that reddish blonde hair, that near perfect face, only younger. It wasn't Silvia. "Tzininha!"

It was her little sister, Tzininha Parra.

Tony jumped up, apologized to Zizi and ran for the door.

"Where are you going?" Rock shouted, extricating himself from Marisa.

"Next door!"

"What for?" Rock said, but Tony was already out the door.

The narrow, airless hallway was hot and humid. A small crowd blocked the way. He waited anxiously for them to pass then burst into Tzininha's box.

She wasn't there.

He looked again.

She still wasn't there.

Tony bumped into Rock in the hallway.

"What's going on?"

"Silvia's sister was here."

"So?"

"She saw me with Zizi. I mean, it was nothing. But she might get the wrong impression. I want to set her straight."

Rock peeked inside the box. "I don't see her."

"I know." He pointed down the long corridor. There was a stairs midway up. "She must have gone that way."

They hurried down the outside stairway past a group of

military men. At ground level, the site was far different than it had been on the opposite side of the Sambadromo. Here it was darker. There were less vendors and high, bare fences kept the riffraff out. Few people wandered about compared to the throngs they'd encountered on the opposite side.

"Do you see her?"

"No," said Rock.

They trudged up and down.

"Hey, look!" Rock thrust out his arm. "Isn't that Yairi?"

"Where?"

Rock pointed through the fence. There was a large square in an island of squalor. Tenements surrounded the backside of the Sambadromo. The square was alive with people.

"I don't see— " And then he did. "You're right." Yairi sat in his Bugre, a passenger at his side. "What the hell is he doing down here? I thought he was up in the box."

"Nah, he took off about an hour ago. I guess you were too busy to notice."

Tony glared. "It was perfectly innocent. I didn't know the girl was going to attack me. It's Silvia I care about."

"Hey, relax, Tony." Rock put a hand on his friend's shoulder. "I'm only kidding. I'm on your side, remember? Let's go see what Yairi's up to."

Tony agreed. They swept past the armed security team at the gates where they were immediately accosted by vendors and ticket scalpers. They fought their way toward the Bugre.

"Hey, hurry!" shouted Tony. "He's leaving."

They ran.

Sure enough, the Bugre had come to life and was inching its way through the crowds. It disappeared between a couple of parked charter buses.

"We're losing him. Come on, Rock, faster!"

Rock led the charge, bullying his way through the thicket of living flesh.

They stopped at a three way intersection. People and

vehicles spread out in every direction. "It's no use. We've lost him." Rock kicked an empty beer can with his toe. It spun into the crowd where it was quickly trampled flat.

"Yeah." For the first time, Tony more closely studied their surroundings and didn't like what he saw. A cloud of beer and charcoal flamed pork seemed to hover overhead. "Let's get back."

"But Yairi was our ride."

"We'll catch a lift back to the hotel with Luis when this is over."

They wasted no time retracing their steps.

Tony flashed his pass to the security guard who stuck his hand out and said something in Brazilian Portuguese. He wouldn't let them in.

"What's he saying?" Rock wanted to know.

"I don't know. Show him your ticket."

Rock pulled his ticket from where it hung under his t-shirt on a slender rope. "What's the problem, man?"

The guard shook his small head from side to side. He made motions with his hands.

A man in a shabby coat and matching beard said, "You are on the wrong side. Your passes are not good here."

"But we're here with Luis Angel," Tony said to the security man as much as he did to the bystander.

Both shrugged.

"He tells you to go around."

A well dressed, middle aged couple hopped out of a taxi and brushed past Rock and Tony. They showed their tickets and entered.

Tony sighed. "Come on, Rock."

"You mean you want to walk around to the other side?"

"What choice do we have?" Tony started walking.

"What if we get lost?"

Tony turned and crossed his arms over his chest. "And just how the hell are we going to get lost with the friggin'

Sambadromo sticking out big as all the world? Not to mention all the fireworks and music coming from the place."

"Yeah, you're right."

Tony took the lead.

The police found Tony and Rock standing alone in the street, shivering in their underwear.

They were escorted into the back of the tiny blue and white police car and driven to headquarters.

Tony squinted. The sun was coming up.

"My feet are frozen," complained Rock.

"Don't start," warned Tony. He wiggled his toes. Even their shoes had been stolen. Who'd have thought they could get so thoroughly lost?

And then the ignominy of being mugged. . .again!

Tony and Rock had made their statements and next found themselves sitting in a small, windowless room on chairs that had long ago lost their last vestiges of varnish. They'd each been given blue wool blankets that smelled like they had last been used to keep burros warm and snugly in some drafty barnyard.

Nearly forty minutes later, by Tony's reckoning, a familiar face passed the door.

"Hey, that's—"

"Yeah, Lt. Lobao. Hey, lieutenant!" Rock waved.

Footsteps stopped then retraced their path. Lt. Lobao stuck his head in the open door. "Ah, yes. Mr. Kozol. Mr.

Bottom." He grinned.

Tony didn't want to know what was so funny. He could guess. The sight of himself and Rock wrapped up in foul, scratchy blankets in a police station could have been funny, would have been funny, if it had been some other Tony. Like Bennett.

"I will be with you shortly," Lobao said before disappearing once more.

"He didn't seem surprised to see us." Rock scratched his head and looked at Tony. "I guess he knew we were here."

"Looks like it."

Lt. Lobao returned with one of the officers who'd brought them in to the nondescript police station on a nondescript block somewhere in the central business district. They spoke in Brazilian Portuguese and the officer left, leaving the lieutenant alone with the two musicians.

He paced several moments back and forth, then spoke. "You will tell me, please, what you were doing wandering around Rio in the middle of the night?" He pulled a Lucky Strike pack from his trousers pocket and lit up, blowing smoke over their heads.

Tony rose through the cloud of death, pulling his blanket up over his shoulders, with as much dignity as he could muster—like a Roman senator. "As I explained to the *policia* here, we were trying to get back into the *Sambadromo* and got held up by a gang."

"They got everything!" Rock shook his head miserably.

The unsmiling lieutenant demanded Tony and Rock go over every detail once more. Tony recounted everything they'd done, though he left out the part about the possible dead guy, figuring that would only make more trouble for himself and Rock.

Rock gave his version of events.

Lt. Lobao seemed very interested in Yairi and insisted on a more thorough description which he jotted in his notebook.

"I do not understand. You mentioned this Alvarez Yairi once before."

"That's right."

"You had dinner with him the night you were mugged and your attacker himself was killed." Lobao chewed his lip like a beef jerky. "What do you know about this man?"

"Who? Yairi?"

"Yes."

Tony answered, "Only that he works for Luis Angel. He's like a gopher."

Lt. Lobao was obviously perplexed. "A gopher?"

"Not the animal."

"No," said Rock. "A gopher like in 'go fer this' and 'go fer that.' Get it?"

After a moment, the lieutenant nodded. "You have an address for *Senhor* Yairi?"

"No," Tony said. "He's moved recently. I'm sure Luis could give it to you or his secretary, Alba Zica. I'll bet she has it."

"Yes," Lt. Lobao said noncommitally.

The lieutenant seemed unwilling to bother the superstar. Tony envied the youth his kid glove treatment. If it came in a bottle, he wanted some. He'd have to look for it on the shelves, next to the hot oil hair treatment. Kid Glove Treatment, $2.99 for a 16 ounce bottle.

Tony came back to earth. There would be no kid glove treatment for him. At best, he could look forward to the leper treatment. "How did you know we were here?"

"You are part of an ongoing murder investigation. Your names have been—" Lt. Lobao paused as if searching for the right word, "distributed."

Tony nodded. Great, every cop in Rio knew who he was. Rock, too.

"Speaking of which," Tony added, "have you found out anything more on the guy that hit me?"

"Regrettably, *não*." The corners of his eyes crinkled slightly. "We will keep you informed. Not to worry."

"Not even a name?" pushed Tony.

"No." Lobao turned his unwavering blue eyes on Tony. "Unless you care to give us one."

"Gee, I'd love to lieutenant, but I'd jotted it down on a piece of paper and stuck it in my wallet and," Tony pulled up his sinking blanket, "the jerk stole it."

Lt. Lobao turned to go.

"Wait!" Rock cried. "What about us? How are we supposed to get back to the Ipanema Palace?"

"Ah, yes." The lieutenant snapped his fingers twice, hard. The pleasant continence of Officer Milito filled the doorway, paper coffee cup in hand. "Milito will see you safely back to your hotel." The lieutenant was looking at Tony now.

Tony squirmed and wrapped his blanket more tightly around his shoulders. A move his nostrils protested. He knew which end of the burro this blanket had kept warm!

"I would ask you to stay out of trouble *Senhor* Kozol—you and *Senhor* Bottom—lamentably you do not seem capable."

Tony opened his mouth to protest but Lt. Lobao stopped him with a raised palm.

"You will tell *Senhor* Yairi to contact me as soon as possible," the lieutenant ordered. "To not do so will have dire consequences." With that, the lieutenant made his exit, sweeping past Officer Milito like he was a speck of dust.

Tony didn't know what Lt. Lobao meant. Would not telling Yairi to contact the police have dire consequences? Or would Yairi not complying have dire consequences?

In either circumstance, Tony was in deep guano. And he was going to drag Yairi down to police headquarters himself if that was what it was going to take to keep the police off his back.

They were stopped at a tiny desk near the front. One of the two officers who'd brought them in was seated behind a stack of yellow papers. He produced two stapled documents and presented one to Tony and one to Rock. "If you please."

"What's this?" Rock asked. It was several pages thick.

"The lieutenant has brought copies of your statements for you each to sign." The officer held out a pen.

Rock took it and laid his papers atop another pile of papers which obscured the desktop. He wrote his first name.

Tony gripped his arm. "Just a sec, Rock. This is in Portuguese. I'm not signing this. You shouldn't either. It could say anything!" Only their names, typed unevenly along the top of each page, made any sense at all.

The officer, whose face looked like it had been squeezed into a vise, frowned.

Rock fiddled with the fountain pen. It bore the name of a local hotel on its shaft.

"I'd like this translated into English, *por favor*."

The officer grabbed back the official documents. "No problem, *senhor*."

Uh-oh, thought Tony.

"I will have these sent out to headquarters to please you. No problem."

"Thanks," said Tony, somewhat warily.

"Of course, I am a lowly corporal and as the lieutenant has insisted that you sign these important statements before you leave, I must ask you to stay until the task is completed to your satisfaction." He was grinning now. He opened a narrow drawer and stuffed the papers inside. "No problem. Only a matter of days. Ah, but it is Carnaval. . ." He held a crooked finger to his lips. "A week at the most." His pinched eyes sparkled. "I'm sure we can find a cell to accommodate you in the meantime."

"Tony," began Rock, "I don't want to check into a jail cell. . .not to mention our jobs. I mean, what would happen to them if we get tossed in the slammer?"

Tony held out his hand and the officer whipped out the

documents. Tony and Rock took turns signing. For all Tony knew, he was signing a confession that he was Jack the Ripper or the wanted leader of a failed military junta. Tony was now too tired to care.

"Thank you very much, *senhor*." The officer's sarcasm and sense of victory were unmistakable.

"Come," Milito said, tossing his half consumed coffee in a trash basket.

Out on the street, Milito escorted Tony and Rock into the back of a small squad car.

"They could have at least got us some clothes," complained Rock, wearing his blanket like a toga. It covered him just adequately from the chest to the knees.

"It's just as well they didn't," Tony replied. "Any clothes they'd have given us would probably come off a couple of corpses found on the streets."

"Ipanema Palace, *não*?" Milito inquired, looking at the two musicians in his rearview mirror.

"*Sim*," said Tony. Tony closed his eyes and settled back. It wasn't only from being exhausted. He'd discovered eyes closed was the best way to drive with any Brazilian at the wheel that he'd met thus far. With the exception of Silvia.

Silvia! He sat up, eyes wide.

Last night's horrible scene with Tzininha came rushing back at him like a ghoulish nightmare. If Tzininha said something to her big sister before he had a chance to speak to her . . .

Tony forced himself to relax. Rock was already dozing, head akimbo. Nobody could fake snores like that. He'd call Silvia and explain everything. Of course she would forgive him. They were to be married after all.

Tony looked at his reflection in the rearview mirror. His face wasn't much to see but the car following them was.

It was Yairi and his olive green Bugre and he was alone. Tony settled back in his seat, risking an occasional look out the back window. Yairi clung to them, maintaining a discrete distance of several car lengths.

Rock and Tony did their best to exit the squad car with dignity, sweeping their malodorous blankets around them like the Roman patriarchs they wished they'd been.

Officer Milito rolled open his window and called to Tony.

Tony leaned over the window. "What is it?"

Milito grinned and fumbled in his pockets. "The lieutenant told me to give you these."

"My wallet and knife!" Tony palmed the red-handled Swiss Army knife, opened his wallet and thumbed through. His driver's license, credit cards, everything was accounted for— except the cash. And he wasn't about to raise a stink about that. "*Obrigado*."

At least he was solvent again. Last night's gang of thieves had relieved him of his MasterCard. Tony had already reported it, though he doubted it had done much good. He was sure he'd seen several of the police officers sniggering.

"*De nada*. It is a bad business you being attacked on the streets and the seaman being killed. Not good for tourism. My father, he runs a small travel agency. Not good for business."

"No, I suppose not. Well, thanks again." Tony turned then did a double take, tapping on the roof of the squad car as Milito made to leave. "Hold on. What seaman?"

"The man who attacked you."

"But I thought— " Tony paused. Lt. Lobao insisted that the dead man, his attacker, had no identity thus far. Why was Milito telling him this? What was going on? What else was he being kept in the dark about?

Officer Milito looked at him expectantly. "Yes?"

"Nothing. Thanks again for the wallet."

Milito nodded and drove off, his little car whirring like a deluxe Singer sewing machine.

Tony mustered all the grace he could manage and climbed

the steps of the Ipanema Palace Hotel, imagining all the time it was the Parthenon. The hot steps burned his bare feet.

Rock was already inside seated next to Yairi in an alcove off the main bar. This early in the day, especially during Carnaval, it was fairly deserted.

"Man," grinned Yairi. "You guys are the craziest Americans I've ever met! Wandering around the slums in the middle of the night, a couple of white faced tourists!" He slapped his bony knees and hooted. "Want some coffee?"

"No." Tony slumped into an empty chair at the small square table Rock and Yairi had taken. "It might keep me awake and I'm going to sleep for about a hundred hours."

Yairi studied his silver watch. "You're going to sleep for about three hours. Then you're going to be at a warehouse two blocks over."

"What?"

"You've got a concert this afternoon. Luis has made me responsible for the two of you."

"Remember?" Rock said glumly.

"Shit." Tony slumped in the chair. A draft rose up his blanket. How the hell did women stand wearing skirts? "We haven't even rehearsed."

"That's Luis' problem, *não*?"

"Yeah, you're right, Yairi," said Rock. "But that doesn't mean we want to look bad."

Yairi laughed. "Look bad? Too late, you both look like hell!"

"Speaking of which, that's exactly what we went through last night. What happened to you? Where'd you go?"

Yairi said vaguely. "I had some errands to do for the boy, Luis. The kid keeps me busy with many things. You don't want to know. . ."

"No, I don't," Tony answered rather quickly.

"How about a *chopp,* men? It'll pick you up."

"Beer? At this hour? Now look who's loco," Rock retorted.

Tony held his head up with both hands. "So how did you know we were at the police station?"

"Luis sent me. He'd been called. Actually, it was that Zica bitch who informed me."

"Is he mad?" asked Rock.

"No, he is glad you're okay, that's all. I was sent to pick you up and was waiting for you outside the station when I saw you get into the police car." Yairi shrugged. "So I just followed along."

Tony slipped into a momentary coma. His head jerked back as he fell forward. "I've got to get some sleep."

Tony started to rise but Yairi held him back. "About this afternoon—"

"What about it, Yairi?"

"You know, Little Armando is expecting our help."

Tony shook his head. "Listen, you've got the acid and the money that Rock accidently took—" They'd turned the stuff over to Yairi the previous morning at the cafe. "You do what you want but leave us out of it."

"I will handle this," Yairi said. "But you must not get in the way. Little Armando must think that we are cooperating. If we don't. . ."

"If we don't, what?" Tony said.

"Yeah, what's he really going to do to us?" Rock slammed his fists together.

Yairi tried another tack. "Listen, men. Little Armando is our friend. We help him and he helps us."

"I don't need his help," Tony said stonily.

Yairi sighed. "I am afraid you have already had his help." He twisted his watch twice around his thin wrist.

"What do you mean?"

"Yeah, what's that bum done for us?" added Rock. "We'll give him the money back if that's what you mean."

"It isn't the money," Yairi said. "It's—"

"Well?"

"Little Armando is an important man. He's used to getting his way."

"You're prevaricating." Tony grabbed a napkin off the table and wiped the grime from his face. "Whatever you're trying to say, spit it out."

Yairi leaned forward, his voice low. "Little Armando has already helped you. He has killed for you."

Tony's hair stood on end. "What the hell are you talking about?"

"The man who mugged you."

Tony and Rock looked befuddled.

Yairi sighed. "Let me explain. That night you left the *Café Bossa Nova* Rodriguez followed along a little bit. To make sure you were okay. He was a block away when you were attacked. Too late to prevent it, but—" Yairi paused, letting the implications sink in, no doubt.

"Are you telling me that Rodriguez killed the guy that mugged me?"

"He—" Yairi seemed to search for a more pleasant phrasing, "assisted you. Then followed you discreetly back to your hotel."

"But that's crazy!"

Yairi shrugged. "You are their friend. Their business associate. Little Armando protects his friends."

"And punishes his enemies," Rock added soberly.

"Precisely."

"And if we don't cooperate. . ."

"Precisely."

9

"What are you doing here? And how did you get in?"

Luis Angel's pretty but unpleasant assistant, Alba Zica, rose from the small writing desk at the window and pushed down a wrinkle that had dared to show itself on the front of her Cabernet-colored silk blouse. The matching silk slacks fell several inches above her ankles. "Gentlemen." She slammed a sharp pencil down on the desktop where it snapped into several jagged pieces. "I've been waiting."

Miss Prissy Pants' hair was done up in a tight coil atop her head, like a cobra poised to strike. Tony wondered if she was venomous.

"For what?" Rock scratched his head against the protruding corner of the hallway. Both hands were busy holding up his blanket.

"For you and Tony, of course."

"We've been tied up." Tony replied wearily.

Miss Zica looked askance. "So I have been told." She pointed to a pile of shopping bags in a neat pile between the bed and the far wall.

Rock grinned. "Hey, what's all this? Christmas time in Brazil already?"

Prissy Pants replied without cracking a smile. "Shoes and

clothing for both of you. Courtesy of Luis." She looked the two men up and down. "I believe you will find them to fit you well. I am a good judge of men."

Tony frowned. The way she said men was almost as disagreeable as the way she said musician. It was like she'd just swallowed a bug. "Thanks," he said, hitching up his stink stitched blanket. "But what's wrong? You don't like our new outfits?"

"Actually," Miss Zica stepped within an arm's length of Tony, "I'd say yours rather becomes you."

Rock laughed.

"Ha, ha," Tony said dryly. He took a seat on the corner of his bed. "You still didn't say how you got in our room."

Miss Zica picked up her rectangular black leather purse from a chair beside the table, opened it and took out a hotel room key card.

"You've got a key to our room?" Tony said, belligerently. "How did you get that?"

"No, I have a key to Luis Angel's rooms. If you will look at the registration you will see these rooms and the rooms of all *Senhor* Angel's employees are in his name."

Rock had crossed over to the shopping bags and was peeking inside one satchel after the next. "It still stinks."

"Not quite so much as some things," quipped Miss Prissy Pants.

Rock laughed again. "You're right, Alba. Want to help me shower?"

"Perhaps some other lifetime."

It was Tony's turn to chuckle.

Her purse snapped shut like the jaws of a twelve foot alligator. A gator that had swallowed their room key. "For now, I suggest you both refresh yourselves and be ready for this afternoon. *Senhor* Yairi has informed you, *não*?"

"Yeah, we know. But I'm disappointed, Alba." Rock said. "I was hoping to see you at the Sambadrome last night."

"I will be there tonight, with Luis. The two of you are free to do as you please this evening."

"Gee, that's mighty swell of you, Miss Zica," said Tony somewhat churlishly.

"You and *Senhor* Bottom are new to the organization, *Senhor* Kozol. You will learn that Luis is more than fair with his employees. In fact, he is quite generous."

Good grief, the woman was insult proof. Tony glanced at Rock, who was preoccupied with holding up a big, colorful cotton shirt. It was a loosely cut hodgepodge of bright parrots and green leaves of many hues.

Rock said, "Think I'll try this one on for size."

"So what happened to the players we're replacing?"

Miss Zica wriggled her brows like a couple of worms writhing on hot pavement. "They were not team players. They also involved themselves in some inappropriate activities."

"Inappropriate activities?"

"I'm afraid there's nothing more I can say." She turned to Rock. The big guy's chest looked like a poster advertisement for the Amazon Rain Forest. "It fits you perfectly."

Rock beamed.

Miss Zica returned her attention to Tony. "As long as you obey the law and your employer, you and *Senhor* Bottom will do just fine."

"What about Alvarez Yairi?"

"*Senhor* Yairi? What of him?"

Tony crossed his legs, carefully rearranging his blue blanket. He realized now that the smell was going to rub off on the bedspread. They'd have to order the maid to fetch a clean one. "What do you know about the guy?"

Miss Zica said quickly, "Nothing. And why should I? He does his job." She added pointedly, "And does it well. I haven't had to go clothes shopping for him."

"Did you hire him? Where's he from?"

"I don't know where the *Senhor* Yairi is from. Why not ask him? As for the hiring of *Senhor* Yairi, that was something that was arranged through one of Luis' contacts, I believe."

"Hey, Alba! How about these slacks with this shirt?" Rock held up a beautiful pair of black jeans. Black was Rock's favorite color.

"Excellent choice."

"Yeah, man."

"Why do you ask about *Senhor* Yairi?"

"No reason. Just curious is all. Don't get me wrong, he's a good guy. I like to know the people I'm working with, that's all. So," Tony ran a hand through his hair, "tell us about you, Alba."

Miss Zica glanced quickly at her watch. "I must go. We meet downstairs at three-thirty."

Tony waited for the pleasant sound of the door being closed behind the woman. "I knew that would get rid of her," he said with satisfaction.

Rock dropped his blanket and stuck a leg in the trousers.

"You know, you really ought to bathe before you put those on."

"Right." Rock tossed the jeans on his bed. "What was all that about Yairi?"

Tony glanced out the window, still clutching his blanket. "I don't know. I'm just trying to figure things out, is all." He tapped the writing desk. "Wasn't this desk over there before?"

Rock looked from the desk to the spot where Tony had pointed. "Yeah, it was. I guess she moved it."

Tony shook his head. "Good old Prissy Pants, gonna arrange everybody's lives whether they like it or not."

"She can help me disarrange the sheets anytime."

"Take a shower, Rock," chirped Tony. "Preferably a cold one."

With Rock butchering Willie Nelson's *Mama, Don't Let Your Babies Grow Up To Be Cowboys*, with his own version, *Mama, Don't Let Your Babies Grow Up To Be Bass Players,* in the shower, Tony took the opportunity to call Silvia.

He'd tossed both blankets and the bedspread out in the hallway, not caring to see any of it again.

On his knees, in his underwear at the night table, Tony dialed Silvia's number. He knew the digits by heart, just as he knew every lovely freckle on her silky skin. It was picked up on the other end on the third ring. "*Bom dia,* Silvia. It's me, Tony."

There was a pause, a muffled sound and light breathing before a chilly voice replied in broken English. "Silvia does not wish to speak with you."

"Who's this?"

"Tzininha."

Oh shit.

"Tzininha, let me—" The line went dead. "Explain." Another disconnection, no doubt. On purpose, no doubt.

"Trouble in paradise?" asked Rock, toweling his damp hair in the hallway.

Tony's lips turned down. "How did you guess? And put some clothes on, will you?"

"Well, let's see. How did I guess?" Rock grinned and wrapped his towel around his waist. "Better?"

Tony nodded.

"You're on your knees, staring into the mouthpiece of that telephone, looking like a lovesick puppy. Sounds like somebody just plunged into Love's Cruel Sea." With his hairbrush as a makeshift microphone, Rock did an impromptu dance. "*Love comes seducing us all. Love lifts us up, love makes us fall.*"

"Will you please—" Tony rose.

"*Love makes us laugh, love makes us cry,*" Rock wriggled his hips and did his best impression of an Elvis impersonator—which wasn't bad—"*Some days we live, sometimes we wonder why.*"

Tony wormed his away around the dancing fool.

"*And I've been cast adrift on love's cruel, cruel sea. Love's cruel sea, love's cruel sea—*"

Tony slammed the door behind him. "I'm taking a hot shower."

"*I've been cast adrift on love's cruel, cruel sea. . .*"

"And tell Elvis I expect him to be out of the room when I'm finished!"

Tony turned the shower up full blast, reducing Elvis to a dull roar.

Tony tried to sneak out of the hotel. He wanted to see Silvia and clear things up. Maybe now that he'd had a whole three hours sleep, he could think and speak rationally.

But Alba Zica would have none of it. She was waiting in the lobby when he came down.

"*Senhor* Kozol."

Her voice shot out at him like a sniper's bullet. He turned. "*Boa tarde.*"

"How nice of you to be down early. Where is Rock?"

"He'll be down in a couple of minutes." Tony gazed longingly at the lobby door; the sunshine, the beach, freedom. "I was just going to go out for a moment."

Miss Zica's head twisted curtly side to side. "We'll wait for Rock and the others. Our driver is already here with our van. I see your new clothes fit you."

Tony tugged at his shirt. It was a gray Ralph Lauren polo shirt, tucked into a pair of blue trousers. "Yes, thanks again." The shoes were brown loafers with tassels and matched the brown leather belt. Tony hadn't had shoes with tassels since he was a kid. He felt a bit silly. Perhaps that had been what Alba Zica intended.

"You're quite welcome."

Once they were all together, Luis Angel's entire band, including his backup singers, piled into the waiting van. Luis was nowhere in sight. Tony figured he'd arrive by limo like the star he was.

"What happened?" asked Rock, squeezing into the narrow seat next to Tony. "I thought you were going to Silvia's house."

"Prissy Pants caught me."

They disembarked behind a stage at a park only a few minutes from the Ipanema Palace Hotel.

"Follow me," instructed Miss Zica. Stepping carefully over long snaking black cables that spread across the ground, they followed Luis' assistant to a cluster of five white trailers set up behind the stage. She barked some instructions and the singers went to the nearest trailer on the right.

"Where's Luis?" asked Rock.

Miss Zica pointed to the larger of the trailers outside of which two security men were stationed. "He is already in his dressing room." She glanced at her watch. "Come, there is no time for questions. You must have hair and makeup."

Hair and makeup? Tony and Rock shared a look of dread. They were led to a long, narrow trailer. Inside was a beauty shop on wheels. The length of the trailer along the wall opposite the door was lighted mirrors. A long white vanity held brushes, rollers, scissors, blow dryers, makeup and all the other tools of the beauty trade. A row of stools was evenly spaced up and down the line.

Alba Zica gave directions in Portuguese, then repeated them in English for Rock and Tony. "You will be seated."

With the drummer, Enrique Lopez, between them, Tony and Rock took to their stools. In a matter of moments, girls in smocks were flitting about their heads. Tony's girl tipped his head back and he closed his eyes.

When he opened them again, Tony realized he'd dozed off. When he looked in the mirror, Tony hoped he was still in the middle of a nightmare. His once wavy hair was now several inches shorter and curled as tightly as a plateful of finger-sized *Slinkys*. Not to mention, it had been bleached unnaturally blonde. His face looked darker. He rubbed his cheek with his finger. Some kind of makeup. "What the—"

Tony looked about.

Rock was laughing.

Alba Zica walked in. "Ah, you are done." She twirled one of Tony's new curls in her fingers. "*Bom. Muito bem.*"

"Good?" Tony shot off his stool like a near-orbit rocket. "Look what they did to me!"

"It is nice, *não*?"

Tony's eyes widened. "Was this your idea?"

Miss Zica turned her attention to Rock. "You look fine, also."

"He looks the same!" shouted Tony. "And answer my question."

Alba Zica gave Tony a hard look. "Luis Angel suggested a more complete make over for you. After all, this is not a recording. It is a live show. He wishes it to have some. . ." she hesitated, then said, "sparkle."

"Sparkle? Christ, my head looks more like a fireworks explosion." Tony sank back onto his stool.

Rock said, "You look like some aging California surfer dude that stuck his hand in an electric outlet."

"Why didn't they do this to you?"

"I dunno." Rock looked in the mirror and rubbed his head. "Though in the first place, I don't have that much hair to screw around with."

Rock and his crewcut, groaned Tony inwardly. He'd have to get one himself when this was all over with. How else would he undo what had been done?

"Besides, Rock's look is quite nice as it is. He only was needing some minor touching up."

"Thanks, Alba."

Luis' assistant smiled. "And now, it is time for the band to take the stage."

"Isn't there going to be any rehearsal?" asked Rock, whose ego seemed to have expanded to the size of the Goodyear Blimp.

"There is no time. Come."

Out in the sunlight, Tony felt conspicuous. Conspicuous and stupid. The good thing, he figured, was that no one would even recognize him. They passed an open door of a trailer backed up to the stage from which cables radiated in every direction. Obviously a command center of some sort for the show.

Crossing the backstage, Tony caught sight of the Four-Star-STA mixing console tucked into one corner. The engineer hovered over it lovingly. Tony wondered how he'd react to a little acid being dumped into its electronic innards. Would Yairi even go through with it? And where was he, anyway?

If Yairi didn't go through with it, what would happen to Rock and himself?

Large stacks of black speakers rose on either side of the stage like miniature pyramids.

Rock swaggered over and picked up his bass.

"Will you please stop strutting about like a goddam peacock," Tony said.

"I'm sorry, Curly" replied Rock. "Do I know you?"

"You're about as funny as this lump on the side of my head." Tony picked up his acoustic and checked the tuning.

The lead guitarist, a serious young dude from Colombia, wearing torn blue jeans, no shirt and a red bandana, walked languorously onto the stage and the crowd applauded. He waved idly and nodded to Tony, Rock and the rest of the group. He was Luis Angel's band leader and arranger as well. His name was Joachim and his father also had been a famous musician in South America. Joachim had scraggly long, dull brown hair. Tony put a hand to his own defaced locks and took solace in the fact that with his receding hairline the kid would be bald in a matter of years.

In Joachim's defense, Tony had to admit that, unlike Luis Angel, this guy was a real musician and not just an act. From what little he'd heard of Joachim live and on CD, he was a ferocious and innovative guitarist.

Joachim conferred with the drummer, Enrique, for several moments then nodded again to Rock. He called out the title of Luis Angel's current Top Ten single, *Your Love Is Reason To Live*.

Enrique tapped out the tempo with his drumsticks and he and Rock kicked in together. By the time the intro had built to the first verse, Luis Angel, in skintight black pants and a formal white shirt and black bow tie had run out across the stage to the excited shouts of the crowd below. He had one of those wireless mikes attached to his ear.

The park bulged and overflowed in every direction with fans standing tightly side by side, swaying to the beat. Vendors had marked out their territories in the distance like wagon trains out of the Old West. Smoke rose in the darkening sky. Green and yellow fireworks went off overhead and the crowd screamed its delight.

By the time the show was over, Luis had shed his bow tie, tossing it to the crowd and pulled his shirttails out of his trousers. When Luis unbuttoned his shirt and exposed his chest, the young girls and the old went wild. Flowers were frantically tossed on stage like offerings to a lesser god.

After his third encore, the band played Luis off. He ran by Tony as he left the stage, a grin of satisfaction on his face. "It is like having sex, no?"

"If you say so!" shouted Tony over the music.

Luis was beaming. "And the hair looks tough, dude." He gave Tony the thumbs-up. With that, the young superstar disappeared into the arms of his handlers. Led away, no doubt to his trailer. Probably where Astrud Pinto or some other sexy superstar counterpart waited for him.

For the real sex.

Tony struck a final chord and waved to the audience, holding his guitar overhead with one hand. He had to admit, it was exhilarating, even when one wasn't the star of the show.

Tony's smile evaporated as he made out the determined faces of Little Armando and his brother, Victor as they pushed up to the stage, bodyguards (or assassins depending on one's point of view) in tow.

Tony made eye contact with Rock and motioned to the men with his eyes. Rock followed Tony offstage.

"You see them?"

"Yeah, man," Rock answered. "What are we going to do?"

A rumble of confusion, unmistakable though it was in Brazilian Portuguese, came from the back of the stage.

"Come on!"

Tony stopped in his tracks several yards from the commotion. The engineer was fuming. So was the Four-Star-STA fully automated mixing console. Tony noticed Yairi standing innocently by sipping a *guaraná*. He grinned in Tony and Rock's direction.

Tony and Rock joined him at the console.

Yairi exchanged words with the chief engineer and his assistant. He shook his head sadly and made clicking noises. He rested a consoling hand on the engineer's shoulder.

Tony didn't dare speak.

More words were exchanged between Yairi and the engineer. Yairi gestured towards Tony and Rock.

The engineer said, "*Sim.*"

"Come," Yairi said, "we need some strong arms to carry this equipment out. It must be fixed, no?"

Tony looked at Rock who only shrugged his big, beefy shoulders.

"Come on," Yairi said, cheerfully. "Work to do. Rock, you

take that side. Tony and I will handle this."

They carried the big board carefully down the steps and out the back. It smouldered from a spot near the front corner. Tony knew it was only cosmetic damage. Yairi would have made certain of that. Little Armando wouldn't pay for damaged goods.

A service truck, with the name of a PA equipment rental company on its side was double parked at the curb near the southeast corner of the park. Oswaldo, wearing a beige jumpsuit with a patch on the chest bearing the firm's logo was waiting at the rear of the vehicle.

Oswaldo lifted up the back door and the four of them gently slid the expensive recording/mixing console onto an inch thick layer of discolored yellow foam which had been spread across the length of the bed.

Oswaldo pulled down the door, masking the musty odor within. He removed a heavy padlock from his pocket and attached it to the door, then jiggled it twice to make sure it was secure.

"There is a lot of crime in Rio," Yairi stated.

"Yeah, so I hear," quipped Tony.

Yairi clapped Oswaldo on the back. Without a word, Oswaldo hopped behind the wheel and the big truck inched its way into the mad traffic that followed the end of the free concert.

The sound of samba came from the intersection ahead. A big sound truck had stopped in the road and an impromptu concert had begun. Oswaldo was going to have a hell of a time getting through that. Unless Little Armando planned on shooting his way out.

And Tony wasn't discounting that plan of action.

10

Silvia wouldn't answer the buzzer so Tony did the next best thing.

He climbed over the iron fence.

Rock gave him a lift up. Yairi was leaning against his Bugre which was triple parked in the street. He was sipping a Skol. They'd stopped at a local *barzinho* on the way.

Fortification.

Yairi had said that Brazilian beer provided, if not courage, at least reckless enthusiasm.

Tony had to agree, why else would he be hopping over the walls of a private residence?

He hit the ground and felt a pang of pain shoot up his legs. A gymnast he wasn't. Lennon and McCartney tried to bark but gave up quickly. Perhaps they were asthmatic. Besides, they liked Tony. He patted them atop their bouncy heads and they shuffled off in search of new adventures.

Tony climbed the stairs.

Repeated banging on the door brought no response. "Silvia. Please, open up. I've got to speak with you."

Cursing under his breath, he descended. There was only one thing to do next, appeal to Mrs. Parra. Reluctantly, he rang the downstairs buzzer.

Mrs. Parra opened the door a crack, spotted Tony and released the chain.

"*Boa noite, senhora.*" Tony bowed his head.

Mrs. Parra wiped her hands on her apron. "Tony?" Her eyes narrowed. She wore a blue dress with a white flower pattern. A thick gold chain hung tightly about her neck. Mrs. Parra had carob brown eyes, unlike Silvia and her sister. "What happened to you, Tony?" she replied in English. She'd already mentioned to Tony that she liked to practice her English, which she'd learned in school as a youth.

"Huh?" Then he caught her looking oddly at his head. "Oh, it's nothing. Is Silvia here, Mrs. Parra? May I speak to her?" He tried to see past Silvia's mother but the door was only partially open and he couldn't see further than a few feet into the entryway. Was Silvia hiding just inside?

"Well," Silvia's mother looked back towards the living room.

"No, she is not here." Tzininha pushed to the foreground. "I will handle this *mãe.*"

Through the thicket of her anger an air of shock was also apparent. What was Silvia going to think of the new Tony Kozol?

"Hi, Tzininha." Tony tried to construct a face that was both pleasant and apologetic all at once.

She scowled. "Get out!"

Apparently he'd failed.

Her hands grabbed the edge of the door and pushed.

Tony pushed back. "Please, just give me a moment. Let me explain!" He looked from Tzininha to Mrs. Parra. Surely Silvia's mother would offer him some sympathy?

Mrs. Parra placed her hand on Tzininha's and removed the girl's grip from the door. "Please, come inside."

Tony looked around. Rock and Yairi were watching between the barred gate. He turned his back on them and took a seat on the lemon colored divan beside Mrs. Parra, who'd now removed her apron. Tony caught the smell of baking chocolate coming from the kitchen. Silvia's mother was always cooking something.

Tzininha stood in the corner of the living room near a built in bookshelf, wearing tight blue jeans and a crisp white blouse. The fury in her eyes matched the arms tightly crossed over her chest.

Tony gave a brief explanation of what had happened at the Sambadrome. "So you see, it was nothing, really," he said after beating around several bushes for several minutes and explaining what had led up to this misunderstanding.

He spoke more for Tzininha's benefit than Ella Parra's, feeling he already had the elderly woman on his side. "And then this woman kissed me. I didn't kiss her." It was the second time he'd said it. This time he tried to say it with even more conviction. "I love Silvia."

Mrs. Parra nodded. "I will tell Silvia all this when she comes home." She folded her hands in her lap.

Tony had a feeling he'd been dismissed. He rose, then stopped at the door. "Do you know where I can find her?"

"*Não,*" said Mrs. Parra. "I have not seen her all this afternoon. Have you, Tzin?" Mrs. Parra rose. She retied her apron about her waist.

Silvia's sister shook her head.

"Well, if you see her," Tony said, humbly, "tell her I'm looking for her, would you?"

Mrs. Parra agreed.

"Well," asked Rock, "what happened in there?"

"Nothing," said Tony sullenly. He squeezed out the gate, careful to keep the dogs on the inside. "I told Silvia's mother and sister what happened, that's all."

"What about Silvia?"

"She wasn't home, Rock. At least she isn't answering and her mother acts like she hasn't seen Silvia. I have to believe her."

Yairi tossed his empty beer can to the floor of the Bugre. "My friend," he clutched Tony by the neck. His hand was cold. "You take this all too seriously. I worry about you, Tony."

"How do you mean?"

"I mean," Yairi waved his hand expansively, "here in Rio every man has at least one girlfriend. Why should you be any different?"

"Even the married ones?" Rock asked. He stuck his thumbs in his belt.

"Sure, even the married ones. Why not?"

Rock grinned. "Gee, maybe I'll apply for citizenship."

"You, my friend, would make an excellent *carioca*." He let go of Tony's neck. "But you, Tony, need to learn to relax and enjoy. That's what we do best. Forget about Silvia. If she doesn't want to see you, you will see someone else!"

"I don't want anyone else," Tony said forlornly.

Yairi tried again. "Women are fickle. They are crazy. They tell you they want you, then deceive you. Trust me."

"What do you know about it, anyway?" Tony looked at the Parra house, wondering where his Silvia could be. Was she out shopping? Was she at the beach? Visiting friends?

He turned to Yairi. "I've never even seen you with a woman."

Yairi grinned large. "I see many women. But I don't let them imprison me." He tapped his chest. "I don't let them imprison my heart."

"Maybe you don't know what you're missing."

"Maybe," conceded Yairi. "But," he said with a pointed finger, "maybe neither do you. Maybe you are missing a lot of things—big things!"

"Now what's that supposed to mean?"

"Hey, guys," Rock butted in, "can't we change the subject? Let's talk about *futebol* or something."

Yairi spat on the pavement.

"I'm waiting." Tony's voice was hard. "You've got nothing to say, have you? Think you know it all, don't you? Well, let me tell you something." Tony enumerated on his fingers. "Here's what I know for sure—about you." He grabbed his finger. "You're a crook. You hang out with murderers and known criminals. Maybe you're a killer yourself. You say Rodriguez killed my attacker the other night. But how do I know it wasn't you?"

"Tony—" Rock looked about nervously and smiled at a woman and child passing on the sidewalk.

"What? They probably don't speak English, anyway."

"Still," warned Yairi, "you must keep your voice down. Someone might hear and understand."

"Hear and understand what? Are you afraid the wrong people might find out about you? Like the police?"

Yairi's eyes were steely.

"Why did you suddenly move out of your apartment, Yairi? And why did that seaman try to kill me?"

Yairi effected a grin. "Conscripts are notoriously underpaid."

"Okay," said Rock. "I think we're all getting carried away here. I suggest dinner," he said, patting his empty stomach, "and drinks. Lots of drinks. You with me?" He looked at his friends expectantly.

Yairi held out his right hand. "I am sorry, my friend. I did not mean to offend. I only mean to help."

Tony blew out a chestful of warm breath. He was shaking. Tony felt like he hadn't breathed in an hour. He took Yairi's hand. "Yeah, me too." After all, he was at an age where he'd come to realize that friends were priceless.

Silvia worked as a dancer at a swank restaurant and nightclub located in the center of Rio named Club Brasil. It was a favorite of celebrities, politicians, moguls and foreigners.

Though Yairi was wholeheartedly against it and Rock himself seemed to think it was a bad idea, they slogged down to the club for drinks after dining at a restaurant Yairi had selected in Leblon.

If the human body's engine ran on alcohol, the three men could have driven up the Pan American Highway to the United States.

A doorman stopped them with a white-gloved hand. The ever politic Yairi muttered a curse and pushed his way past. "Come on, men." He marched up to the maitre'd and demanded a table. "If we're going to be here we might as well have good seats for the show." Yairi's head swivelled side to side.

"Looking for someone?" Rock asked. The place was packed. Many were in elaborate costumes, some in skimpy costumes. Some in drag.

The air was thick with smoke.

"No." Yairi nervously tapped the tabletop. He called to a waiter two tables away. "*Moço, um chopp*!"

The waiter glanced in their direction and nodded.

"You boys want beer or something harder?"

Tony and Rock agreed to the beers and Yairi ordered two more.

The stage was thirty feet away and barely four feet off the ground. Somewhere back there, behind the heavy brocaded purple curtains, Silvia was preparing for the show. Soon she would come out, with the others, wearing one of the sexy little outfits that were expected in a samba show. Often she was topless.

At first, Tony had thought this would bother him—with all those other men staring at her body in general, her bare breasts and round exposed derriere—but surprisingly, he'd come to accept it. Maybe he was becoming a *carioca* after all, and Yairi was wrong, he was loosening up.

Yairi bought a Cuban cigar from a passing cigarette girl, bit off the end and lit up. "If you ask me, this still isn't a good idea, Tony."

"I know, you've said that a hundred times."

"I'm with Yairi. You ought to wait and see Silvia after she gets off. She's working now. She may not be too happy to see you here."

Tony held his head up with his fists, elbows firmly planted on the hardwood table. The pink table cloth shifted and Yairi grabbed his glass."Careful, Tony."

Yairi craned his neck toward the right. It was the third time he'd done so.

"What is it that's so interesting over there?" Tony looked over Yairi's shoulder.

"Nothing, only a pretty lady in a black dress." Yairi winked. "I think she likes me."

The curtains opened and a small troupe of dark-skinned musicians came forward with drums and tambourines. The show had begun.

A dozen girls came out prancing, amongst them and most beautiful of them all, was his Silvia. Her green eyes shined like precious jewels and her lithe body never stopped moving.

Tony tried not to think about his friends Rock and Yairi and what they might be thinking of his girlfriend's naked body. Besides, it was Yairi who'd brought him to Club Brasil in the first place and introduced him to the girl. So he'd seen her naked maybe a thousand times before. Tony had not asked and had not wanted to know.

Tony turned his chair to face the stage directly. Silvia must have seen him, but she gave no indication. When she left the stage, Tony complained. "She never even acknowledged me."

"What did you expect? This is a choreographed show, man. She can't just stop and wave to you." Rock waved his hand and said in a high-pitched voice, "Hi, Ton-ee!"

"All right, all right." Tony pushed Rock's arm down. "I get the picture."

"Why don't we go?" Yairi suggested. "The next show here isn't for nearly forty minutes." He rose from his seat. "I know a place where we can hear some authentic Brazilian folk music—"

"Forget it," Tony said firmly. "You guys can go if you want to, but I'm not leaving until I've seen Silvia." He held up his glass and ordered another beer. "And talked to her."

Their waiter appeared. He set three beers on the tablecloth and handed Tony a folded slip of paper.

"What's that?" Rock leaned forward.

"It looks like a note." Tony unfolded the paper. He brightened. "It's from Silvia!" He scanned the words in the low light. "She says, 'I am sorry to miss you at the house earlier. I spoke with mother. Don't worry. All is forgiven. I will phone you at your hotel when I am free. Love, Silvia.'"

"Yeah, man." Rock raised his glass. "All's well that ends well."

"Yes, that is good news, Tony. I told you not to worry." Once more he rose. "Perhaps we should go now? I will show you some of my favorite places."

Tony refolded the paper and put it in his pocket. He was thinking. "Okay."

"Great." Yairi placed some bills on the table. "Drinks are on me."

"Thanks." Tony wasn't about to fight it. After all, Yairi was flush with the five grand they'd taken from Little Armando. He looked towards the stage. There was a side entrance that led toward the kitchen. "First I'm going to go say hi to Silvia. Then we can go wherever you guys want. Okay?"

Yairi was craning his neck again. He looked dubious. "Well, I suppose it will be alright now."

"I'll be right back."

"Can I come?" Rock asked.

"What for?"

"Are you kidding? You're going back to the dressing room with all those Brazilian babes and you gotta ask?"

Tony rolled his eyes. "Come on."

The three men threaded their way past the tables, dodged scurrying waiters and found their way to the dressing area. It was a large room which all the dancers and musicians shared. With all that nudity on stage, what was the point in pretending any modesty offstage?

Laughter and the chatter of several disparate conversations filled a brightly lit room with scattered tables and mismatched chairs. There were large mirrors on the longest wall.

At first Tony didn't see Silvia and wondered where she might have gone.

A silver haired man in the corner in a dark blue suit was holding a woman's arms. He was leaning close. Tony took him for an old lech getting a cheap feel of some young girl's bare breasts.

But when the man shifted and the girl looked over his protective shoulder it was Silvia that he saw. The blood drained from his face. Hers seemed to do the same as if some invisible beast had suddenly sucked the corpuscles right out of the both of them.

"Silvia—" he croaked and felt as if he were falling down an elevator shaft, hurling inexorably, hopelessly to the unseen black ground below.

Silvia's eyes had gone wide.

The man turned. "You!"

It was Silvia's uncle! Tony felt suddenly relieved and a smile began to form on his face.

"Shit," Yairi said.

"What?" Rock asked.

"Get out of here, Tony!" Yairi grabbed Tony roughly by the arm and yanked him to the side.

Silvia's uncle reached into his coat.

"Help me, Rock!"

"Let go of me!" insisted Tony, struggling vainly to free himself. "Silvia, what's going on?"

She looked from Tony to her uncle. "Fidel, no!"

He'd pulled a dangerous looking pistol from his inside pocket and held it at arm's length.

A shot was fired.

A mirror exploded six inches from Tony.

Men and women alike began shouting and fleeing in all directions. Tony was dragged from the room and shoved through the back door out into the sidestreet.

Tony pulled himself free of Rock and Yairi and grabbed for the door handle. It was locked. He turned about and faced Yairi. "What the hell is going on?"

Yairi lowered his eyes. "I am sorry, my friend. I didn't want you to see this."

"See what?" Tony looked at Rock for answers but saw only confusion. "Silvia and her uncle?"

Yairi's little brown eyes looked into Tony's. "This man is not Silvia's uncle, Tony. She is his mistress."

"Liar!" Tony lunged at him.

11

The waves hit the shore with a docile rhythm that belied the danger that could lurk beneath. The sweet odor of marijuana came from a small fire a hundred yards upwind from where they sat.

The sound of the samba came even to the beach at night. The moon had already passed the midway point. Somewhere out there, millions of Brazilians were partying, losing themselves to the music and magic of Carnaval.

Somewhere out there Tony had lost his heart. He dug his toes into the damp sand. He'd stuffed his socks into his shoes and tossed them aside. "Sorry about your eye."

"No problem." Yairi tenderly rubbed his left eye. "It is good to let go of your anger."

Rock was walking at the shoreline, his pants rolled up to his calves to keep the water from dampening them. "Yeah, I'd say you let it go pretty good, Tony. Man, I didn't know you had it in you!"

"Neither did I." Tony had lashed out at Yairi as if he was the one hurting him and not just the messenger of his pain. Rock had pulled him off. Yairi hadn't even tried to defend himself. And now Tony felt guilty as hell.

He stood and walked the few short steps to the ocean. A

homey smell of salt dosed sea air filled his lungs. Damn, he wished he was in Florida. And that made him chuckle. What a joke! Here he was—Carnaval in Rio—and wishing himself back home in Florida.

Tony pulled Silvia's folded note from his pocket. A scent of gardenias came with it. He tossed it into the Atlantic Ocean. The tiny piece of paper caught on the wind, fluttered like an injured butterfly, then connected with a small wave.

Tony watched it bounce and bob before losing sight of it in the inky darkness of ocean. He turned. "Tell me about him."

"Tony. . ." Yairi sat crosslegged on the sand, a stub of cigar hung from his lips.

"I want to know. You knew he was there all along, didn't you?"

"Yes, I knew. I saw him when we entered the club. He was sitting with friends in the corner."

"There was no girl smiling at you, was there?"

Yairi grinned. "A man can hope."

"Hey, if it wasn't for hope, I'd have no sex life at all," interjected Rock.

"Anyway, when you wanted to go see Silvia between shows I thought it would be okay. I thought he'd departed." Yairi shook his head. "I didn't think he'd gone to—"

"—see Silvia," Tony finished bitterly.

Yairi nodded his head.

"So? Who is he?" Tony thrust his hands in his pockets. He felt cold. The fine hair on his arms bristled.

"His name is Fidel Salu. He is an important man, a colonel in the Brazilian Navy. Well-respected."

"And he and Silvia are not related?"

"No."

"That explains a lot." Tony told Rock and Yairi what had happened the other day when Fidel had burst into Silvia's apartment and threatened him. "When I asked her afterwards, she told me he was her uncle and she didn't want to talk about it. She said he was old fashioned and resented my sleeping with her when she wasn't married."

"He resented you, all right. Salu is quite jealous. He comes to see her at Club Brasil every night that he can and threatens anyone who dares speak to her."

Tony couldn't blame him.

"Then you came along. I didn't know the two of you would start seeing one another."

Tony looked at the glowing lights of the highrises along *Avenida Atlantica* in Copacabana. They, too, were like jewels. Coming into Rio that first night, looking down on the city from the plane it had looked like a city he could fall in love with.

Instead it had become a city he had fallen in love in. Damn Silvia! Didn't she know how she'd hurt him?

"Salu must have become insanely jealous."

Tony rubbed the slowly healing Mount Kozolus on the side of his head. "I remember now. . .when that fellow hit me, the night I walked home from dinner with Yairi and his friends, the guy said 'Stay away from Silvia'. . .or something to that effect."

Yairi nodded. "He was one of Salu's men. I warn you, Tony. The colonel wants you dead."

Rock said, "We've got to go to the police. Let's get this bastard arrested!"

"I wish it were so simple," Yairi said with a sigh. "But, my friends, the police would never believe you. Why should they? Colonel Salu is a very powerful man. Who is going to believe that he is behind a simple mugging of an American? Besides, even if they did believe it, do you think they'd bother? After all, Salu is protecting his mistress. No man here would deny him that."

"Even if he tried to kill me?"

Yairi shrugged and traced a jagged line in the sand. It

looked like the line Tony had seen running along the neck of the dead man who had attacked him. "Even if he tried to kill you. You slept with his woman."

Tony's face tightened. "She was my woman." He kicked the sand and a broken shell splashed into the water. "At least I thought she was."

"You must forget Silvia," Yairi said.

"I can't," he replied in a voice as soft as the retreating waves.

12

Tony put the mouthpiece back in the cradle.

He'd taken it off the receiver before going to bed. Tony couldn't bear Silvia calling.

He didn't want to hear any lies. He didn't want to listen to any excuses.

Tony ran his hands through his hair and gave a start, then remembered the make-over he'd undergone at Luis Angel's behest. Those ridiculous bleached blonde ringlets. His head fell back on the thick feather-filled pillow. There was only one thing in the whole world that he wanted to do now.

Sleep.

Tony closed his eyes and put a tentative hand on his scalp. The bump on his head had shrunken to the size, and possibly the shape, of Vermont. Geography had never been one of Tony's strong suits in school.

He'd leave a wake-up call for when it was the size of Rhode Island. He'd wake up, have a late breakfast, grab a towel, rent an umbrella and spend the afternoon sleeping on the beach. . .

"Hey, you're awake."

Tony cracked open one eye.

Rock in his jailhouse pajamas gave the curtain cord a

yank.

"Cut that out!" groaned Tony. His mouth was dry and cottony. He'd been too depressed to even brush his teeth the night before. Of course, he also hadn't felt like seeing himself in the vanity mirror.

"Warn a guy next time." Tony's eyes were open now and he was faced with the surreal spectacle of a black and white striped monster against a brilliant white light background. "Move away from the window."

Rock laid a white, letter sized envelope on the covers.

"What's this?" asked Tony, propping himself up with a couple of pillows.

"I found it under the door when I got up. It's got your name on it."

"I can see that." Tony frowned. It looked like Silvia's handwriting. "It's from Silvia." The flimsy envelope fluttered in his hand.

"Aren't you going to open it? It's not a draft notice, you know."

"It may as well be." Tony rose and ambled slowly to the bathroom. The envelope fell from his fingers and landed with the trash in the wastebasket beside the desk which was still before the window where Prissy Pants had left it.

He turned on the cold water and splashed his face. Rock's booming voice came from the other room. "Dear Tony. Please, please, please, forgive me. It is not—"

"Rock, you had no business opening that!" Tony shouted through the door. "Will you—"

Rock's voice only bellowed louder. "—what you think. I saw Alvarez Yairi with you. I'm sure he has told you by now the sad story of me and . . .I cannot say his name. . .this other person. This person was in my life, I admit, yes. But it has been over for a long time. You must believe this. I only wish he would. He has been following me, you see. Though I have told him time and time again that it is over between us. He refuses to take no for an answer and intimidates any man who shows even an interest in being my friend. I love you, Tony."

Tony shut off the spigot. His heart beat loud and erratic in his chest. He stepped into the hallway.

Rock glanced up and continued reading. "I love you and want to be with you. To be your wife, if you still want me? We will even go to America." Rock shot Tony a startled look.

"Keep reading, Rock," Tony said quietly.

Rock's eyes returned to the paper. "I tried to phone you but you did not answer."

Tony groaned.

"So I write you this note and speak you my heart. Please, please, please call me or come see me. I will not leave the house until I have heard from you. And please watch out for you-know-who. He is a dangerous man. I am still mortified that he might have killed you last night." The big guy wiped a tear from his eye. "You will always have my heart. You can have all of me if you will."

Rock stumbled over the next couple words. "*Seu amor*, Silvia." He presented the letter to Tony. "I think that last part means 'your love.'"

"Yeah," rasped Tony. He grabbed at his wrist and remembered he didn't have a watch. "What time is it?"

He picked up the phone, got an outside line and dialed up Silvia. It rang twenty times before he hung up in frustration. "Damn." He looked at Rock. "I don't get it. She said she'd be home. That she wouldn't leave until she'd heard from me."

Rock could only shrug. He dropped to the floor and went on with his morning exercises, doing pushups on his fists. "Maybe," he huffed, "she's downstairs at her mom's."

"Yeah!" Tony punched the pillow. "Why didn't I think of that?"

"Guess that makes me the brains of the outfit, Curly," Rock replied, launching into a series of abdominal crunches, the sight of which made Tony's own poorly toned abs ache in empathy.

"Curly was one of the Stooges. And if you ask me, you look more like him than I do."

"Did you know Curly was Moe's little brother?"

"Can't say I did."

"Well, he was. You know, they even get *The Three Stooges* here. I saw them on TV speaking Portuguese the other afternoon. What a trip. When I was a kid, my parents got me a record of *The Three Stooges* singing nursery rhymes, like *Mairzy Doats, The Alphabet Song, Three Little Fishies, The Merry-Go-Round Broke Down. . .*" Rock scratch the stubble on his chin. "Amazing the stuff we remember, huh, Tony?"

Tony had given up listening. "The problem is, I don't know Mrs. Parra's number." He grabbed the local phone directory and started searching. There was an abundance of Parras.

But no Ella Parra. "Not even a Tzininha Parra," said Tony in disgust.

"How about E. Parra? Did you think of that?"

Rock was doing jumping jacks now and Tony feared for the guests in the room below. They were probably evacuating right now, alarmed that the hotel was collapsing. The bed was vibrating and he hadn't had to stick a quarter in any box.

Tony's answer was a what-do-you-take-me-for look. "I'll try the operator." Five minutes of broken English and incomprehensible Brazilian Portuguese later, Tony was no closer to a number for Silvia's mother. He had been connected to a dentist and a barber, however. The barber he could have used and getting a number for Mrs. Parra was like pulling teeth, so maybe there was some serendipity to life after all.

Nonetheless he was no closer to speaking to Silvia.

"So, go see her already," Rock suggested. He was sitting cross-legged on the floor now, playing scales on his electric bass.

"I plan on it." Tony went to the bathroom, brushed his teeth and hopped into the shower. As he soaked his head under the jet force shower head trying to obliterate both the hair color and his godforsaken curls, there came a rap at the door.

Rock called, "I've got it."

Tony quickly shut off the faucets, whipped open the shower curtain, twisted a towel around his waist and jumped out of the tub. He slipped on the tile, caught himself in the doorway and collided with Rock. "That could be Silvia!"

Rock stepped aside.

Tony opened the door.

"Ah," clicked Alba Zica, "foul blankets, wet towels. . .you are quite on the cutting edge of fashion, Tony. I see Rio has much to learn about *haute couture*. Here we wear merely clothes so simple as shirts and slacks."

"I thought you were someone else." Tony notched his towel tighter around his waist. "Besides, I was in the shower."

Miss Prissy Pants stepped around him, careful that he didn't drip on her white linen outfit and waved a newspaper in front of Rock's nose.

"Hi-ya, Alba." Rock ran a hand over his head.

"You are made up for a Carnaval ball?"

"Huh?" Rock tugged his pajama top. "Oh, these. They're my pajamas."

Miss Zica rolled her eyes.

"You'll excuse me." Tony grabbed a pair of shorts and a tank top and dressed in the bathroom. When he came back he asked, "So what brings you to our humble abode?"

Whatever it was, she'd better make it quick. Tony had to see Silvia right away. There was so much he wanted to tell her. It didn't matter about Fidel Salu. None of the past mattered. All that mattered was that they were together.

Married. They'd go to the United States where Salu would never bother them again.

"You have seen this?" Luis' assistant slapped the newspaper down on the desk where it unrolled.

"It's a newspaper," Rock said matter-of-factly.

Tony leaned over the table. Drops of water fell from his damp hair to the paper and quickly soaked through. He couldn't even understand the headline.

Alba Zica was watching him. "Turn it over."

Tony obliged. There, on the lower half of the front page, was a picture of Luis Angel, the boss, cuddling with a knockout young girl with short blonde hair.

Tony looked at Miss Zica. "So?" The picture looked like it might have been taken at the Sambadrome.

Miss Zica folded her arms under her ample chest. "There has been an incident."

"What sort of an incident?"

Rock studied the picture. "Looks like a good one to me."

"Unfortunately, Luis has had—" she paused, "how do you say—relations with the girl in this photo."

"Good for him. Now, if you don't mind?" Tony motioned towards the door. "I was just on my way out."

A small smile came to Miss Zica's lips. What the joke was, Tony didn't know.

Yet.

She picked up the newspaper and hurled choleric looks at the image. In obvious disgust she said, "The young woman is the daughter of a prominent banker from Rio."

"Is there more to this story that you've got to tell or do I have to wait for the book?" Tony sat in the closest chair and began putting on his socks and shoes.

"Yeah, what gives?" added Rock. "Hell, if you're jealous, all you've got to do is go out on a date with me, Alba."

Miss Zica turned on the boys angrily. "The young woman—should I say girl— is underage. Fifteen."

"Shit," whistled Rock.

"And, though Brazil may seem quite an open minded country, the girl's father, in this case, is not so liberal. He is furious and insulted. He wants retribution."

"What's Luis doing?" Tony asked. He couldn't help himself. Suddenly this was getting interesting.

"What he does best," Miss Zica said as she paced the narrow space between the window and the beds, "running."

"Running?" Rock repeated.

"*Sim*. He has charted a private jet and is already on his way to the airport."

"That doesn't give us much time." Tony had sudden visions of being torn apart by two horses, one being his love for Silvia and the other is obligation to his job.

Miss Zica was smiling wanly again. She looked at her slender gold watch. "That doesn't give *me* much time."

Tony said warily, "What's that supposed to mean?"

Prissy Pants pulled two envelopes from the same leather purse that had swallowed their room key the other day. One bore Tony's name, the other Rock's. "Luis has decided that a vacation is in order."

"But what about the tour?" demanded Tony, feeling yet another rug being pulled out from under him.

"The tour has been canceled indefinitely. You understand. I have been instructed to give you your severance pay." She shook Tony's hand, then Rock's.

Rock looked like he'd just had a rock dropped on his head and only said, "But. . ."

Luis' assistant stopped in the open doorway. "The room is paid up through tomorrow. Enjoy it, gentlemen. *Tchau*."

Tony stared at the back of the door then looked at Rock, who himself looked dumbfounded. And whether it was from their losing the tour, their jobs and their hotel room or rather his abruptly losing Alba Zica, Tony couldn't tell.

"Shit." Rock tore open his envelope. "Well, I got fifteen

hundred bucks anyway."

Tony ripped open his envelope. It was a check for the same. "This stinks. They can't do this. We were guaranteed a minimum of ten weeks' work!" He threw the envelope across the bed. "We've got an iron clad contract. Where is it? Let me see it."

Rock scratched his head. "Well. . ."

"Luis Angel is not going to get away with this. I used to be an attorney, after all!" Tony pushed the desk away from the window and back to the wall where it belonged.

"Don't just stand there, Rock. Get me the contract." Tony had given Rock power-of-attorney to sign their contract before they'd left the States while he'd been taking care of his passport. They'd been hired as a duo and everything had been done in a mad rush.

"I'm thinking." Rock went to the closet and pulled out his suitcase. "I think I got a copy here someplace." He tossed the suitcase on his bed and began rummaging around. He pulled out a long manilla envelope. "Ah, this might be it."

Rock stuck in his hand and produced a document several pages thick.

"Great! Let me see it." Tony snatched the contract from Rock's hand. "If Luis thinks he can run out on us and get away with it he's got another thing coming. When I'm through with him—"

"Uh, there's just one thing, Tony. . ."

"What's that?"

Rock was fidgeting. "Well, it's just that. . .well. . ."

"Oh, for crying out loud, Rock, if you've got something to say—" Tony looked at the first page of the contract.

Time froze.

Tony quickly rifled through the remainder of the pages. His eyes were twice their normal size.

Rock backed up.

"It's in Portuguese!" Tony screamed madly. "Are you

insane? You signed a contract in Portuguese?!"

"I'm sorry, Tony. I'm sorry." Rock wrung his hands. "I didn't think it would matter none."

Tony opened his mouth to speak but couldn't find a solitary appropriate word; though a fusillade of invectives would have done his soul good. He flung the useless contract to the floor.

"We could get somebody to translate it for us, maybe?" Rock suggested hopefully.

Tony shook his head no. "By the time we pay some local lawyer to do that, what little money we've got will be spent."

Rock let out a short sigh. "So what are we going to do, Tony?"

13

"Okay, okay." Tony paced. "No need to get all worked up about this. We're going to tie up our loose ends here, get Silvia and book ourselves on the first available flight out that we can manage. You like Florida, Rock?"

"Sure, had a good time there when I was down touring with Clint Cash and the Cowhands, anyway. And that's where you and I met."

"Yeah." Tony took a deep breath. It was all about not getting excited. Maintaining control. "At least we've got our return tickets, huh?"

Rock looked surprised. "We do?"

Now it was Tony's turn. "What do you mean, '*we do?*' You told me it was in our—" Tony's voice rose as his eyes fell on the useless contract fallen on carpet the color of Rio's beaches. Someone might have rolled up a swath of beach and spread it out again in the small room. Quietly he said, his lips barely turning, "You don't have any return tickets to the States, do you, Rock?"

"No, Tony."

Tony grabbed his head. He rubbed and he squeezed and he wished he hadn't. Head wounds, even the size of Vermont, were slow to heal and hurt like hell.

Tony headed for the door.

"Where are you going?"

"I'm going to try and catch Prissy Pants." Tony stormed out.

"Wait for me!" hollered Rock, bounding after him like a leviathan mastiff in striped pajamas.

Tony was already at the elevators, stalking anxiously. When the middle elevator opened he jumped in.

"Hold it!" Rock squeezed through the closing doors. "Oh, excuse me," he said to a rotund, pink-skinned, middle aged woman with half a dozen gold chains around her neck. He hit the button for the penthouse. "Up?"

"No," Tony said. "The lobby. Don't you remember? Alba said Luis has already gone." The elevator began its descent. Fortunately the woman had initially selected the lobby.

"But Alba might have gone back up to the room," said Rock.

"Maybe, but if Luis is already on his way to the airport, Prissy Pants can't be far behind."

"Not unless she wants to get left behind."

"Nah, Luis wouldn't leave without her," snapped Tony. "Who else would the kid get to change his diapers?"

Rock laughed.

The plump woman in sneakers and a frock the color of pink Impatiens compressed herself as best she could into the corner. She was muttering under her breath in what sounded like German.

As the elevator doors came open at the lobby level, the deceptively fleet of foot dame drove past Tony and Rock like a three hundred pound bowling ball, buffeting the boys away like six ounce bowling pins.

"Hey!" Rock shouted indignantly. "Lady! Didn't you ever hear of—"

Tony pulled down the big guy's arm. "Forget it, Rock, we've got bigger fish to fry."

"Hell," replied Rock, "I ain't never seen a fish bigger than that."

"Never mind." Kozol pushed his way through to the front of the line at the check-in counter. "Pardon me."

A kid in a red blazer tapped away at an ivory colored keyboard. His eyes went from the screen to Tony and back again.

"Excuse me, but I'm in a hurry. I'm looking for Alba Zica." He spelled it out. "Can you tell me if she is still registered here? She may have been staying in Luis Angel's suite."

"I'm afraid I cannot give out this information, *senhor*." He made eye contact with a man in a tan colored suit. "Next, please!"

"Just a second," Tony said. "I'm Tony Kozol. I'm with Luis Angel's band."

Fingers clickety-clacked and the kid in the suit came to a decision. "Luis Angel has checked out."

"I know that," Tony said in exasperation. He looked at the time on the gold clock behind the counter. Its hands were sweeping away his life even as he watched. Alba could be halfway to the airport by now. But he was hoping she was still in the hotel somewhere. "I'm trying to find out if *Senhorita* Zica has also left."

The clerk beckoned a bellhop. Words were exchanged in sing-song Portuguese and the clerk waved the bellhop on his way. "Miss Zica has hired a radio taxi." He raised his shiny black eyebrows. "She is departing now. Is there anything else, sir?"

"Hey, I see her!" called Rock. "Hey, Alba!"

Tony looked out the window. Miss Zica was in the backseat of a small black car, one of Rio's unmarked radio dispatched taxis. "Thanks!"

Tony ran. "Don't just stand there, Rock! She can't hear you. Get her!"

"Right!"

The big guy, closer to the lobby entrance than his partner, leapt into the revolving door only to be shunted out by a young mother and daughter coming in from the beach with armloads of towels and toys.

"Excuse me," he said, as he waited for the child to go twice around the revolving door.

Tony cursed under his breath and went out the side entrance. The car was slowly inching its way into the heavy traffic. "Hey!" Tony ran into the street and waved his arms. "Stop! Hey!"

The little car disappeared, one of the cogs in the snake-like motion of traffic flitting down *Avenida Atlantica*.

"Now what?" Rock folded his arms across his chest.

Tony watched Alba's taxi dwindle in size to that of a Matchbox Racer. They could hire a taxi and try to chase her, but what would be the point? Even if they caught up with the woman or even Luis Angel himself, would it make any difference? "Back to Plan A. Let's clear up our business here and get the hell out."

"Agreed." Rock turned his head from side to side. "Uh, Tony, why is everybody looking at me?"

"Gee, Rock, I don't know. Maybe they think you're a rock star. Or a motion picture celebrity. Of course," Tony said, bringing his hand to his chin and making a show of studying his friend, "it could be those neat PJ's of yours."

Rock wiggled his toes. "Oops."

Rock dressed and met Tony at the rooftop restaurant where Tony was already breakfasting on eggs and fruit. He was on his second cup of coffee. Tall windows enclosed the roof on three sides. A small pool, occupied by a woman in her mid-twenties sat center stage. The blonde haired girl looked Scandinavian and could have been a runway model. She had a light sunburn and stood half-submerged in the clear blue water.

Rock smiled and said hello. She smiled back and Rock took a chair facing her. "Nice view."

"Yeah," Tony said. "Don't you ever stop?"

"Why should I? I'm not the one who's in love." Rock ordered orange juice and told the waiter he'd be having the buffet.

"Speaking of which, I'd better try and phone Silvia again. I'm beginning to worry about her."

"Relax, Tony. You think too much." Rock stood. "I'm gonna get some grub." Rock disappeared inside. When he returned, he was balancing two platefuls of food; exotic fruits, sausage, ham, toast, pastries and a bowl of cereal nested in his scrambled eggs.

"What's wrong, Rock? Not hungry this morning?"

Rock set down his dishes. "Very funny. Look, everything's paid up until tomorrow and I'm getting my money's worth. Thought I might even call home. Haven't talked to Mom and Dad since before we left the States."

Home was West Memphis, Arkansas. Rock's father was a preacher in a small church. Tony wasn't sure he remembered which denomination, but thought it was Southern Baptist.

Rock layered a spoonful of runny eggs on top a slice of toast and took a bite. "They worry about me, you know."

Tony shook his head. "So do I." Tony wiped his lips with a linen napkin. "Look, when you're finished—if you finish—" the twin peaks of food on Rock's plate looked insurmountable, "call your mom and dad and anybody else you like. Hell, you can phone New Zealand and leave the phone off the hook for all I care. But," Tony fished in his wallet and pulled out a slip of yellow paper, "first I want you to call Yairi. I wonder what he's going to make of all this and if he's been paid off the same as us."

"I doubt if he's worried. He's still got Little Armando's money."

"Yeah, well, if he's smart he'll give it back." Tony unfolded the paper and slipped it under Rock's knife. It was the new number Yairi had given him the night before. "You just call Yairi and tell him what's happened. Tell him we're leaving tomorrow. Oh, and call the airlines and see what you can find."

Rock sized up a fresh fig and popped it into his mouth. "And just what are you going to be doing while I'm doing all the work?"

"I'm going to phone Silvia again. I've got to straighten things out with her and let her know what's going on. Get Silvia a ticket, too."

"To Florida?"

"That's right."

"Are you sure she'll go?"

Tony rose. "I'm sure." He wasn't.

"But what about visas, passports. . ."

"Never mind all that. You said I like to worry, so let me worry about all those details. I'll marry her today if that's what it takes." And he would.

Rock grunted and scooped up a buttery-scented croissant. "Man, I don't know if it's the sun or the bump on your head, but you're getting crazier every day."

"I'll worry about that, too."

"I would if I were you."

Tony left the table. "I'll check back with you later. If you're not in the room leave me a note and let me know how things stand."

"Will do, boss." Rock gave a full croissant salute, leaving crumbs pressed into his forehead.

To save time, Tony dialed up Silvia from the lobby. Was the phone going to ring forever like last time? His heart skipped as the receiver at her end was picked up on the fourth ring. "Hello, Silvia, it's me!"

Silvia said nothing.

"Silvia, please. I got your note."

"*Quem é na linha*?" demanded an unrecognizable and gruff male voice.

"Huh? Silvia? Is this Silvia's house?" Tony looked at the receiver as if he could peer through the wires and identify the speaker at the other end.

"*Como é seu nome*?"

Tony hung up. He was confused. Who was that man? Could it be Fidel Salu? It didn't sound quite like him. With trembling fingers he dialed Silvia's number again, more slowly this time, not missing a digit.

The phone on the other end was picked up on the first ring.

"*Oi*." It was the same menacing voice.

Tony gave a start. "Who is this? May I speak to Silvia, *por favor*?"

"*Aqui é a policia. Como é seu nome*?"

Tony quickly hung up the receiver and backed away. The phone started ringing accusingly and he ran outside. It was a knee jerk guilty reaction and he didn't even know why. He'd heard the word *policia* and understood they were asking his name. That was enough to make him run.

Traffic whirled around him. Beach goers, tourists and locals alike, swam past. Tony felt as if he was running against a watercolor background in the rain and what was true one instant was false the next as each color bled into the succeeding one. Reality seemed to have taken a quick jump to the left while he'd been going to the right. Tony didn't know what was real anymore and what was counterfeit.

But he knew one thing. . .he had to get to Silvia's house.

Some minutes later, lathered in sweat, Tony found himself on Silvia's street. How he'd gotten there he couldn't remember and it didn't matter. Traffic was thick.

As he got closer, Tony spotted two police cars parked

bumper to bumper in the road, virtually blocking the street at this end. Their small lights flashed and whirled yet were all but washed out in the bright light of the midday tropics. Another car was double parked at the curb near the garage.

A small crowd had gathered and spilled out from the sidewalk to the road. Probably another impromptu celebration in honor of Carnaval.

"Excuse me," repeated Tony over and over as he shouldered his way through men, women and children. He expected to hear the infectious sound of samba but heard only indecipherable talk and saw only nervous eyes looking about.

The throng suddenly thinned at the sidewalk surrounding Silvia's home. A police officer was at the front gate and another at the side.

Tony paused and wiped his forehead. The guard glanced at him then turned his attention to a young boy who was trying to squeeze his head through the iron bars. The boy's mother grabbed his hand and hurried him off.

"*Por favor.*"

The officer rested a hand on his baton.

"Um, *com licença.*"

The officer attempted to shoo Tony away with a look and a shove.

"Wait," said Tony, planting his feet against the sidewalk. "Wait." He pointed at the house. "*Senhora* Parra. I am an *amigo.*"

The police officer pushed him more firmly this time. An audience was watching.

What was going on? Had the elderly Mrs. Parra suffered an accident of some sort? A heart attack? Silvia had earlier mentioned her mother had a weak heart and that she had suffered a mild heart attack the previous year. Poor Mrs. Parra.

Tony smiled at the officer and stepped back to the curb.

He walked to the corner closest to Silvia's front window. The curtains were open but there was nothing to see. He cupped his hands and called out, "Silvia! Silvia! It's me, Tony!"

She didn't appear. If only he could stick his fingers in his mouth and give with one of those Olympic-sized whistles like Rock was capable of blowing.

Then a man in a short sleeved white shirt stuck his head out the open window and barked. Tony didn't even see the officer at the front gate as he suddenly grabbed him with two hands, one on the shoulder and the other on his left arm.

"Hey!" Tony tried to get loose but as the officer led him inside the Parra gates he decided to give in. After all, that was where he wanted to be in the first place. "Alright, I'm going, I'm going," complained Tony as the officer rough housed him towards the outside stairway.

Tony jogged up the steps while the officer reclaimed his post at the front gate. There was neither sight nor sound of Lennon and McCartney.

The front door stood open.

"Silvia?" Tony stopped dead in his tracks. The sound of an ambulance drifted closer as if it was rising from a hole that had opened up in the earth. A hole that now threatened to dart Tony's way and swallow him whole.

The small apartment was astir with men, some in suits, some in uniforms. The man in the white shirt, with the parrot- like tuft of brown hair atop his head, stood with his arms folded. A cigarette was clenched between his down-turned lips.

But none of that mattered.

In the center of the room sat Silvia, in one of the kitchen chairs. Someone had moved it there, away from the table where it belonged.

Silvia, her hair twisted and unkempt, didn't move. The scent of mango rose unbidden, as if she had just showered and washed her hair and hadn't had the time to comb it out.

Her white terry robe gaped open, exposing freckled breasts. Silvia's long elegant legs were askew. Her neck was limp and Silvia's chin rested against her chest. Silvia's arms had been tied behind her.

A thin white rope, like the kind used for a clothes line, twisted several times around her waist.

Another wound tightly about her limp neck.

Silvia's face was streaked with dried tears and her dazzling green eyes were closed.

Forever. . .

Tony shouted.

14

It took two police officers to subdue Tony and wrestle him to the ground.

The man in the white shirt with the tufted hair passed to the door, mashed his cigarette out on the guardrail and let the butt fall to the bushes below. He looked down at Tony, his round face expressionless. Tony couldn't help noticing a resemblance between this man and a particular cartoon character. For, in fact, this fellow looked like a grown-up, middle aged version of Herge's *Tintin.*

In a low but commanding tone, the man said something to Tony's captors and the smaller of the two searched Tony's pockets. He removed Tony's wallet from the back pocket and handed it over to the man in charge. All the while, the more corpulent of his opponents held Tony down, gripping him by the wrists with his arms held painfully behind his back.

The man who seemed to be in charge opened the wallet, studied the driver's license, looked at Tony and studied it some more.

"It's me," Tony said.

The man looked at him with interest. "American?"

Tony nodded. His Silvia was just a few yards away and he avoided looking in that direction as if to do so would be to face Medusa herself. Though at this point, being turned to salt might be an improvement. It might even end the endless heartbreak that was waiting inside, like an overloaded dam on the verge of bursting.

"You look not like your photo." The man dropped Tony's wallet open in front of him.

"I've had a haircut." So, this guy spoke English.

"The color is also much changed and, of course, the curls. Perhaps you are trying to hide your identity?"

"No. Look, it wasn't even my idea. It's for my job. . .or, it was for my job. . .which I don't have anymore. And what's my hair got to do with anything, anyway?"

"You carry no passport. That is a crime for tourists in Brazil."

"It's back at the hotel because pickpocketing is a crime, too, but that doesn't seem to stop the crooks around here."

"What is the name of this hotel?"

"Ipanema Palace." Tony squirmed and his keeper squeezed harder. "You want to tell this goon to let me up?"

The man nodded and Tony felt his hands being released. He rubbed his wrists and slowly rose from the floor. Tony turned towards the open door.

"I would not suggest running, Mr. Kozol."

Without turning around, Tony replied. "I wasn't thinking of running. I just didn't want to have to see. . ." He couldn't finish his sentence.

"I understand." The man came forward and blocked the doorway. He lit another cigarette and tossed the match carelessly outdoors. "Of course, there are many reasons for not wanting to see. A woman is dead, a beautiful woman at that. Such a shame."

He shook his head in a gesture of sadness, but what could he know of sadness, wondered Tony.

"That is always hard to see, even for I who am supposed to be used to such things." The round faced man inhaled deeply, sucking up his fix of nicotine and releasing a cloud of death into the air.

"You know, Mr. Kozol. Sometimes it is quite difficult for a murderer to see one's victim. It can be quite disturbing. If one has any moral fiber at all, it can be nearly impossible, especially if the murder were an act of passion. . ." With cigarette in hand he wiped back his crown of hair. "One experiences remorse."

"Are you accusing me? I didn't kill Silvia. I love her!" Tony balled up his fists. Ready to fight the entire force of the police but unable to fight back the tears that proceeded to fall.

"I am Captain Paolo Fausto. It is my sad duty to investigate this young woman's death. I suggest we sit and talk, Mr. Kozol." He motioned to Silvia's small sofa.

Tony wiped away his tears and turned. Silvia! He ran to her. Officers hurried to stop him and Captain Fausto ordered them to stand down.

Tony gently pulled Silvia's robe closed over her chest. He ran his hands over her head and whispered. "I love you," and more softly, "and I'm going to kill whoever did this to you. I promise."

"Mr. Kozol?"

Tony took a seat on the sofa across from the captain. He rubbed his arms and legs. Why did it feel so damn cold in here? Why was his skin freezing even as his heart was burning?

"Mr. Kozol, I asked you a question."

"Huh?"

Captain Fausto played with his cigarette which was now half its original length. "I ask how you come to know the victim."

"Her name is, was, Silvia Parra."

"I am aware of this, Mr. Kozol. I only thought it less painful to you if I were to be less precise."

"And we were friends. More than friends. We were going

to be married."

"That is so?" Captain Fausto straightened and sucked the remains of his cigarette. Finding no ashtray he deposited the butt in a clay pot that held a fern of some sort. Why not? Silvia wasn't going to mind.

Tony rubbed his arms again.

"You are cold? It is quite warm in here."

Tony shrugged.

Captain Fausto said something to one of his officers who grinned and pulled a flask from inside his jacket and handed it to Tony. "Drink."

Tony opened the silver flask and sniffed.

"Whiskey."

"Trying to get me drunk so I'll confess? Is that how it's done here?"

Captain Fausto shook his head. "If you'd rather not—"

Tony tilted the bottle and put it to his lips. The whiskey burned going down. But maybe that was what he needed.

Captain Fausto waited patiently.

Tony lowered the flask and handed it to the captain who drank slowly and wiped his mouth with the back of his hand. "So, you will tell me, please, how long you have known," he paused, "the young lady."

Tony explained.

"And these people you mention can vouch for your whereabouts this morning?"

"Sure, even the people at the hotel. I mean, I was just talking to them before I came here. You can ask at the front desk."

"You will write the names down of any persons you might remember."

"Sure. Listen, do you mind if I stand? I'm going crazy."

"Of course." Captain Fausto took a drink of whiskey. "Another drink, perhaps?"

Tony agreed. He took the cool flask in hand and tipped it

back. He glanced out the window. The crowd was no smaller, if anything it had grown. An ambulance had arrived and a crew was working its way forward.

And then Tony spotted a familiar face, in brown slacks and a white t-shirt. Yairi! He leaned against the side of a tree across the street, like a smaller secondary trunk, casually sipping a beer and watching the house. What the hell was Yairi doing here?

Tony gulped and swallowed fire. Yairi had finished his beer and stomped the can underfoot. When Yairi looked up, there was an unmistakable grin on his face.

And then Tony understood. "You son of a bitch!" he shouted and threw the flask out the window. Tony bounded for the door and half-ran, half-tumbled down the stairs.

He was only barely aware of Captain Fausto's angry shouts behind him.

Tony charged out the gates, past the startled sentry and into the crowd, screaming all the while. "Yairi? Yairi, you bastard! I'll kill you! I swear, I'll kill you!"

He pushed his way through the startled onlookers but when he got to the tree he was alone. Had he imagined it? Tony looked wildly up and down the street for a sight of Alvarez Yairi. There was nothing.

Perhaps he had been hallucinating. Crestfallen, he paused to catch his breath.

Rough hands grabbed Tony and pushed him up against a car. It was the police.

Captain Fausto, apparently as physically fit as Tony, was wheezing and coughing. "What the hell are you doing, fool!"

"I-I thought I saw someone I knew." Tony groaned. His back was pressed into the door handle. "I thought he might be the murderer. I didn't kill Silvia, I swear, Captain."

The captain pressed his hands against his knees and coughed. He spat against the wall of the house at the corner and straightened his back. "You idiot. You run from the police?! You could have been shot!"

"I don't care," Tony said defiantly. "The woman I love is dead. So what's the use in living?"

"Perhaps to live to see her killer brought to justice?"

"Very funny, considering I'm your number one suspect."

Captain Fausto forced a laugh. "Are all you Americans this *louco*?"

"If there's a joke, I wish you'd let me in on it."

Captain Fausto said, "I will ask my men to release you so long as you pull no more stunts."

Tony agreed and was free once more.

"Mr. Kozol, I am a police officer. I don't know how my colleagues in the United States work, but here I follow all trails, gather all details." The captain wiped a line of perspiration from his flushed and mottled forehead. "But as far as Silvia Parra's murder is concerned, we already have a good suspect."

"You mind telling me who?"

The Captain shook his head no. "I am afraid that might compromise my investigation. Though I must insist you inform me who it was you were chasing."

Tony hesitated then said. "His name's Alvarez Yairi. He's a friend of mine."

Captain Fausto's thin brows went up. "And so you pursue him as a murderer?"

"Is he?"

"Again, I cannot say."

The captain's poker face was unreadable. Tony looked at the stained, uneven sidewalk. A crushed beer can lay beside the tree. So at least he hadn't imagined that part.

The captain might not be willing to talk and Tony couldn't make him. But he could track down Yairi and he would make him talk. . .at any cost.

15

When Tony and Captain Fausto returned to the house, the ambulance crew was bringing Silvia's body down the stairs in a black body bag. Mrs. Parra stood at the bottom of the stairs, her face blanched, the tears unrestrained.

"Mrs. Parra," Tony began, "I am so sorry. Believe me, if there is anything I can do. . ."

"You can leave!" Tzininha said fiercely coming round from the front of the Parra home. She grabbed her mother and led her away.

Mrs. Parra remained silent and allowed herself to be shuffled off. Tzininha had her arms around her mother's waist.

"Tzininha!" Tony pleaded. "Please, listen to me— "

"I don't want to see you here again. We don't want to see you here again."

"Mrs. Parra, please, you must— "

Captain Fausto pulled Tony back. "Poor Mrs. Parra. It is she who discovered her daughter's body." Captain Fausto released Tony's shoulder. "I think it is best for you to go now, *senhor*. If we have further need, we will contact you."

Tony watched as Tzininha led her mother into the house and shut the door. Mrs. Parra looked so frail now, where only a day before she had seemed so strong. Lips trembling, Tony fought back fresh tears.

The ambulance drivers had shut the rear door of their vehicle and turned on their flashing lights. Why, he couldn't imagine. What was the hurry when you were dead?

Rock wasn't in their hotel room. Tony took it out on the walls. "Goddam it! Where the hell are you, Rock?" He picked up a pillow and threw it at the wall, knocking a picture from its hanger. It fell to the floor, the frame cracked.

Not even a lousy message. Tony had told Rock to leave word if he went out and he hadn't. How the hell was he going to find Yairi? He'd given Rock the only clue he had, the slip with Yairi's telephone number. Now there was no way of tracking the miscreant down until Rock got back and Tony didn't even know where the big guy had gone or when he'd return.

Tony left the hotel and hailed a cab. On the third try, he found a driver who spoke English. At least enough. Tony didn't know the address, but he was pretty sure he remembered the way.

He was going to the *favela*. He would find Little Armando or his brother, Victor. They would know where to find Yairi.

The taxi driver refused to drive up the mountain. He refused to go even as far as Rodriguez and Oswaldo had taken Tony and Rock on their previous visit to the slums.

He paid off the driver at the main road and marched up without hesitation. Tony had no trouble finding the run-down market where the truck had dropped them. There was the same worn-out, wary looking shopkeeper; the same wooden bars, worn smooth in spots where countless hands had tried to pilfer the fresh food within. Yet it was out of reach.

It was always out of reach.

Tony looked up the mountain. Somewhere up there was

the lair of Little Armando. But now that he was standing in the *favela*, his goal seemed unreachable, like a mirage shimmering on the road ahead. Which tiny road led to the samba hall? This one or that?

Tony jogged up to a woman garbed in a tattered red dress. She had a scarf wrapped around her hair. Only a wisp of fine dark hair lightly touched with gray dared show itself.

"Little Armando?"

Her brown eyes widened as if he'd aimed a gun at her stomach. She bent her head to the ground and hurried off.

Tony ignored the stares of the young men on the street and headed upward.

After a time, he noticed that he'd drawn a crowd. A growing parade was following the American stranger up the mountain. He turned and faced them. "Armando?" Tony pointed up the hill.

Hungry faces made no reply. But when Tony renewed his steps so did they.

A thin youth, no more than nineteen stepped out from the shadows of two leaning buildings and stood in Tony's path. He made beckoning motions with his right hand.

Tony hesitated.

"*Pouco Armando, não?*"

Tony studied the speaker. He didn't look armed or particularly dangerous, but there could be a knife in those bagger trousers and Tony could find his throat slit around the next corner.

Tony looked over his shoulder. The entourage was still in tow. He took a chance and nodded his assent.

The stranger grinned and hurried forward, darting down a narrow, uneven track to the right. They snaked upward through tiny streets that stunk of human waste. The sun barely touched the ground here on these tiny paths between buildings so close together people could reach out and shake hands between the windows. The buildings themselves looked unsteady on their feet.

Tony's followers had had to proceed in twos through some of the tighter spots. He was beginning to think he was being led in ever widening circles when the decaying walls suddenly gave way to open space. He'd reached the plateau!

There ahead of him was the practice hall and seeming headquarters for Little Armando. Tony carefully removed twenty *reais* from his wallet.

The young man snatched it from his hand and ran across the courtyard, disappearing down one of many little streets.

The armed guards at the doors had no problem letting him in. He didn't even have to ask. They'd opened the doors as if reading his mind.

Had he been expected?

The great cavernous hall was empty. Victor, wearing an olive colored suit that could have passed for a Brooks Brothers, stood at the top of the stairs. "*Senhor* Kozol, how good to see you again."

Tony hesitated.

"Please, come up. My brother is waiting for you. He has a gift."

Tony climbed to the landing and asked, "You knew I was coming?"

Victor laughed. "While there are few telephones here, you will find that our people make quite the—how do you say—grapevine." Victor laughed again. "Besides, a white man coming alone up into the *favela* is as notable as the coming of Christ!"

"I'm looking for Alvarez Yairi."

"*Sim*?" Victor opened the door to the office. "Come. We shall discuss this."

The office was cool, cooler than Tony remembered. Perhaps Little Armando had had air conditioning installed in the meantime. Tony wouldn't put it past him.

Little Armando rose from his chair behind the table as

Tony entered. He leaned forward and held out his hand. His one eye seemed to study Tony as well as any microscope lens.

Tony had no choice but to take Little Armando's hand and shake it.

There were no guards present. But Tony wasn't about to be fooled by that. They could be hiding behind the door or lurking someplace close by. Tony had no doubt that they would be.

"Sit, please, Mr. Kozol."

Tony sat. "Look, I'm sorry to bother you," he began, suddenly realizing the perilous position he'd put himself in, "but I need to get a hold of Alvarez Yairi." Little Armando sat and, in English, asked his brother Victor to bring them some beers. Victor obliged by plucking three ice covered cans of Skol from the same cooler Tony remembered seeing on his last calamitous visit.

Victor handed Tony a can. Tops were popped.

"*A nossa bom fortuna,*" said Little Armando.

Tony tipped his beer and drank. He didn't know what Little Armando's words meant, but he could guess. Tony gripped the cold beer in his hand, his fingers stinging from the cold but he was afraid to set the wet can down on the lustrous table. "About Yairi. . ."

"This is no problem." Little Armando swung his chair around, opened a wooden cabinet, removed pen and paper. He wrote quickly. "This is his address. Alvarez has moved to Copacabana."

"*Obrigado.*"

"It's nothing. In fact, I have something for you and your partners."

"We're not—"

Victor wagged his finger and Tony shut up.

Little Armando reached into the cabinet once more. He set a stack of worn American bills on the table top. Tony didn't need to count it. He knew what it was. Another five thousand dollars. For a job well done, no doubt.

"We are much grateful to you." Little Armando pushed the pile forward. "Please."

Tony's mouth had gone dry. He nodded and picked up the money.

"I suggest you put it someplace safe until you can dispose of it properly. There are a lot of thieves around here."

Sure, thought Tony, and not all of them are in your employ.

Little Armando handed Tony a crumpled brown paper bag. "This will help."

Tony pulled open the bag and put the money inside. He felt like a kid on his way to school with a sack lunch. Except this lunch was worth a small fortune. There'd be no trading sandwiches with his friends with a meal like this.

"Perhaps inside your shirt?" Victor suggested.

Tony stretched out his collar and dropped the wad of dollars down inside. It presented him with an unsightly bulge like he'd just swallowed a brick. The rough paper scratched his belly and he stood and adjusted it to look as natural as possible. Which it didn't.

"You would like a ride back to Ipanema?" Little Armando asked.

Tony didn't want any more favors from these crooks but neither did he want to walk down that mountain. "Please."

Little Armando told Victor to escort Tony on his way. And Tony was anxious to get out of there before Little Armando enlisted him in any more thievery. He set his beer on the ground, was forced to shake hands once more and hurried after Victor.

Outside, Victor called to a youth sitting against a low stone wall. The boy wore torn jeans and a torn t-shirt and he hadn't paid top dollar in some high priced boutique for his. Those holes had come naturally. The young man waved and disappeared. He returned pushing a battered motor scooter.

Tony wondered why he saw so many young people. Was it because no one lived long in the slums?

"Sergio will take you wherever you want. I have instructed him to take you to your hotel. This is okay?"

"Can you have him take me to Yairi's instead?"

Victor shrugged. "Certainly." Victor gave Sergio instructions in Brazilian Portuguese. "*Até logo, Senhor* Kozol."

See you soon? Tony hoped not. Victor waved and returned to the samba hall. The doors shut behind him. Sergio waved for Tony to get on back.

Tony held up his finger. "One minute, *por favor*."

A boy, with thick black hair that looked like his mother had chopped it back with dull edged scissors stood several feet away. He was doing nothing. Just watching. Why not? He had no TV, Tony was sure, and probably didn't even attend school, though he was old enough. His juvenile teeth already looked uneven and broken, giving him the mouth of a fifty year old and not the kid that he was of no more than a handful of years. The boy wore pants that had been torn off at the knees and no shirt. His ribs showed through his nearly translucent skin.

Tony smiled at the kid and he responded with a lopsided grin of his own. Digging down into his shirt, Tony pulled up the brown paper sack, stepped forward and handed it to the boy. "*Vai*," he whispered.

Tony clambered onto the torn seat of the little scooter and felt a warmness in his heart as the youngster cautiously opened the bag, peeked inside, lit up about five thousand watts, gave Tony a grin-to-die-for and ran off.

"Okay," said Tony, clutching the underside of the narrow seat as best he could, "v*amos*."

The motor scooter sputtered up *Avenida Atlantica* as the sun settled down to the west, preparing for a dip in the far off Pacific. Tony could easily have been a tourist on a pleasant sightseeing expedition. Like the hoards of tourists they passed. There was Sugar Loaf in the mists ahead which is really two hills connected by cable cars; the first being *Morro da Urca* at 220 meters and the second and far more familiar from its prominent display in postcards the world over, *Pão de Açucar* at nearly 400 meters. Silvia had promised to take him there. . .

The majestic Copacabana Palace was to the left and the adjacent outdoor market was swelling with browsers and buyers who easily outnumbered the sellers, which wasn't always the case.

But Tony wasn't a simple tourist out on an adventure, enjoying life's distant pleasures.

He was a man who had been robbed and beaten. A man without a job. Without a future. A man who had had his lover's life taken and been forced to see her lifeless body bound and defiled. Nothing he'd ever done or ever learned or ever heard could have prepared him for that.

The young man suddenly swung to the left and came to a lurching stop in front of a sleazy looking club on *Rua Duvivier* in the heart of Copacabana. That is, if the heart of Copacabana was the Red Light District. And Tony was certain that while that may not be strictly true, certainly an argument could be advanced in that direction.

His driver killed the motor. The heretofore silent fellow rested a worn sneaker on the curb and spoke. He pointed to a brick-faced edifice. The ground floor was an establishment with the delightfully quaint English name *Club Sex Machine*. Somehow, Tony couldn't imagine that name bringing in the tourists. Not unless they were randy sailors on shore leave.

The lone window was blackened. A tall white sign beside the door bore a silhouette of a naked woman in red. Decals advertising various liquors and beers had been plastered alongside.

Tony slid off the scooter. His legs were stiff. He stretched.

"Here?"

The young man nodded eagerly.

"*Obrigado.*" Tony reached into his back pocket and pulled out his wallet.

The young man waved his head no vigorously.

Tony said, "Are you sure?" He held out several dollars.

The young man said something Tony couldn't comprehend, restarted his scooter and took off.

"Well," muttered Tony, stuffing the money back in his billfold, and ignoring the outreaching, opportunistic hand of a passing woman, "that's a first."

As the sound of the motor scooter's tiny engine babbled ever more faintly on its way back towards the beach and the smell of fuel dissipated, the foul odor of urine took over. Human or dog, Tony couldn't tell and it wasn't an expertise he cared to cultivate.

He stepped out of the street and onto the sidewalk. Tony hesitated only a moment before pulling open the heavy door and stepping into the dimly lit establishment. His eyes adjusted to the purple glow. There was a bar along the near side with a dirty mirror behind it. Across from this, two women lazily danced on a narrow stage barely eighteen inches off the ground. They were naked. Neither was particularly attractive. One was way too skinny.

That didn't seem to bother the half dozen or so casually dressed men who sat at the tables closest to the platform and dully drank their whiskeys and beers. They looked like *Cariocas* and appeared mesmerized. Only the bartender seemed to notice Tony's entrance.

Oddly, there was no music.

The barkeep wore black slacks and a white shirt. He should have worn an apron. His shirt, even in the low light, was evidently stained. He probably wiped his hands on it, Tony figured, just as the sour looking man obliged, setting down a lime and brushing his fingers up and down on his chest, leaving a fan-like pattern of lime juice and pulp on his sorry shirt. He looked up at Tony with lugubrious, yet questioning, eyes.

"Boa noite."

The man picked up a filthy rag, probably yesterday's shirt, Tony speculated, and wiped the spot of the bar in front of Tony.

"Uh, no. *Não.*" Tony waved his hand. It fluttered like a pinkish dove in the odd lavender light. "I am looking for someone. Yairi. Alvarez Yairi." He pronounced each syllable slowly and clearly and still the man looked befuddled. "Meu a*migo,* Alvarez Yairi?"

The barkeep broke his silence. He said something in Portuguese and pointed towards the back where Tony noticed a plastic beaded curtain hanging to the tiled floor. The man's voice came from a throat doubtless ravaged with whiskey and cigarettes.

Tony thanked him and pushed through the blue beads. A narrow, unlit stairway led steeply up and to the right. The ceiling was low.

How odd, thought Tony as he climbed, that in a bar filled with spirits, the bartender himself should seem so dispirited.

Tony knocked on a door so thin he thought his fist would go through. A low susurrus of voices came from within. After a moment, Tony detected a creak and then slow steps.

"*Sim*?" The voice was flat, noncommital, but unmistakable.

"Yairi?"

No reply.

"Yairi, it's me, Tony Kozol." There was the chinking sound of a chain being released and the door opened.

Yairi, shirtless, welcomed him. "Tony, come." He stepped aside and Tony entered the meager, tomb-like room. There were no windows. There was a small, crooked bed on the opposite wall. A tiny TV, droning at the foot of the bed, was perched on a broken molded plastic chair. An orange crate served as a bedside table. A yellowed light fixture in the ceiling gave off a hundred watt glow.

A middle aged woman in a vulgar red teddy sat on the bed, her legs crossed. For modesty's sake?

She smiled at Tony.

"Sorry, I didn't realize—" Tony took a shallow breath. The room was rank and overly warm.

"No problem." Yairi said some words to his friend. She pouted, rose, took a sip from a glass tumbler on the floor, smiled for Tony once more and shook her *bunda* for Yairi, kissed him briefly, her tongue licking his cheek, then departed.

"*Opa, e ái?*"

"What's up? You know what's up." Tony noticed a pistol lying atop the orange crate. "Is that thing loaded?"

Yairi shrugged. His baggy brown trousers barely hung on to his bony hips. He grabbed a cigarette from the pack on the bed. "Why? What's it matter?" Yairi lit up and inhaled, billowing smoke as he replied. "Should it be?" He laughed coarsely. "Am I going to need it?"

"That depends," Tony answered, his voice hiding the rage and pain that was churning like a twisting, storm broiling sea inside him.

"On what?"

"On whether or not you killed Silvia." Tony took a step closer.

Yairi glanced at the gun then returned his attention to his cigarette. "You going to shoot me?" he said evenly.

"You bastard!" shouted Tony. "Why did you do it? Did Little Armando order it? Did you all think you were doing me a favor somehow? Like when Rodriguez killed the guy that mugged me?"

Yairi threw his cigarette on the floor and crushed it

underfoot. He spat. Flecks of tobacco stuck to his lip. "That prick that mugged you wasn't just some cheap hood."

"What's that supposed to mean?" Tony rolled the pistol around in his hands. He didn't even remember picking it up. It was cool and had an oily scent.

"It means that the man who attacked you worked for Fidel Salu. In fact, Salu was his commanding officer."

"What?"

"That's right. Salu sent him to rough you up. Kill you maybe."

"All right, so maybe he was trying to keep me from Silvia."

"I told you he was jealous. Didn't his shooting at you last night convince you of that?"

"Okay, so what's all that got to do with Silvia being dead?"

Yairi paced like a caged bear. The room wasn't big enough for more. "Don't you get it?" he said sorrowfully. "I didn't kill Silvia. Why would I?"

"But I saw you there. Outside the house."

"Yeah, sure. That was me. Rock telephoned me. He said you told him to call me, so surely you must believe that?"

Tony nodded.

"Anyway, Rock told me you were maybe going to Silvia's and I was going there to meet you. Of course," said Yairi, picking an open bottle of brandy from a small collection of liquors on a narrow shelf nailed to the wall, "when I got there I discovered the police and the ambulance."

"But when I went after you, you were gone. You ran."

"*Não*." Yairi took a swig, offered the bottle to Tony, who refused, then continued. "I don't know anything about that. I didn't see you, Tony."

Tony frowned. That part could be true. "But if you didn't kill Silvia, who did? The policeman I talked to told me they already have a suspect."

Yairi grinned. "And they do."

Tony waited expectantly.

"Fidel Salu."

"What?!" cried Tony.

Yairi shook his head. "He was seen in the neighborhood shortly before Silvia's body was found."

Tony's grip tightened around the gun, his finger on the trigger.

"You mind putting that down before one of us gets hurt?" Yairi said nervously.

"Huh?" Tony, with a look of surprise, noted the weapon in his hand. He threw it down on the bedsheets. Fidel Salu. Colonel Salu. He was going to pay. . . "I don't get it. How do you know all this? How do you know half the shit you know? Let's face it, Yairi, you're as slippery as a greased pig."

"I hear things."

"I'll bet you do." Tony looked about the claustrophobic room. There was nothing personal about it. Alvarez Yairi seemed to be everywhere, yet never left a trace of self behind. "The woman I love is dead. You say you didn't do it. Then you tell me Fidel Salu is the killer. But how the hell do I know that's true? Maybe you killed her because she'd betrayed me and you thought you were doing me a favor? Is that it? Huh, is that it?"

"I told you, Tony—"

"Yeah, you told me." Tony shrugged him off. "You've told me lots of things. It doesn't make any of them true. Let's face it, you're a cheap hood yourself. One of Little Armando's boys. But guess what," Tony grinned maliciously, "that five grand you're expecting from Little Armando—I got it. And I gave it to some child in the *favela* that I've never laid eyes on before." Tony beamed. "So what do you think of that?"

Yairi chuckled. "I think you are very generous. You've changed someone's life."

"And you're out five thousand dollars."

Yairi pursed his lips. His eyes looked like tiny stones. "What will you do when you learn the truth?"

"I promised Silvia I would avenge her."

Yairi smiled. He pulled a thin brown billfold from his back pocket. He lifted the cover and held it in front of Tony's eyes.

"What's this?" stammered Tony. "You're—"

"A cop."

16

Tony knocked Yairi's ID aside.

"I don't believe it," he said. "That thing's as phony as you are." He turned, took two steps and slammed the flimsy door behind him.

"Tony, stop!"

He ran down the steps.

Night had fallen. Hookers had taken up their positions on the street. The evening's madness had begun and Tony was in the thick of it. Tonight he was its ringleader.

Tony wasn't thinking straight or walking straight. Music that throbbed like a rampaging heart, hot, sweaty bodies and the smell of beer running along the gutters engulfed him. It was all a blur. Still none of it was enough to block the pain.

A couple of hours later he was sticking his keycard in the slot and entering his hotel room. It was dark.

The only light came from outside. Tony pressed his face up against the cool glass and watching the mute passage of headlights. He thought of Silvia. . .

Then the door burst open and Rock came bounding into the room. He hit the light switch. "I got the tickets!" He was beaming from studded ear to ear.

Tony looked at him sullenly then turned back to the

window where he was confronted with his own reflection. His face looked like it had gone to the Netherworld and back.

And it had.

Tony said, "Where the hell have you been?"

Rock held the airline tickets in his left hand. "I got the tickets, like you asked. For you, me and Silvia."

Tony removed a ticket from Rock's hand. Silvia Parra's name was typed across its face. "Thanks, Rock."

"It wasn't easy. I had to go all the way across town to the airline office just to find someone who spoke English and understood what we needed."

Tony nodded.

"Everything okay?"

"No." Tony's hand crumbled the ticket.

"Hey, what are you doing?"

"We won't be needing this one." Tony twisted the ticket in his hands as if he could wring his misery out of it like water from a rag.

Rock stepped back.

"Silvia isn't coming with us."

"She's not? Gosh, I'm sorry, Tony." He patted his friend lightly across the back. "But like they say, life goes on, huh?"

"Not always," Tony mumbled.

"What?"

Tony looked his friend in the eye. "Silvia's dead, Rock."

Rock grunted nervously. "No, you're kidding, right? You guys had a fight and—"

Tony shook his head. "No, Rock." He began shaking. "She's dead. Somebody killed her."

Rock stood silent as a monolith while Tony recounted his afternoon. When Tony got to describing the part about how Silvia had been apparently been killed, Rock ran to the fridge, rummaged around for drinks and came back with two little bottles of vodka.

They drank them straight.

Tony told Rock of his meeting with Little Armando and Victor.

"You're crazy," Rock had said, with a shake of his head. "Even I wouldn't go up in that *favela* again."

Tony shrugged it off. "Then I went to see Yairi. You called him, right?"

"Yeah, after breakfast like you told me to."

"So, I guess that lets him off the hook." Tony sat on the bed.

"Lets him off the hook for what?"

"For killing Silvia."

Rock seemed stunned. "You think he did it?"

Tony rubbed his head. "I don't know. I don't know anything anymore."

There was a loud knock at the door.

"It's probably the maid to turn down the beds. Tell her to go away, Rock. Please."

"Sure." Rock padded to the door. "Who's there?"

Yairi's muffled voice replied from the other side.

"It's Yairi," said Rock. "What should I do? You want me to let him in?"

Tony nodded and turned to face the door.

Yairi had put a shirt and shoes on. He bowed to Rock and said softly, "You have heard?"

"Yeah."

"What are you doing here?" demanded Tony.

"I wanted to make sure you were okay." Yairi glanced uneasily about the room, his eyes never resting long in one place.

"Yeah, just peachy. Right, Rock?"

Rock looked helplessly at Yairi and shrugged.

"Have you told Rock my identity?"

"Your identity?" echoed the big guy.

"Go ahead," Tony said, belligerently. "Show Rock your fake ID."

Yairi pulled out his wallet. Rock studied the identification card within. Yairi flipped it over. On the opposite side was a badge.

"I don't know, Tony." Rock scratched his nose. "That badge looks real to me."

"I assure you both. My credentials are real. I work for the federal government." He held his identification under Tony's nose.

"Do they know you're a part-time crook in your off hours?" Tony asked.

"My dealings with Little Armando are part of my cover."

"Luis Angel, too?" inquired Rock.

"That's right." Yairi stuffed his ID back in his pocket. "I have had to work my way into the local underworld here in Rio de Janeiro."

"You ripped off Luis Angel!" Tony had risen from the bed and returned once more to the window.

"It is a small thing," explained Yairi. "I am going to be honest with you, though I risk my cover and my life to do so."

Tony crossed his arms. "I'm waiting."

Yairi's eyes shot from Tony to Rock and back again. "I have been charged by the government to investigate police and military corruption. I am working on a particularly sensitive and complicated case."

"Tell me, Yairi," cut in Tony, "does any of this have anything to do with Silvia's murder? Because if it doesn't—"

"It does. I told you, Tony, Silvia died at Colonel Salu's hands. And Fidel Salu is—how do you say—the fish I am after."

"That maniac from last night? He killed Silvia?" Rock looked stunned.

Yairi nodded and said, "Help me catch Salu and you will have Silvia's murderer."

"Help you?" Tony shook his head. There were too many

thoughts floating around inside, like logs jamming a narrow river. Something was going to give and it was likely to be his sanity.

"No," answered Tony finally.

"No?" stammered Yairi. "You refuse to help? You who stood in my room only a couple of hours past and vowed to avenge your lover's murder?!"

"No. You're the police, Yairi. Catch him and shoot him when you do. I can't stay here any longer." How could he survive if he did? Tony turned to Rock and asked, "What time does our flight leave tomorrow?"

"We've got to be at the airport at two. Non-stop all the way to Miami."

Tony nodded.

"Talk to your friend, Rock. Fidel Salu is a criminal and a murderer. Surely you are willing to assist the authorities of Brazil in apprehending him?"

Rock only said, "I have to go along with Tony, whatever he says."

Yairi's face turned hard. "I was hoping to avoid unpleasantness. You two gentlemen are guests in our country. I have offered you my hospitality and protection on many occasions and really I must insist."

"Insist?" scoffed Tony.

A grin twisted across Yairi's lower face. "Yes, insist. You will find that your passports are no longer in your hotel lock box. But not to worry, they have been removed to a safe location. You will—"

Tony rushed to the closet, pulled open the door and punched in the code to the electronic lock box. "Empty! Where the hell are our passports? How did you get them?" And how would they get out of Brazil without them?

Rock bent and peered inside the tiny box built onto a low shelf along the back of the clothes closet. He had to see for himself.

"It was any easy thing, I assure you." Yairi stuck his hands in his pockets.

"We'll go to the local police. Tell them everything we know about you. Everything you've told us."

"And then I may forget completely where I have sequestered your passports. You may be in Brazil a very long time."

"You son of a—"

"Tony, Rock, I regret that we must speak to one another in this way. We are friends, *não*?"

Rock and Tony made no reply.

"Help me. I have been after Salu for a long time. A matter of days, no more. Then I will return your passports and you can return to the United States."

Yairi crossed to the mini-bar in the hallway and snatched up a cellophane wrapped package of peanut butter crackers from the basket atop the refrigerator. Three bucks American. "Talk it over, gentlemen. I will be in the downstairs bar."

Rock kicked the door shut afer him. "You okay, Tony?"

"Yeah, I'm okay."

"You want me to go kick Yairi's ass and get our passports back?"

"No. It probably wouldn't work anyway. Those passports could be anywhere. Besides," said Tony, staring at Silvia's crumbled airline ticket on the carpet, "Yairi's right." And Tony was taking his anger out on him. Again.

"He is? About what?"

"I made Silvia a promise." He picked up her ticket and straightened it out. "And I'm going to keep it. Or die trying."

Rock nodded his assent. "I'm with you all the way."

True to his word, Yairi was waiting for them at a small corner table of the downstairs bar, his hands wrapped around a drink. He'd polished off the crackers. Only the plastic exoskeleton remained.

Tony and Rock pulled up chairs and ordered a round of beers. "Charge it to our room," Tony said, jotting the room number down on the bill.

"So," said Tony, after the beers had arrived and he'd drained half, "you want to tell us what is going on?"

"I've told you much already."

"Nothing that makes any sense," complained Tony. "For instance, why did Salu kill Silvia?"

Yairi slid his beer mug round and round, in tiny circles. "I expect he was jealous. He killed her to keep you from having her, no doubt. And perhaps to cover his tracks. Perhaps his wife had found out about his," Yairi hesitated, "indiscretions."

"His wife?" Tony leaned forward. "That bastard was married?"

"Yes," said Yairi. "Though I am sure Miss Parra did not know this. After all, it is unlikely that Salu would mention such a thing, *não*?"

Tony's hatred for Fidel Salu had reached a new depth. Not only had he been hounding Silvia, according to her, refusing to let her go, but he'd been married to boot!

"This guy's a real scum bag," Rock opined.

"Agreed," Tony said, "but none of this explains your interest in him, Yairi. At least, not before Silvia was murdered and yet you said you were after him." Tony finished his beer and said softly, "Why?"

Yairi cleared his throat. "There is much to tell. But—" He looked cautiously about the bar. It was quite busy and conversations were going on all around them. "Not here. There have already been two attempts on my life this week. I fear my cover has been somewhat compromised."

"Someone's tried to kill you?" Rock said somewhat overly loud.

"Shh," admonished Tony. "The other night at your apartment. I did see you fighting, didn't I? Through the curtains."

"Yes," admitted Yairi. "My assailant was waiting for me in my apartment. It was quite a struggle." He pulled up the front right leg of his trousers. "A souvenir."

"Some souvenir," Rock remarked.

"Yes. I was forced to find new accomodations."

Tony leaned over the table and looked. A six inch gash ran unevenly up Yairi's leg. Tony shivered as he remembered how he'd helped Yairi get rid of what had been a fresh corpse. If he'd known. . . "And that guy at the Sambadrome—the one I thought had been hurt—he was another one, wasn't he?"

"He had a gun with a silencer. Not that such a device would have been necessary in all that noise. Nonetheless, I was fortunate to spot him before he was able to fire. In the struggle, the weapon discharged."

"But why all the obfuscation? Why hide the body?"

"Yeah," chimed Rock, "why not let the police handle it?"

"All will be made clear to you, I promise. For now, I can only tell you that I must maintain a low profile. To bring in the local police would only draw unwanted attention and dangerous whispers. The police are not beyond corruption."

"But somebody's trying to kill you." Rock pointed at Yairi's fresh wound.

"Yes, someone wishes to assassinate me. And I have no doubt who. I am certain it is Colonel Salu. He is on to me."

"Shit," Rock said. "Why don't you call in some back up?"

Yairi grinned and drained his *chopp*. "This is precisely why I have enlisted you, my friends." Yairi rolled down the leg of his trousers and stood. "Come. Let's find someplace less conspicuous to talk."

17

"You are familiar with W. Mercer?" Yairi pulled three loose cans of beer from under the bed. They were warm and covered with dust bunnies.

"The jewelers? Yeah," said Rock. He picked Yairi's television set, which looked older than the medium itself, off the chair that served as its stand, set it on the floor and took the seat for himself. "I see them all over town. We've even got a small one in our hotel."

"What about them?" Tony stood, beer in hand. He wiped the lid with the inside corner of his shirt before taking a sip.

Yairi was seated on the uneven, lopsided bed. Yairi's idea of a less conspicuous place to talk had been that ever so charming new apartment of his in the bowels of the Club Sex Machine. Quite a comedown from his last residence. Tony wondered if his old landlady and her husband would ever see the two months rent Yairi owed them. Probably not.

Whatever Yairi was paying for this place, no matter how little, it was too much. When they'd entered the dark strip club, Tony could have sworn he recognized the same faces, whose hands probably clutched the same beers at the same stained little tables, in attendance. Not even the bartender had changed. Nor had he changed his shirt.

The only difference this time around was that some less vacant soul had hit on the brilliant idea of adding music. A tiny, tinny, boombox balanced at the edge of the narrow stage was thumping out American rock and roll while the less than erotic dancers did their lackadaisical humping.

"They are Brazil's best known jewelers," Yairi was saying." "The highest quality. An impeccable reputation. They've been in business more than a century. But now there is a problem."

Rock echoed, "Problem?"

"I am speaking of their headquarters in Ipanema." Yairi wiped a trail of beer foam from his upper lip.

Tony still couldn't get used to the idea of this *malandro* being a federal cop of some sort. "The highrise on *Rua Visconde de Pirajá*." He'd passed it many times. There was always a different guy, way overdressed for the heat, in a dark suit, handing out passes to anyone that dared make eye contact. "What about it?"

Yairi pulled several newspaper clippings from a shoe box at the foot of the bed. "There have been three high profile robberies in as many months. Most recently two weeks before."

Tony glanced at the pictures. The articles were written in Brazilian Portuguese. "So?"

"Fidel Salu is the mastermind behind these thefts."

"Are you sure?" Rock asked.

"I am certain of it. There has been an informer. Unfortunately he ended up dead, washed up on the beach out by the *Aeroporto Santos Dumont* about a month ago. Colonel Salu uses enlisted men under his authority as well as accomplices in the local *policia*."

There was a knock at the door. Quicker than Tony could blink, Yairi had his pistol in hand and an alert ear to the door. He said nothing and Tony held his breath. If there was going to be a shoot-out, there was nowhere to hide.

A woman's voice broke through from the other side and Yairi turned the handle. It was the woman from earlier. This time her hair was fixed back behind her ears and she had slipped into a tight fitting purple micro-dress. She looked in the room, whispered something plaintively to Yairi, who grudgingly let her inside.

She smiled wanly to Tony and Rock, went purposely to a small chest of drawers and removed a red sequined G-string and matching bra.

When she was gone, Yairi continued. "I'm sorry, Valeria needs her costume." He cleared his throat. "As I was saying, W. Mercer's headquarters have been hit three times. This is not only bad for them but bad for Brazil."

"How's that?" asked Rock.

"The tourists," explained Yairi. "Tourism is a large industry as is the mining and sale of precious stones. Fidel Salu is attacking both. This is why I have been sent to investigate." He smiled proudly. "It didn't take me long to figure out who was behind the crimes."

"But why?" Tony finished off his beer. "I mean, if Salu's such a big shot, why is he pulling jewelry heists?"

"He has an expensive lifestyle. Several homes, including an apartment here, a villa at the seashore. A wife and children. Mistresses. Luxury cars. . ."

Mistresses? Plural? Tony decided to let that statement pass. As far as helpings of pain were concerned, his plate was as full as a Pilgrim's at a Thanksgiving feast.

"Still it takes a lot of balls to rip off a big place like that," Rock commented. "It's got to be a fortress."

"But this is the beauty of it. He does not actually rob the W. Mercer building itself. This would be, as you say, Rock, nearly impossible. It is well guarded and protected with alarms of the most state-of-the-art."

Tony was confused. "But you said he was robbing them."

Yairi shook his head. "And he is." Yairi raised a finger.

back his chair, stuck his thumb in his shorts and pushed outward to gain an extra inch. "I'll check us out."

"It's a little early, isn't it, Tony?" Rock was wearing that crazy shirt Alba Zica had given him, the cotton hodgepodge of bright parrots and green leaves of many hues with a pair of black shorts and black sandals.

"That's okay. We'll haul everything over to Yairi's in a taxi. Afterward, I'm going to Mrs. Parra's house."

"You sure that's a good idea?" Rock wiped up his scrambled eggs with the remainder of his toast.

Tony shrugged. "I have to try. I want you to see what you can do about our tickets. Maybe we can get our money back?"

Rock shook his head. "No way. Not according to the airline clerk who wrote them out."

Tony frowned. A light went off and he snapped his fingers. "I know! Remember that kid, Officer Milito?"

Rock said yes. "What about him?"

"He told me his uncle or his father, somebody, was in the travel business. Maybe he can help us."

"And just how am I supposed to find this guy, whoever he is?"

"Come on, Rock. All you've got to do is find Officer Milito."

Rock raised an eyebrow and waited.

Tony looked heavenward for inspiration. There was none coming. Perhaps it wasn't in the day's forecast. Mostly sunny with only a ten percent chance of inspiration. "I don't know," he grumbled, "you'll have to call around. Check the precincts, if that's what they call them here."

Rock said he would, though he didn't sound happy about it.

Tony rose. "Finish your breakfast and I'll meet you back at the room."

Rock, his cheeks stuffed with figs and sweetbread, said

something that sounded like "Mumphydumphoster," and nodded.

"Will you say that again, please," Tony said, his jaw set, a wave, no a tsunami of anxiety threatening at the stern. He was in a lifeboat with no land in sight.

"I am sorry, sir." The pretty young clerk tapped her keyboard. "But we have no instructions here for paying for your room. I am afraid you are responsible for the bill."

Tony laughed nervously. She was looking at him like she expected some money. Good luck, *senhorita*. "But this is crazy. I work for Luis Angel. He is responsible for our hotel bill. Hell, he's responsible for the rooms of everybody in the band. Surely I'm not the first to complain."

Her ridiculously long fingers worked the keys. "You and Mr. Bottom are the last of Mr. Angel's block of rooms."

"A-ha! You said it yourself. 'Mr. Angel's block of rooms.' I'il bet nonc of the others are going to like this or go along with it."

"Everyone else has checked out previously."

"Oh." That was a surprise. "And did they pay for their rooms?" Tony laid his hands across the cool granite counter.

"I couldn't say, sir."

"Look," said Tony, determined to try again, "there has got to be a mistake here somewhere. I," he jabbed his chest, "did not reserve this room. I didn't sign anything. I only work for Luis Angel." Okay, so that part was no longer true. There was no reason to confuse or complicate the issue or the girl; on that account, Tony was certain.

"I am afraid the *Senhor* Angel has checked out."

"Yes," said Tony, grimly. "You told me that. And I knew that already." He tried another tack. This boat was sinking. "How about Alba Zica?"

The clerk's lovely little blonde eyebrows did a two-step.

"Did she leave any instructions or some sort of credit card

number for you to bill our room to?"

"Zica? Z-I-C-A?"

Tony nodded.

Fingers did their finger thing. Apes should be so lucky. "I'm sorry, *Senhor* Kozol, but the *senhorita* has checked out yesterday."

"I know that, too!" Tony chewed his lip. "Okay, how much exactly is it that we owe you?"

The girl got busy with that finger thing again—way too busy, in Tony's opinion. It only got worse when he heard her answer and a computer spat out the verse. "Five thousand—"

Tony eyes started to glaze over.

"—seven hundred and twenty four dollars and twelve cents." She shoved a copy of the bill in his face.

"You mean *reais*, don't you?"

"No, this is U.S. dollars. I thought you would prefer it, but if you like I can recalculate this into *reais* for you, *senhor*."

"Nearly six thousand dollars?" stuttered Tony. It was incomprehensible.

"Yes." She ran a hotel pen along the page. "Each night's stay plus taxes, room charges, meals, movies—"

Movies. That had to be Rock. How had he found the time to order a dozen pay-per-view films?!

"Would you like to convert this to Brazilian *reais*?"

"No," Tony clutched the bill, "that won't be necessary. Look," he said struggling to maintain his composure, such as it was, "is there a manager I can speak to?"

The perky blonde looked left to right and held the pen to her lips. "One moment, please."

She said some words to a young man who in turn spoke to a cohort, who disappeared behind a thick oak door, only to return moments later with a black-suited gentleman in tow.

Tony's clerk whispered to the man in the elegant shirt. He glanced in Tony's direction, nodded, tugged on his cuffs and approached. "There is a problem, sir?"

Tony leaned over the counter. "There is a problem, yes." He laid out the printout. "It's this bill."

Cool grey eyes scanned the long page of items and charges then locked in on Tony. "Are you questioning the entire bill or a particular item? Perhaps the exchange rate is confusing you?"

"I'm questioning the whole darn thing. I'm confused by the entire situation and I'm beginning to question my entire confusing reason for living."

"Please, sir." The manager glanced nervously side to side. "We don't wish to create a disturbance." A set of muscles in a suit had silently stepped forward. The manager shook his head no and the ape man departed back to his position at the front doors.

"Look," Tony rang his fingers through what was left of his hair, "when I checked in here I was under the impression that Luis Angel was paying for my room. In fact, I'm certain he was. That was our deal."

The manager's tongue was clicking. He returned the printout to Tony. "Yes, I can see this is inconvenient for you. Of course, once you have explained the situation to *Senhor* Angel, I am certain he will reimburse you, *não*?"

Tony closed his eyes and counted to ten slowly. When he opened them, the manager was still there. The clerk was talking on the phone and the bill was still facing him. So much for the power of positive imagery. "What time is checkout?"

"One o'clock, sir. Will you need some help with your bags?"

"That would be great. I tell you what. Please send someone up around quarter till one. We'll handle this then."

The manager nodded.

Tony pocketed the hotel bill with mock confidence and strolled off.

"Hurry up, Rock! Are you packed yet?"

Rock lifted his skull from the headboard. The Three Stooges was running on the television. "Sort of."

"Sort of?" Tony looked around the room. Shirts and underwear littered the floor. Rock's bass and amp were near the table along with Tony's acoustic guitar and Roland JC-77 amplifier.

That left the suitcases. Tony pulled them out of the closet. They were virtually empty. "Come on, get up, will you. Help me pack up all this garbage." Tony darted around the room picking up shoes, socks, underwear, shirts, shaving gear and anything else that wasn't locked down. He tossed it all into the suitcases not caring who belonged to what.

Rock rose. "What are you doing? What's the hurry?" He looked at his watch. "We've got a couple of hours before we've got to be out of here. Let's enjoy it. Maybe watch a movie."

Tony vigorously shook his head no. "No more movies. We're getting out of here. Now."

"But they even refilled the minibar. We've got lots of time."

Tony was shaking his head again.

"We don't?" Rock shuffled back and forth. "I wish you'd stop shaking your head like that and just tell me what's going on. I feel like I'm thirteen years old again. My mother used to stand there like that shaking her head at me and I never even knew what I'd done wrong. She'd just keep on shaking and I'd keep on standing there. If I asked her what was up, she'd just shake it some more and tell me that if I didn't know she wasn't going to tell me. Drove me nuts."

"Look at this." Tony dug into his pocket and pulled out the bill.

Rock scanned the bill. He laughed. "Wait until that punk Luis gets a hold of this!"

"That's just it, my friend. Luis is gone and we're stuck

with the bill. He never paid it."

Rock's eyes grew as big as the moons of Jupiter. "But, Alba said— "

"She was either lying or didn't know. In either event," Tony wadded up the statement and hook shot it into one of the two open suitcases, "we can't cover it and have to get out of here without being seen."

"But the bill— "

"Forget it, Rock." Tony slammed shut one suitcase. It had reached its max. "Once they've discovered we've run out on the bill, they'll go after Luis Angel." He locked it down. "And that's who's supposed to be paying after all."

"Or they can call the police and have us arrested for fraud or something. Does Brazil have firing squads?"

"No way they'll call the police," replied Tony with false bravado. "Besides, we don't have that kind of money and having us locked up isn't going to get it for them. And they'd have to find us first and not even we know where we are going to be." As for the firing squads—he didn't want to know.

Tony checked under the beds and came up empty. "No, they'll take the path of least resistance. I mean, they know Luis has got the bucks. I say let him pay."

"I guess you're right." Rock glanced out the window. There was no fire escape. Not to mention they were on the twenty-third floor. "But how are we going to get out of here with all our stuff and not get caught?"

Tony looked at the door and their pile of gear. "Very carefully, Rock. Very carefully."

While Rock scoured the bathroom and pocketed a couple extra bottles of shampoos and conditioners, Tony filled him in. "So the manager isn't going to send the bellhop up until nearly one. I scoped out the lobby before coming back up to the room. There's a side door near the back. We'll take the elevator down to the second floor. There's a stairway that runs from the first floor to the third. We'll take it down to the ground floor. It comes out in the lobby, so we'll have to be careful we don't get spotted. But it's right next to the side door I'm talking about. That door empties out on *Rua Joana Angelica*. From there we'll hop in a taxi and be long gone before they even notice."

"There's a maid's cart in the hall," Tony said sticking his head around the corner. "So be quiet."

Rock nodded. "Maybe you should run push the button so we're not just standing around where anybody might see us. I mean, what if the manager comes?"

Tony frowned. Why did Rock always have to envisage the worst? Still. . ."Good idea." Tony padded up the hall, pressed the down button and ran back for his luggage. The middle elevator opened quickly and they were off. The back wheels on Tony's amp were squeaking and he was forced to carry it with one hand. Every third step it knocked him in the leg, pushing him to the left and threatening his stability.

The doors were closing quickly. But Rock was quicker. He stopped their advance with a well placed suitcase. Tony hurtled his own gear in after him.

They had an elevator to themselves. Rock hoped there weren't any hidden cameras. Tony told him he was being paranoid.

"I've never been a criminal before," complained Rock.

To Tony's annoyance, he found himself compelled to look into the corners of the elevator car for signs of a camera lens.

A couple of minutes later, during which neither one spoke, they'd exited on the second floor. Someone in hotel garb glanced at them from an open office then went back to her telephone.

"Hurry," urged Tony. It took two trips to get all their gear to the bottom steps and Tony was out of breath and sweating. He stuck his neck out. The lobby was bustling. That was good. They'd blend in. "You go first." He gave Rock a push and whispered, "Make a sharp right and you can't miss it. I'll wait a minute, then meet you outside."

"Right." Rock gathered up the bulk of their luggage and music gear and nervously stepped into view. A moment later he was gone.

A moment after that a teeth-rattling alarm sounded.

"Shit!" Tony muttered, picked up his things and sprinted around the corner and out the door. He didn't have to understand Portuguese to understand now what was written on the door. No doubt something of a warning that the door was to be used only as a fire exit and that an alarm would sound.

He should have expected that!

Tony hit the sidewalk and the heat hit him back square in the face. He paused, letting his eyes adjust to the painful glare. There was no sign of Rock. "What the—"

A horn beeped twice, like the burp of a soprano in mixed company. Tony looked for the source. Rock stuck his head out of the back of a taxi. He was waving.

Tony picked up his suitcase, his guitar and his amp—a feat which heretofore he would have considered impossible—played dodge'em with two lanes of traffic, tossed his belongings into the open cab, shut the door and hollered breathlessly. "Let's go!"

The driver may not have understood English but he got the message. The little taxi shot out into traffic.

"Well," said Rock, turning to see if the chase was on, "it's official. We're on the lam."

Tony stole a look himself. At least there was no sign of a posse.

18

The cab dropped them off outside the Copacabana Palace Hotel. Yairi had insisted no one know where he was staying, not even a cab driver. Talk about paranoid.

They had a good block or so to walk, pushing their effects slowly ahead of them.

"Let's go to Brazil, you said," Tony said, giving his amp a kick forward, "it'll be fun, you said."

"Hey, I'm not the one who got us into this mess," Rock answered dourly. "You're the one with a knack for stepping in it. Lucky for you that you don't live on a farm."

Tony huffed. It was unfortunate, but the big guy was right.

The distant sound of a siren set them to walking faster, much faster.

Inside the bar, they found Yairi sitting at the counter sipping a *cafezinho*. "Ah, my friends. You are early." He pushed his empty cup forward and rose.

Except for the bartender, the club was empty. Apparently its patrons did have beds somewhere. Of course, they might have been sharing bunks with the ersatz exotic dancers.

"Come." Yairi shoved past Rock who was halfway into the process of lugging all their gear inside. "This way."

Rock groaned and reversed the process. Tony lent a hand. Yairi's hands remained free. Maybe he needed to be unrestrained in case of gunfire or an ambush assault.

It was a quick trip to the little building next door with the crumbling facade. They climbed a stairs that had more sags and creaks than Tony's great-aunt Matilda. It was a toss-up which was older.

Not a creature was stirring, as the story goes. They plodded up to the third landing. There were three doors on each side. Yairi removed a key from his pocket and opened the first door on the right.

Tony followed him in. He pinched his nose. The smell of urine, beer and sex made his eyes all watery. He ran to the window and pulled. With a second tug, he managed to raise it up. A welcome breeze wafted in. At least they were on the street side with a view, such as it was. An opportunistic fly buzzed in, took one look around, then retreated.

"Bathroom's in the back, down the hall." Yairi was fanning the front door. "Don't worry, once you air the room out, it'll be good as new."

Rock stood a couple of feet inside the threshold. "This room wasn't 'good as new' when it was new."

Tony had to agree. "I'm beginning to feel homesick for the Club Sex Machine."

Yairi shook his head no. "There was no room. But this is good, *não*? Very close. Many of the girls live here."

"Girls?" Rock echoed, his hormones honing in like sonar.

"Yes, the dancers from next door."

"Cool."

Tony kept his mouth shut. Of course, that was partly defensive. The air was so thick and so foul he swore he could taste it. Take a bite out of it like an old shoe leather which would have gone down like French pastry by comparison.

"And you haven't heard the best part, yet."

"What's that?" Tony in his most vivid fantasies couldn't

imagine a passable part, let alone a best one.

"It's free," replied Yairi with a wave of his hands, as if he'd created some magic. "No charge."

Tony could think of several answers, none of which were worthy of friendship. So he said, "Wow, that's great, Yairi."

Rock stepped out into the hall and started fetching their bags. He set his bass against the nearest wall which was stained with things Tony didn't want identified.

Yairi looked at his watch. "Well, gentlemen, I must go. You get settled in. Have some lunch. There's a good *boteco* up the street and a *Bobs* a little further." Bobs was like a local version of MacDonald's. "We'll meet back here this evening to formalize our plans."

Tony and Rock agreed. Yairi stepped out into the quiet hall then stuck his head back inside. "Oh, there is one other thing."

"Let's hear it," Rock said. He had chosen to sit on his amplifier rather than one of the two bare mattresses or the filthy floor. A good choice, in Tony's humble opinion.

"One of the conditions for your free rent is that I informed the landlord that you gentlemen would act as bodyguards."

"Bodyguards?" Tony and Rock said in unison.

"Yes." Yairi grinned. "It is nothing really. A small thing."

Interesting, thought Tony. It's nothing and it's a small thing. In Rio, that probably meant 'it's a big thing.' He waited for his friend to elaborate.

"As I explained, many of the girls from the club next door, and some of the other dance clubs nearby, live here. They often," he wiggled his fingers in the search for words, "supplement their income by bringing clients to this establishment."

"You mean they're working girls? Prostitutes?" Rock was on his feet.

"Well—"

"You got us a room in a whorehouse?" Tony said

incredulously.

"Gentlemen, please. This is only temporary, remember? Once we've nailed Colonel Salu you will return to America. Is this not worth a little discomfort?"

Tony and Rock begrudgingly agreed.

"Just what is it we're supposed to do?" demanded Rock.

"Nothing. Everything is usually very quiet. If there is any trouble, it comes at night."

"And what do we do if there is trouble?" pressed Tony.

"Yeah, I don't really want to get mixed up in—"

"Not to worry," Yairi insisted. "If there is any noise, calm the patron down and escort him to the front door. The girls are good at their trade. I'm sure you will find there is nothing to be concerned about." He was out the door again.

"And if there is any shooting, just close your door!" he shouted as his footsteps echoed raucously down the stairs.

"Well, this is fun." Tony shut the door shut and locked it. "Let's plan on keeping this thing closed. And locked. No matter what we hear out there." He pocketed the key Yairi had tossed him.

"What do we do now?" Rock stood near the window.

"We do like I said. You find Milito and see if his father can help us with our ticket troubles. I'm going—"

Tony stopped mid-sentence. Someone was knocking on their door.

"Now who could that be?" Rock inquired.

"Who knows? We just won't answer it. Keep your voice down."

But even as Tony spoke, the front door opened. A voluptuous young vixen in a baby blue kimono popped inside. Her feet were bare. Her toenails purple. She smiled and said something that Tony and Rock were at a loss to understand. The only thing Tony caught was *'oi'*. Hi.

"No," said Tony, shaking his head. "English, speak

English. *Não falo portugués,"* he said slowly.

The girl started babbling again in a lilting tone. She pointed to the room across the hall, made sipping motions bringing her hand to her lips.

"I think she's inviting us for a drink," Rock opined.

"You could be right." Tony stepped forward. "Later. *Obrigada*. Later." Tony nodded his head up and down in exaggerated movements.

She pointed to her chest, whose majestic peaks were more than teasingly revealed. "Maria."

"Maria," repeated Tony, feeling quite the well-practiced myna bird. "*Sim*." He pointed to his friend. "Rock," then to himself, "Tony. *É um prazer encontrando*." Tony scrounged up one of the few handy phrases he knew or at least hoped meant 'It is a pleasure meeting you.'

Tony smiled and nodded at her next remark, whatever it was. His Portuguese couldn't have been too bad because she wasn't huffing and seemed rather pleased herself. He only hoped he hadn't just arranged a date with her for later.

Maria blew them each a kiss and waved cheerfully goodbye. "*Tchau*."

"She seemed nice enough," remarked Rock after the girl had entered the room across the hall from theirs.

"Yeah. Don't forget what she does for a living." Tony closed the door with himself on the outside. "I know I locked this. You lock it, Rock."

Tony waited while Rock pulled the door tight and turned the lock.

"Okay," shouted Rock.

Tony tried the handle. The door practically fell open on its own power. "Oooo-kay," said Tony. He tossed the pointless apartment key across the floor. "I'm out of here. Don't forget to lock up when you leave."

"Funny. Very funny."

Funds being what they were, Tony relied on his tootsies to get him to the Parra's house across town. Way across town, now that he was hanging or hiding out, in Copacabana.

The crowds were gone, the gate unlocked, but latched. On impulse he went to the side, then remembered. Silvia wasn't home. He followed the sidewalk back around the corner to the front of the modest house and knocked lightly. A scent of jasmine came from the garden.

Silvia's little sister, Tzininha opened the door. Her face looked puffy and her eyes dim and red.

"May I come in? Please?" Tony asked softly. He heard Mrs. Parra's voice in the distance asking who was there.

Tzininha looked into Tony's eyes and seemed to be sucking his essence straight from his soul. Finally, she said, "Come inside."

The house was warm and humid. The windows closed. Mrs. Parra, in a simple black frock, sat in a wooden rocker before the big window overlooking the back porch. She turned to get a look at her visitor. Probably expecting another well-wishing neighbor.

Tony stopped somewhere between Tzininha and her mother, unsure of his next move and then it was decided for him. Mrs. Parra opened her arms. "Tony."

He gave himself over to her embrace and she told him to sit.

Ella Parra's brown eyes had seen better days. Better days and better times. Silvia had gotten her beautiful, now closed, green eyes from her father. She had often said it was the only thing he gave her.

Tony looked into dark pools of despair. Somewhere underneath he suspected there were whirlpools threatening to drag her reality under. Maybe that was a good thing. Who could say?

Tzininha took hold of her mother's hand.

"I'm so sorry." He sat on the edge of a foot stool. "If there is anything I can do, please ask."

"You will come to the service?" Mrs. Parra inquired, her voice a dry whisper.

"Yes, of course. When will it occur?"

Mrs. Parra shrugged wearily.

Tzininha answered. "We are waiting for the police to give us word. They promised us it would be only a matter of a couple of days."

Tony nodded soberly. "Mrs. Parra," he began hesitantly, "I know how difficult this must be for you and, believe me, I wouldn't ask you this if it was not important." He glanced at Tzininha whose face was beginning to show her displeasure. "But I wonder if you can tell me what happened?"

"You know what happened, Tony," Tzininha said sharply, squeezing her mother's hand.

"I know, yes." He ran his fingers through his hair and was surprised to find that he was shaking. He returned his attention to Silvia's mother. "The police said you found the body—that you saw. . ." He didn't want to utter the name, for his sake and for Mrs. Parra's, but there was no way around it. "They say you identified Colonel Salu leaving Silvia's apartment."

"Tony!" Tzininha scolded.

Mrs. Parra patted her daughter's arm. "It is all right." She turned to Tony. "Yes, I saw Salu." She pointed towards the front. "I was in the garden, tending the flowers." Her eyes seemed detached and unfocused as her memory led her down one of life's most unpleasant trails. "I heard a clamor, you know? I turned around. I looked up. I saw that man running off. *Bastardo*."

Tony agreed. "What time was this?"

She seemed to consider. "I don't know. I'm sorry, I don't know anything. It was early. The sun was not yet so strong."

"What did you do next?"

"Nothing," she said, remorsefully.

"Nothing?"

"Silvia was a grown woman. She could handle herself." Mrs. Parra began to sob. Her hands hid her face. "At least, I thought so." She wiped her nose with the back of her hand. "Later, I called her. I thought she might come to the market with me. She did not answer, yet I knew she must be home."

Tzininha interrupted. "That's enough, *mãe*."

Mrs. Parra's eyes were fixed on the backyard where a pair of *beija-flors*, hummingbirds known as flower kissers, flitted in and out of a small tree from which hung a small birdfeeder. "That is when I went upstairs."

Tony watched the shimmering birds fly off.

"Can't you see what you're doing to her?" implored Silvia's little sister.

"I'm only trying to help," Tony explained.

"How can all the pain you are causing help?"

"My Silvia was dead." The sobs wouldn't stop now.

Tony rose to leave. Tzininha followed him to the door. "I really am trying to help," he said.

"There is nothing anyone can do. Salu has murdered Silvia and the music goes on."

"I don't understand," riposted Tony. "According to the police, Salu was seen not only by your mother but by your neighbors. Surely he'll be arrested and tried for murder?"

Tzininha scoffed. "American," she said with disgust. "You think there is justice in everything? In everyone's lives?"

"But, if he's guilty—"

"They say there is not enough evidence. That they are looking into the matter. This is Brazil. There is much corruption and men like Fidel Salu are at the heart of it. He will never see justice."

"But what did Salu say? How did he explain himself to the police?"

Tzininha laughed an unhappy laugh. "The Colonel said he came to talk to Silvia, to beg her to take him back. Probably to offer her more money, who knows?"

"And he killed her?"

"Salu says he only discovered the body. That she was dead when he arrived." The look in Tzininha's eyes was all hatred. "And he ran."

Tony's hand clutched the door handle. "I can't explain it," he began, "but I am going to help. You'll see."

"Can you bring my sister back to life?"

"No," Tony admitted slowly. If only he could. . .

"Then there is nothing you can do to help," snapped Tzininha.

Mrs. Parra spoke from her chair. "Enough, children. I won't have you fighting each other."

Tony and Tzininha looked guiltily at one another.

Mrs. Parra spoke unsteadily. "You must understand, Tony. Fidel Salu is a powerful man, from an influential family." She folded her once strong hands in her lap. "We are no one."

19

"I feel ridiculous," grumbled Rock, walking unsteadily out from the elegant Copacabana Palace hotel to the van on elevated sneakers and clutching a man's purse.

"How do you think I feel?" replied Tony, hitching up his pastel yellow trousers. The lilac shirt only added to his discomfort. "Where on earth did Yairi come up with these ridiculous outfits? Everyone is staring at us."

"I think the hookers in our building had a hand in it." Rock tried stuffing the leather purse in his front pocket. It was way too large. "I never even heard of a man's purse." His own outfit was a pair of balloonish white linen slacks, matching shirt, unbuttoned to the middle of his stomach at Yairi's insistence, and brown open toed sandals.

Tony rolled his eyes. It didn't look like a man's purse. In fact, he was pretty sure he'd seen one of the ladies around the building carrying it earlier. He kept his opinions and observations to himself.

Three long days had passed since he'd promised Silvia's mother and sister that he would help. In that time, Rock had taken care of the tickets, so he said. Though it had been Tony who'd finally tracked down Milito and then given Rock directions to the small travel agency the policeman's father ran in Ipanema.

Life in the new Copacabana apartment had been colorful to say the least. And to say it was uncomfortable was still being over generous. At least they hadn't gotten into any serious fights with the clientele. The girls themselves proved hard as nails and much more adept at dealing with the more belligerent gentleman callers than Rock or Tony could ever have managed.

And the one time they heard gunfire and reluctantly ducked under their fetid mattresses it only turned out to be champagne bottle being uncorked. Maria and the other girls were celebrating a thousand dollar tip from a swaggering Swiss diplomat. Tony and Rock had been invited to join in the celebration.

Now, a sharply dressed gentleman with a perfectly coiffed head of hair pulled open the side doors of the blue Dodge van and they stepped inside. It wouldn't do to be picked up outside the Club Sex Machine or a known hooker hostel, so they'd instructed the W. Mercer van to pick them up at the pricey Copacabana Palace where they pretended to be staying.

The plan that Alvarez Yairi had hatched was that Tony and Rock were a rich, American 'couple' on a shopping spree. The wild clothes and gay attitude were supposed to draw attention. At least that part was working. And it annoyed the hell out of Tony and Rock.

The driver said nothing. The radio didn't play. Rock and Tony fell into the silence. Fifteen minutes later they arrived at the tall, white headquarters of W. Mercer, Jewelers, in downtown Ipanema. The van rolled to a stop under the covered entrance and the driver hopped out efficiently and opened the side door.

An equally hirsute middle aged man greeted them in pleasant, yet formal, Portuguese, escorted them to the main doors and whisked them inside.

The lobby of W. Mercer was cool and quiet. "All right," murmured Tony, "from here on we stick to the act."

Rock nodded. "Yes, dear." Rock settled his arm over Tony's shoulder.

"Cut that out!"

Rock feigned a hurt, pouty look. "What's wrong, darling?"

"You're overdoing it, don't you think, Rock?" Tony said between tightly drawn lips.

"Oh, I don't know, honey. Yairi told us to play up this gay couple routine."

"Yeah, yeah." It had made sense at the time. Of course, a few drinks could make any plan sound good, like defending the Alamo. Sam Houston and Daniel Boone had probably shared a few bottles of whiskey before deciding to hold off the Mexican Army. Tony could just about hear it, Sam's arm over Dan's shoulder, "Come on, Dan, we can do it. I know we can. . ."

A young woman in a tan business dress approached. "*Boa tarde*."

"Hello," said Tony.

The young woman smiled and immediately shifted to English. "I am Carmen. May I help you?"

Before Tony could form a response, Rock said, "My lover and I are interested in taking the tour."

The girl smiled warmly. Then again, it could have been a smirk. "Of course, the museum. Come this way."

Tony made a note to kill Rock later.

They were led up the red rug to a spartan desk where another well-dressed young woman was seated. She asked them their names and wrote this on the back of a form. She tore off the top, stuck it in her bin and handed them the bottom. She pulled two visitors passes from a drawer and instructed them to wear them around their necks.

Carmen led them through yet another door to an elevator.

A guard stood opposite in front of a wide stairway that led up. "The tour starts on the next floor," Carmen informed them as she pressed the button.

"I can't wait," bubbled Rock. He tugged on one of his earrings. Yairi had wanted Tony to get an earring for himself, but Tony drew the line at piercing body parts.

Tony and Rock followed Carmen to a reception desk where two more young women stood. They wore matching blue blazers and slacks. W. Mercer seemed to have cornered the market on beautiful people as well as gemstones.

Carmen said some words to the girls, then turned to Tony and Rock. "Have a very nice time. If you have any questions, please do not hesitate to ask anyone."

"Thanks," said Tony. One of the girls tapped his shoulder and handed him a portable cassette player and headphones. The other girl offered Rock the same.

"What's this for?" Rock asked.

"For tour, sirs," the girl who tapped Tony's shoulder answered. She pointed down a long dimly lit corridor. "You begin here."

Tony stuck the headphones over his ears. Rock did the same. "*Obrigada*."

Large glass windows covered both sides of the hall. The boys stopped in front of Number One and listened.

By the time they'd reached Number Fifteen, Tony was yawning. He'd learned more about gems and mining than he cared to know, or would ever remember. They'd stood through several minutes of watching some guy in a white lab coat polishing a diamond.

"Let's skip ahead," suggested Tony.

"But the tape will get out of sync," complained Rock.

Tony looked at Rock's watch. The English narration on the tape was synchronized with the windows, but at this rate the tour was going to take better than an hour. "So what? We're not here to learn about the history of W. Mercer and gemology. We're here to catch the thieves who've been preying on Mercer's customers. And to catch a killer."

"Okay," Rock grudgingly agreed. They moved on to Number Thirty. Several minutes later they turned in their tape players and headsets.

"Now what?"

"According to Yairi, this is where we get the sales pitch."

"But I don't see anybody trying to sell us anything. You think they didn't take us seriously?"

"Who knows?" Though the thought was annoying. After all, who were these people to judge?

The girl at the counter had pointed to the right and to the right they went.

This corridor opened up into another that spun off in three directions. A woman, this one in a canary yellow jacket with a white blouse and matching yellow skirt that fell short of her knees, welcomed them. She caught Tony's eye "*Como vai o senhor*?"

"*Vou bem, obrigada*. Do you speak English?"

"Certainly, gentlemens," she responded quickly. "Would you come in, please." She extended her hand.

Tony and Rock followed the woman to a small, open cubicle. The room was a catacomb of the same. Sales personnel fawned over the dozens of well-healed customers who themselves fawned over a fortune in gems and jewels.

"I will bring to you an associate. Sit, please." She motioned to the two leather chairs in front of the narrow table and soundlessly departed. There was a glass case at the side where it attached to the cubicle wall. It held a small collection of rings and matching earrings.

The glass case wasn't locked, but Tony had a suspicion that any attempt to lift a jewel or two would not go unnoticed. For all of its pleasantry and the benign, elegant facade, there were probably dozens of watchful eyes upon them and the rest of the customers. And probably a well-oiled gun or two.

Tony watched a middle aged man and woman seated nearby as the woman fondled one expensive necklace after another. The man patted her knee and smiled benevolently.

Not for the first time, Tony wondered what it must be like to be rich. He felt for his wallet. It was still there. Yairi had given him a fake ID and a credit card good for a half million *reais*. That was over a quarter of a million dollars. It sounded like the fortune of a lifetime to Rock and Tony, but would it be enough to tempt Salu and his men?

They could only hope so.

What would happen if they spent a half million of the Brazilian government's money on jewels and it didn't lead to an arrest?

Tony squirmed in his chair. Just one more thing he didn't want to know. He and Rock were on the hotseat no matter how he looked at things.

And he didn't care. Perhaps he should, but he couldn't. Not so long as Silvia's cold-blooded killer was loose. Tony wanted the animal exposed and led to justice. He did worry about Rock though, the poor guy was in over his head and it was all Tony's fault. Rock trusted him. Tony was going to have to see to it that that trust was not misguided.

A small, bent woman in her sixties, with hair as gray as it was black, introduced herself. "I am Trina. Good afternoon, gentlemen." Tony and Rock gave their names.

Trina took up a seat in the matching black leather chair on the opposite side of the table. The old woman's eyes were sharp and black. The wrinkles that pinched at the sides were probably the result of a lifetime's squinting expertly over precious stones. "Would either of you care for a drink?"

"Well—"

"I'll have a *guaraná*," Rock said quickly. "Go ahead, darling, have something."

Tony blushed and looked at the floor. "I'll have the same."

He kicked Rock under the table.

Rock's only response was to lace his fingers through Tony's atop the desk.

Tony looked into Rock's eyes and smiled. He only hoped Rock could read his mind and know what he was thinking of doing to him later, something to do with sharp sticks and burning oil.

Trina called to the woman who'd led them to her station and ordered drinks which were brought moments later in tall glasses borne on a silver tray.

"To your health," Trina said, raising her glass.

"To love," added Rock, looking into Tony's eyes.

Tony choked, spilling soda down his shirt front. He swallowed the rest in one gulp and set his empty glass on the table.

Trina, all smiles, folded her small hands in front of her and asked, "There is something special you are looking for today?"

Yeah, a killer, Tony wanted to say. Instead, what came out was, "Nothing in particular. We just felt like shopping! After all, that's what vacations are for, aren't they?"

"Yes, indeed." Trina cast a thoughtful look their way. "You are from America?"

"Yes, Palm Beach." At least that was the address on the false ID they'd been provided. Tony couldn't afford to use a parking meter in Palm Beach.

"Ah, yes. Palm Beach. We have many visitors from Palm Beach. It is beautiful, no? Like Ipanema, perhaps?"

"Yes, we like it. Don't we, dear?" Rock squeezed Tony's hand.

Tony carefully extricated his fingers and surreptitiously shoved his chair sideways some inches from Rock.

"Where do you stay in Rio?"

"The Copacabana Palace," Tony answered.

"Yes, very nice." Trina's eyes looked thoughtful and Tony

figured the price of the goods just went up.

The sales associate rose. "I tell you what. I will go bring some selections of many things and we will see if we can find some pieces that you like, no?"

"Sounds great," Rock said.

"Yeah, great." After she disappeared, Tony turned to Rock. "Will you cut it out, already?"

"Cut what out?"

"All this touching stuff and dear garbage."

"Hey, we're supposed to be a couple. I'm only trying to play the part. Who knows? There could be somebody watching us right now."

Tony swallowed his tongue. Rock could be right, of course. Yairi said there had to be an inside man, or woman, and he was inclined to agree. "All right. But let's not overdo it, okay?"

Rock grinned. "Yes, darling." He squeezed Tony's knee.

Tony punched him in the shoulder.

"What's this?" Trina had reappeared. She carried a small tray.

"Oh, ah, nothing." Tony patted Rock affectionately on the arm.

Rock pulled Tony's chair closer and said, "Just a lover's spat. Pay us no mind."

Trina beamed. "Love must be fiery to be worthy. My husband and I are the same way ourselves. And married over forty years. My daughter is studying for the foreign service. Though my son—"

"What's that you've brought?" demanded Tony, eager to do anything to change the subject.

She laid the white tray on the table and sat. "I have brought several rings. Some fine chains and some bracelets." Trina glanced at Rock. "Even some earrings as I see you are fond of them."

Rock tugged his ears. "Guilty," he said.

Tony asked, "How much are those?" He was pointing to a pair of opal studs.

Trina pulled out a pocket calculator. "Twelve thousand U.S. dollars."

"Nice." Rock picked them up and fondled them. "Do you have anything more expensive?"

Trina grinned. "How much did you have in mind to spend?"

"Well—"

"Money is no object," Tony boasted.

"Yes," agreed Rock, "not when love is involved."

Trina excused herself and returned with yet another tray. This one held diamonds, many cuts and sizes.

Rock grabbed a pair of diamond earrings.

"You have excellent taste. These are fifty thousand dollars."

"He'll take it," Tony said quickly. It was about time to finish up this little shopping trip and move on to the hoped for stick up.

"Thank you, love," cooed Rock.

"You're welcome, darling." Tony figured two could play at this game.

When the dust had settled, diamond in this case, they'd bought up the store, or at least their own little corner of it. There were earrings, matching 'his and his' bracelets, jeweled necklaces and ridiculously expensive matching rings for their fingers.

"We'll call them our commitment rings," cooed Rock, admiring the one on his own outstretched hand.

As far as Tony was concerned, Rock was ready to be committed.

Every selection was carefully boxed and wrapped and each piece further came with a four-color computer generated pedigree. "And you pay no customs returning to the States."

"Really?" Tony was skeptical. But no matter, he wasn't

going anywhere with the stuff.

"That's right. We have an agreement with your country. You must only fill out these forms."

Tony signed the documents quickly.

Rock was the last to rise. Tony carried the bags.

Trina held out her hand. "Thank you very much."

"Thank you," replied Rock. "You've such lovely, lovely things."

"Please, you will follow me." Trina led the boys out of the cubicles to another area of the W. Mercer complex on the same floor. This looked like a more traditional jewelry store with spotless glass cases laid out for casual viewing.

"More?" Tony said.

"You must allow my colleague to show you some of our special pieces."

The guys balked.

"Please, it is necessary. It is my job to bring you here," explained Trina. "I could be dismissed. You only have to look, *não*?"

"Come on, dear. Just a little lookie?" Rock pulled Tony's hand.

"Certainly, darling."

They were introduced to yet another of the infinitely pretty and, apparently ubiquitous, W. Mercer girls. She asked them if they were searching for anything in particular.

Aware of the time, Tony was anxious to move on. The shopping trip combined with the museum tour had taken twice the time they had calculated on with Yairi. The plan was unraveling fast.

"How much are those?" asked Tony. He pointed to a pair of topaz encrusted necklaces. They had nearly fifty-thousand dollars left on their credit card in spite of their best efforts to spend wantonly.

The sales assistant stepped behind the counter and slid open the case. "Yes," she laid both atop the counter, "they are lovely, are they not?"

Tony held one up to the light. Very lovely.

"Twenty-two thousand."

"A piece?"

"Yes, sir."

Rock whistled.

"We'll take both."

The clerk smiled and filled out the paperwork. Tony added the necklaces to his bags. "Can you tell me where the restroom is?"

"Of course. Follow me."

Around the corner was a bathroom. "You coming, Rock?"

"No, I'll wait here." Rock smiled at the clerk, no doubt hoping to squeeze a phone number out of the unsuspecting girl. "Want me to hold those bags?"

"No, I've got them. I'll be right back." Tony went into the men's room and entered a stall where he carefully pulled out the two topaz necklaces, stuffed them in his underwear, re-wrapped the boxes and put them back in the shopping bag.

Finished, he rejoined his partner. "All set."

They were escorted to the elevator and back down to the ground floor where they turned in their visitors badges.

"Thank you for coming," the girl at the desk commented. It was the same girl who'd greeted them. A row of vans and cars stood in the covered drive. Drivers, otherwise unoccupied, stood in small clusters idly passing the time.

One driver, a small man with a hitch in his step and half a cigarette in his left hand, hurried over and offered to carry their bags.

"*Obrigado.*" Tony casually handed over the small fortune in jewels. They were led to a blue van. For all he knew it was the same that had taken them to W. Mercer. The vehicles very nearly all looked the same. Tony counted five blue vans and six blue sedans.

The driver hopped behind the wheel. He was grinning.

"*Copacabana Palace, não?*"

"*Sim,*" Tony said, settling back on the benchseat. He and Rock were not the only passengers. Two other couples, middle aged and speaking German were already in the back seats.

Tony's hand went to the strap of one of the bags which were on the seat between himself and Rock. He knew better than to hope that things went well. They never did. Instead, he only hoped they wouldn't go too badly.

The driver forced the van out into the heavy early evening traffic.

"Here we go," murmured Tony. The van lurched forward, like the first tentative advance of a rollercoaster car.

Rock nodded.

Tony stole a look behind. There was no sign of Yairi or the Bugre. And they were already more than an hour and a half later than they'd expected to be getting out of the building.

Something told him there was going to be trouble.

20

Tony didn't know too much about Rio de Janeiro, but he knew this wasn't the way to the Copacabana Palace. Instead of heading towards the beach, the driver had turned further inland. Before long they were skirting the edges of Ipanema towards Copacabana. "Keep your eyes opened," he whispered.

Rock grunted and stretched. The big guy had been dozing off. So much for reinforcements. And there was still no sign of Yairi. If he didn't show up soon. . .

The German tourists were lost in their own conversations, happily oblivious to any signs of danger.

The van twisted up a small road in some disrepair. A worker in dirty overalls had been standing at the corner, waving a white handkerchief. The street was unnaturally devoid of traffic and pedestrians. Most of the storefronts themselves had been boarded up. There wasn't a soul in sight. Even the birds seemed to be shying away from the little throughway.

A blue two door Renault came towards them from the curb. Its dull grey twin came up behind. The van was forced to stop.

Tony glanced at the Germans and smiled reassuringly.

They'd stopped talking and were looking at one another with universally recognizable, quizzical faces.

Men with dark masks over their faces jumped out of the cars, guns in hand. The driver of the van said something in Portuguese to his passengers and held up his hands.

There was no telling whether he was in on the hijacking or not.

"Remember, Rock," Tony said, forcing himself to maintain some semblance of calm, "we don't resist. Smile and give them the jewels."

"You see those guns?" Rock commented. "No problem."

One of the gunmen yanked open the side door and gestured with his weapon. Tony and Rock stepped down followed by the Germans. The men looked understandably shocked and the women near tears.

"Where the hell is you-know-who?" muttered Rock.

Tony shrugged and looked over his shoulder. The van was boxed in. Their driver was standing next to his door with another of the masked gunmen beside him. Still, there was no way of telling if he was an accomplice. His hands were held lackadaisically in the air. Was it all an act for their benefit?

One of the German women had sunk to the ground. Tony wanted to reassure her, tell her to relax. The robbers had never killed anyone, only robbed them of their valuables. At least, so far.

The Germans handed over their packages and were then summarily stripped of their watches and jewels. The younger of the two men protested and a gun was thrust into his ribs. A smile appeared in the hole of his attacker's mask. "Bang-bang," he said ominously.

The German got the message and shut up quickly.

One of the men entered the van and removed the merchandise Tony and Rock had just purchased. He grabbed Rock's arm and looked at his watch, muttered a word that even Tony understood as contempt and let the big guy keep it.

Tony could see Rock fighting to keep from lashing out and laying into the little man with the big gun.

A tall fellow who'd stayed some feet from the fray barked a command and the hijackers retreated to their cars with their spoils.

The Germans stood in the road like deer in the headlights, frightened and disoriented.

The lead car was backing up and turning around. The car behind them had pulled forward. The man at the corner in overalls had disappeared. Part of the plan?

So far, the crooks seemed to have a better plan than the good guys.

"They're getting away," said Rock. "Where the hell is Yairi?"

Tony looked up and down the street. The two Renaults were heading up the hill. There was still no sign of Yairi or the little Bugre. For that matter, there was no sign of anyone else either.

Their own driver was leaning against the nearest storefront. He'd extracted a cigarette from his pocket and was smoking feverishly.

Tony ran around the front of the van. "Get in, Rock!"

"Huh? What about them?" Rock pointed to the German tourists.

"They'll be okay." He hated to leave them behind but couldn't be responsible for dragging them into further danger. "Besides, they've already been robbed. What have they got to lose? Tell them to call the police!"

The driver made a move in Tony's direction. "*Ai, sao fazendo?*"

Tony grabbed the wheel and checked the ignition. The key was still there. He slammed the door shut and pushed down the lock. The driver grabbed the handle and pulled. He was screaming.

Rock jumped in the back as Tony put the van in gear and floored the gas pedal. "Hey, wait for me!"

They bounced and lurched up the road. Tony cut the wheel sharply to the right and they slid around the corner, neatly missing a fire hydrant and continuing. The van was no match for the smaller and more maneuverable autos, but Tony didn't want to catch them, he only wanted to follow from a distance.

Rock had pulled himself up into the passenger seat. His hands gripped the dash. "Don't lose 'em."

"I won't," vowed Tony. If the thieves got away, it would be the end of everything.

Out of the corner of his eye, Tony saw a familiar sight. It was the little Bugre bouncing up into the air as it cleared a ridge in the road. "Yairi's back there!"

"It's about time." Rock turned his head. "He's got somebody with him."

"Good." Tony weaved in and out of traffic. The Bugre was catching up.

"He's waving." Rock waved back. "I think he wants you to stop."

"Stop?" Tony twisted around and back again. "Is he crazy?"

"You already know the answer to that."

The Bugre had pulled alongside the moving van. Yairi was honking and pointing to the curb.

"Better do like he wants," Rock said. "It's his show."

"Sure." Tony slowed to a stop. The two Renaults dwindled and disappeared. Now what?

Yairi had parked behind them. Tony and Rock climbed out of their borrowed van and approached.

"Hey, that's the van driver," Rock noted.

"Yeah." Tony studied the little driver. He was sitting morosely in the passenger's seat, his left hand clutching his right. On closer inspection, his middle finger was twisted unnaturally back. It was swollen like a steamed Polish sausage and just as red.

"What's he doing here?" Rock asked.

"And what's the idea of stopping us?" Tony was visibly upset. "We could have nailed those guys and now they've gotten away. With a quarter million dollars and more worth of jewels to boot."

"No problem," Yairi said. He pulled out a pair of handcuffs and cuffed the van driver to the steering wheel.

The man flinched in understandable pain.

Yairi climbed out of the Bugre. "Our friend here will help us to his cohorts."

"He will?"

"Yes." Yairi was grinning mischievously. "He is most cooperative. Well, not at first, but—"

"After you broke his finger?" Tony suggested.

"A small accident." The way Yairi said it made Tony sure there had been no accident.

Tony put his hands on his hips. Traffic flew by, paying the small group no heed. "Where are the rest of your men?"

"Ah, well," Yairi scratched his ear. "Actually, a small lie on my part, I am afraid. There are no other men."

"No other men?" Rock echoed slowly.

"No, Rock. You see, Colonel Salu has many spies, infiltrators. How else has he been able to be so successful and brazen, *não*?"

"But you said you would have a whole team with you," reminded Tony.

"Yes, you and Rock are my team, eh? Besides, I have worked hard for this case. It's mine. I've placed my life at risk."

"Your life? How about ours?" Tony complained.

Yairi ignored this. "I do not want some local official coming in and claiming my victory."

"Oh, great. Just great." Rock shook his head. "Maybe we

should wait. . ."

"I have told you, Fidel Salu has members of the police on his payroll. Who could I trust? That's why I have you men. Our friendly driver will lead us to Salu's hideout. There we will catch him with the stolen jewels. Today. Tonight. Tomorrow," Yairi whistled and rubbed his hands, "will be too late. The jewels will have been moved. Far from Rio. Perhaps far from Brazil."

Tony asked, "So what kept you, anyway? None of this would have happened if you'd have shown up on time."

"I had a bit of trouble. Someone was tailing me. It was quite an effort to lose them, I must tell you."

"Any idea who?"

"No. The authorities, Little Armando's men or underlings of Colonel Salu. I've no idea."

"But you did lose them?"

"Yes, I am certain."

Tony nodded. "Good."

"And now, gentlemen, time is precious. I suggest we take the van and get moving." He reached into his vehicle and, after a quick exchange of words—mostly pained grunts and nods on the part of the van driver—unlocked the cuffs and guided the wounded man to the van where he was secured to the post of the center seat.

Tony drove. Rock road shotgun. Yairi sat next to his prisoner and extracted directions as they went.

Nearly forty minutes later the sun was down. The little van driver muttered a few words to Yairi and Yairi instructed Tony to stop. "Our friend says we are near." He pointed up a narrow road, barely wide enough for one vehicle. It was heavily wooded on each side. "According to our friend here, Salu has a small villa there. Probably one he keeps only for such business. I am unaware of any property listed in his name in this area. And I have done a thorough search."

Tony nodded. He was sure Yairi had. Traffic was light. Tony pulled the van off the road and onto the sandy embankment.

"Turn off the headlights," ordered Yairi.

Tony cut the lights and the engine.

Yairi prodded his prisoner in the chest. Whatever he was saying sounded and looked threatening. He turned to Rock and Tony. "If the bastard isn't lying, the house is a couple hundred meters up. The only home in the area. No trouble finding it." He turned his hard eyes back to the driver whose finger had swollen beyond all normal proportions. "And if this *bastardo* is lying, I'll cut his tongue out."

"What are we going to do with him? Leave him here?" Rock asked.

"We must, Rock. He can't come with us. He might give us away. And if he has misled us, we will need to come back and question him," Yairi's eyes narrowed, "more exquisitely, *não*?" Yairi tied a handkerchief around the van driver's mouth. "In case he decides to get noisy."

Rock gulped.

"Come on," urged Tony. He quietly opened the driver's side door and climbed out. He took the keys with him. "Let's get this over with."

Under cover of darkness, the three men marched up the steep road. There was no traffic. They didn't even see any lights. It was like a road through the wilderness.

They stuck to the sides of the tiny lane. Branches tore at Tony's clothing. He glanced over his shoulder from time to time. No one was following.

A noise to the left froze them. Yairi held a finger to his lips. "Quiet," he mouthed. The thrashing started then stopped again just as suddenly.

A small, dark animal burst from the bushes and darted across to the other side.

Rock let out a startled cry and Yairi's face showed his

alarm. He urged Rock to control himself.

"Sorry," apologized Rock.

They resumed their climb.

Shortly, the road intersected with a narrow, channeled dirt track.

"Stay here." Yairi loped quietly ahead, his back bent towards the ground. He returned just as noiselessly and short of breath. "There's a small villa around the bend, one hundred meters."

"Salu's?" Tony asked.

"Who else?"

Still, it wouldn't do to go bursting in on innocent people. There was a plain bulge beneath Yairi's coat and Tony had no doubt that the special agent was armed and dangerous. Very dangerous.

"Let's take it slowly," Tony suggested.

"Of course. There is no sign of a sentry, but I expect no less." Yairi led them forward. "Stay low and keep your eyes open. If you see anyone, signal me by stopping. I'll understand. And," he said, ominously, "leave them to me."

Rock and Tony nodded silently. Picking off criminal lookouts hadn't been in their deal and neither intended it to be now. Rock was looking less and less sure of their plans and their situation with every step. But like Tony, he had to know that there was nothing left to do but go forward.

Tony stole a last look over his shoulder before rounding the curve in the dirt road, sweeping them out of sight of the larger lane. They were alone but for the enemy ahead.

Suddenly, Tony stopped in his tracks. A two-story home, longer than it was tall, sat in the clearing. There was a wide veranda along the front that looked like it might have continued around the back. Trees sprinkled the yard, but crowded the edges. The villa itself was a colorless gray in the darkness. There were stone chimneys on each end. One was smoking. Tony guessed it was on the east side of the house, though his sense of direction had probably been hopelessly compromised in their quixotic travels.

Two lit windows were visible upstairs and one big one was illuminated downstairs. Curtains hid the view within.

Tony was certain he had seen a shape moving beside a tree nearest the house.

Yairi dropped to his knees and crawled over. "You see something, my friend?"

"There," murmured Tony. He dared not raise his voice or his arm. "The tree nearest the front porch. I thought I saw a man." At least he assumed it would be a man. Who could tell in the darkness?

"Thought I saw something, too," Rock said softly. He stood stiff as one of the trees. In the distance, he'd probably pass for one.

"Both of you," Yairi whispered, "slowly, slowly get down."

Tony bent his knees and did a slow motion descent. Rock followed.

Yairi crept to the right of Tony and headed forward in a large arc. Soon he was lost from view.

An eternity passed in which Tony reflected on his life and every decision that had led him to be standing in a desolate forest in the environs of Rio de Janeiro, waiting to possibly fight for his life while exposing a jewel thief and a killer and avenging the death of the woman he loved.

Nothing. Nothing he could remember. Nothing he could trace a line or pattern to led to this.

Still, here he was. . .

Tony gave a start. Yairi was back and he hadn't even seen him. The special agent tugged at his sleeve. "*Tudo bem.*"

"Did you find someone?" Rock asked.

Yairi nodded. "Our friend is sleeping." Yairi stuffed a short, thin rope in his pocket.

Handcuffs, ropes, the guy was a regular secret agent

supply shop. "What did you do, strangle him?"

"No, Tony. I only coaxed him to sleep. We may not have much time. I suggest we create a diversion and catch them by surprise."

"Got anything in mind?" Rock wondered.

"Yes."

"Mind sharing?" Tony said.

Yairi pointed a nicotine stained finger. "You see? There are the cars, to the left, near the house."

"Yeah, we see them, so what?"

Yairi pulled a disposable cigarette lighter from his trousers. "Know how to use this, Rock?"

"Of course."

"What are you trying to get at, Yairi?"

"Boom," the agent said smugly. "Rock will blow up the cars. At least one of them. Salu and his men will come running out and we will go running in. Perfect, *não*?"

Tony had long ago learned that nothing was perfect. Most things never even came close. "Close enough."

"*Bom*. Rock, you go first. Get in position. Tony and I will then proceed. I will signal you like this." Yairi raised his arm and lowered it. "You drop the lighter into the gas tank. Okay?"

Rock fiddled with the lighter, a mere speck in his big hands. He gave a thumbs up and, head low, ran towards the hulking vehicles. Once he was in position, Yairi and Tony worked their way silently forward, threading their way between the trees cautiously until they were at the edge of the porch.

There had been four men in the Renaults. And, according to Yairi, Colonel Salu wouldn't have been one of them. Too smart to dirty his hands, according to Yairi. Tony figured that was correct. One man was down, maybe permanently. That meant there were four men inside, possibly more.

Searching his pockets, Tony realized his only weapon was

a light gauge guitar pick. Yairi had drawn his pistol. It only now dawned on Tony that Yairi was insane. They were woefully outnumbered and probably outgunned. The best Tony could do was scratch someone. And even then, only lightly. If only he'd packed his heavy gauge guitar picks. . .

And then it struck him. He was just as crazy as Yairi who was even now raising his free hand and lowering it to his side before Tony could form or voice a reason to stop.

21

It all happened in slow motion.

Rock twisting open the gas cap on the blue Renault nearest the villa. Rock flicking the lighter to life. Rock slipping the lighter into the hole and realizing too late he'd have no time to run for cover.

The explosion rocked Tony off his feet. The house shook. Pieces of metal, large and small hurtled through the air and Tony fell face down, covering his head reflexively with his hands.

Feet stamped across the porch as loud as a herd of mustangs crossing a bridge. They were shouting in Portuguese. Tony pushed himself up. Yairi was already on the move. The two men who'd come were unarmed. Yairi waved his pistol at them with deadly precision and they shut up quickly. He cuffed them beneath the same tree that their accomplice was now lying unconscious under.

The house was on fire, a victim of the spreading car blaze.

"Rock!" Tony hollered. There was no sign of the big guy. A shot rang out from the upstairs window and Yairi pushed Tony down. Bullets tore into the tree inches from his head. Yairi fired back and the shooting stopped. Either the shooter had retreated or been hit. There was no way of knowing without going up and that's just what Yairi was doing.

Tony tore after him. He had to.

Tony paused in the poorly lit hallway to catch his bearings. A stairway was dead ahead and Yairi was already halfway up. Leaving Yairi to deal with the shooter, Tony headed into the main room. It was a large, though poorly appointed living room. A fire was burning low in the hearth.

Tony heard shots upstairs, then silence. He didn't know which of the two was more frightening. A rustling sound coming from behind closed mahogany doors made him jump.

Tony approached slowly, his footsteps muffled on the Turkish rug covering the tiled floor. He put his hand on one of the knobs and twisted slowly. Two shots rang out, splintering the door. A long fragment lodged itself in Tony's cheek. He winced in pain, pulled it out and kicked the door in. "Salu!"

The Colonel stood behind his desk, gun drawn. "You!" The W. Mercer bags from the latest heist were spilled out on the desk. A leather briefcase lay open beside them, now half full with stolen jewels. He aimed the small revolver at Tony's face and pulled the trigger.

Tony jumped to the side. But the gun hadn't fired. It was empty.

Salu reached into his desk and pulled out a fresh box of cartridges and Tony lunged over the desk, bringing the colonel to the floor. They tumbled and fought. The old guy was tougher than Tony had figured. And he fought dirty, kicking, biting and scratching.

Tony couldn't hold on and Salu broke free and took several steps back. His eyes crisscrossed the room, probably looking for an adequate weapon. His pistol was on the ground near Tony.

"Give it up, Salu."

Fidel Salu laughed maniacally. "Give it up? Fool." He wiped his battered and dripping brow. "I gave up when I lost

Silvia."

"Right, that's why you hijacked another van load of W. Mercer customers."

Salu said plaintively. "It was the last time. I only wanted enough money to leave here. To leave Brazil. To-to escape my memories." He stepped closer, a look of pleading on his face. "Let me go and the jewels are yours," Salu said, gesturing towards the open briefcase. "Take them. You'll be a rich man."

"I can't do that," said Tony. He picked up Salu's revolver and held it loosely in his hand. In the open drawer, he spotted a box of cartridges.

"But I did not kill Silvia, I swear! I loved her. Loved her with all my heart. I could never do such a thing."

"Mrs. Parra saw you running away. Others spotted you in the neighborhood."

"Yes, yes. I ran away. I was disturbed. Heartbroken." He trembled. "Scared. I wanted Silvia for myself. I admit it. I admit I wanted you dead." He shook his head forlornly. "But not my Silvia. You must believe me." His outstretched arms were pleading.

"I do."

Colonel Salu looked baffled, then repeated his offer. "Then, let me go. With or without the jewels."

"I can't do that," Tony said. "It's too late."

"Then shoot me," implored Salu. "Shoot me, please!" His troubled eyes fell on a photo in a silver frame atop his desk. It was a picture of Silvia. "I cannot live without her."

A sound came from behind and Tony spun around. It was Yairi. Smoke had begun to fill the house and Yairi was coughing.

Yairi yelled. The sound of shattering glass came from Tony's back. Tony turned yet again. Salu had leapt through the window behind the desk.

Tony raced to the edge. Despite the darkness, Tony

discovered something new. The house was built on the edge of a vast precipice and Colonel Fidel Salu had chosen the easy way down. The easy way or the hard way, depending on how you looked at things. Tony was of mixed feelings. In some ways, it had certainly been the easy way out. Tony hadn't even heard Salu cry. The colonel had gone silently to his fate.

Was it the breeze breaking in through the broken window, or was Tony shivering for other reasons?

No matter, he turned his attention back to Yairi.

Yairi set his weapon on the desk. "So, we have the jewels and we have our killer." He turned the briefcase around and fingered the jewels. "Very nice, *não*?"

Tony had edged himself between Yairi and his gun. Salu's gun was still in his own hand and he slipped a couple of cartridges into the well-oiled chambers. "I know who killed Silvia."

"Yes, of course." Yairi held up a necklace. "Colonel Salu. And now he is dead. It's a shame really. I was hoping for a criminal trial. The publicity would be good for the justice system."

"You did it."

Yairi set down the necklace, his eyes scanned the desk. "Did what, Tony?" He smiled, hands open at his sides.

"Killed Silvia."

Yairi laughed. "Are you crazy? Did you get bumped on the head again, my friend? Fidel Salu murdered Silvia Parra."

Tony shook his head no. "I've known for some time. You see, do you remember when you showed us the jewels from one of the previous W. Mercer robberies?"

"Yes, of course." Yairi had stepped away and was pacing. "So?"

"You had something in that box that never belonged there."

Yairi was still grinning. "And what might that be?" he inquired, though his voice was losing its friendly edge.

"Silvia's engagement ring. I bought it for her," Tony declared stepping forward. "She'd only had it delivered the day she was murdered. And it was from her cousin's jewelry shop. I'd noticed it missing from her finger when I saw her body. I couldn't figure out where it had gone. Who would take it? Why?" He was toying with Salu's revolver.

"You strangled her, like you did that sentry outside, and you couldn't resist taking the ring. What were you going to do with it? Sell it, you bastard?"

"Now, now, Tony, relax. You're crazy. You're imagining things. Salu was crazy jealous and he killed your girlfriend."

"No, you did. And you wanted it to look like he'd done it. What I want to know," said Tony, waving the gun in Yairi's direction, "is why?"

Yairi coughed and laughed. He ran his fingers through his hair. "All right." He stuck his chin out defiantly. "If you want to know the truth, Tony, I did it, yes."

Tony took a threatening step in Yairi's direction.

"But I had to. There was no choice. Silvia and Salu had been lovers and you and she were lovers. I needed your help to catch Salu and I was afraid that you would let something slip to her of my designs once I told you of them and she would then tell Salu about our plans to trap him."

"Silvia would never have done that. She loved me and wanted nothing to do with Salu."

The cop shrugged, remorselessly. "Perhaps. Still, I could not take that chance." Yairi grinned evilly. "She may have yet felt a sense of loyalty to him. Besides, with her dead and you thinking Fidel Salu her murderer, I was certain that you would help me catch him and break up this ring of thieves."

Yairi's right hand fell to his side and he said smugly, "And you did."

"You inhuman bastard."

Lightning quick, Yairi's hand slipped under his trouser leg and pulled up a devilish looking knife. He swung it towards Tony's nose. "So," he said, "what are you going to do? Shoot me?" Whoosh! Yairi's swing came closer and Tony's neck snapped back. "I don't think so."

"No," admitted Tony. He stepped back as far as he could, up against the desk. End of the line. "But he might."

"A poor ploy, my friend."

"Drop it or I'll shoot your balls off!"

Yairi's shoulders tightened. His hard eyes bore into Tony's. He turned and threw.

Poor Officer Milito caught the knife in the left shoulder. For the second time, Tony was forced to perform a tackle and he'd never been one for football.

He leapt in the air and came down on Yairi who himself was going for Milito's gun. Tony's fist came down against the side of Yairi's face. Milito was struggling and kicking out and still Yairi was a more than worthy opponent. Tony was being elbowed in the ribs. Everyone was yelling. The black and white smoke was making it hard to see. Hard to breathe. . .

Tony was beginning to wonder if they'd all die like this, up in flames, locked in mortal combat, when the weight of the world fell on him.

Tony grunted and felt the air escape his lungs like a beachball being landed on by a hippo. Something seemed to be giving in, breaking. Probably his bones. He heard groaning and couldn't figure out if it was himself, Milito or Yairi. Maybe all three. Painfully, he twisted his neck, vainly trying to see over his shoulder.

Rock was lying atop him. The big guy's eyebrows had been burnt to crispy little doodles. The hair atop his head, sparse as it was, had been singed and he stank like a roasted cat. Rock's face was black. But then he'd probably like that, black being his favorite color. Scratches cut grooves of red in his arms and cheeks.

Rock was grinning.

Tony struggled to rise, but his arms collapsed like willow

sticks. "I don't remember calling dogpile," he moaned.

22

It was a small funeral, in a large, empty cemetery on the outskirts of Leme. The rains had returned to Rio. Even now, a light drizzle fell on the tiny group dressed in black.

Tony laid a wreath on the small stone and paid his last respects with a prayer to Silvia. He nodded to Mrs. Parra and Silvia's sister, Tzininha and they took his arms. It took all three of them to hold themselves upright. Around their necks, Silvia's mother and sister wore matching necklaces whose stones shone blue and green; green the color of Silvia's eyes. A gift from Tony and the government of Brazil, though they'd be unaware of their contribution.

Head down, Tony returned to the limousine. They drove in heavy silence, the four of them, Tony, Rock, Tzininha and Mrs. Parra. He said goodbye to Tzininha and Mrs. Parra at their door, then rejoined Rock in the back of the limo. Lennon and McCartney were keeping themselves dry under the front awning.

"Ready?" Rock leaned forward and patted Tony's arm. They both wore dark suits bought specially for the service.

Tony nodded. Rock's hair was just beginning to grow back from the explosion, while Tony's hair had been deliberately cut to the bone. He was finally rid of Luis

Angel's hair stylist's creative ministrations. His hair would grow back. Silvia was gone forever.

Yairi was in custody. Salu was dead. Officer Milito had come to the funeral, his shoulder in a sling. Good old, Milito. The way he'd come up on Yairi from behind, shouting some crazy phrase he said he'd picked up from some American cop show, that was something!

Tony had secretly filled Milito in on everything he knew, and arranged for him to tail he and Rock from the moment they left for W. Mercer. Tony hadn't even let Rock in on the secret for fear he might accidently let something slip to Yairi. And Yairi could never know.

And how close they had come to disaster! Milito had been following Yairi. Yairi had said he'd lost whoever was tailing him. At that point, Tony thought all hope was lost of succeeding. Every time he looked over his shoulder, he expected, hoped, to spot Milito, and hadn't.

But Milito was good. And determined. He'd followed them all the way to Salu's hideout and with his help the ring had been broken and Silvia's murderer caught. Milito had been promised a promotion. Tony was glad. Sometimes people got what they deserved.

Tony looked out the window. The limo moved slowly. The tinted windows gave the day an even darker look than it already bore. "So, where are we going? This isn't the way to the airport."

"No, it's a surprise. You'll see."

"I've had enough surprises," said Tony, his eyes yet swollen from the tears he'd left behind. "I just want to go home."

"This will be good. Trust me."

Tony opened his mouth then shut it just as quickly. He could have reminded Rock that his statement was almost word for word what he'd said before they left for Brazil.

The black stretch limousine belonging to the funeral home

rolled into a harbor and pulled up along the docks. The windshield wipers played slowly side to side; one step forward, one step back.

The story of Tony's life. "What are we doing here?"

"Okay, here's the thing," Rock said nervously. "I got us another job."

"Oh, Rock. I don't want another job. I want to go home."

Rock leaned forward. "And do what, Tony? Sit around and mope? That won't do you any good and it won't bring Silvia back."

"So what are we supposed to do? Work the loading docks? I don't think so, Rock."

"No," said Rock. "Nothing like that at all. This is a music gig. It's only a lounge act, but— "

"A lounge act?" Tony imagined playing Brazilian jazz standards for longshoremen or their *Carioca* counterparts at some salty dive. "I don't think so. I'd just as soon get out of Brazil."

"Hear me out, Tony. We would be getting out of Brazil."

"Sorry," said Tony firmly, "I don't know what you're going on about but I don't want to stay here and I don't want to go out on the road. At least, not now. Not yet."

"Will you just listen?" Rock gave his friend a look of exasperation and continued. "We won't be on the road exactly."

Tony started to respond and Rock held up his hand. "Look over there." Rock pointed towards the water.

"What am I looking for?"

"You see that big ship?"

"Kind of hard to miss." A large ocean liner stood tied to the docks. Passengers were boarding and the deck was half-filled with tourists waving goodbye.

"That's the King Leopold."

"So?"

"So that's it."

"That's what?" Tony's eyes narrowed warily.

"That's our job. On a cruise ship. They've got a small band and a lounge singer. We'll be doing our backup thing six nights a week."

Tony forced a laugh. "You mean you'll be doing your backup thing. I'll be on a plane to the States."

"Come on, Tony. It's not like being on the road. We'll be on a ship. Free room and board plus a small salary. Sleep in our own beds every night. What could be better than that?"

Tony could think of about a million things. "I don't like boats."

"Why not?"

Tony hesitated. Some things he didn't like to talk about. This was one of them. "My mother and father died on a boat."

"I'm sorry, man." Rock bit his lip. "What happened?"

Tony shrugged. "I was really too young to remember much. All I know is that it was a boating accident. It happened in the Intracoastal in the Pompano Beach area. My mom and dad were out on the boat. We owned a boat at that time. I was spending the weekend with a friend." Tony's eyes unfocused. He was seeing the past now. "I heard about it later. Some joker in one of those cigarette racing boats. Out joyriding. Smashed right into them. They didn't have a chance. The guy that did it was drunk. Spent all of two years in jail."

"I'm sorry, Tony. If I'd known—"

"That's okay. You didn't know." Tony held out his hand. "Just give me my plane ticket." Tony grinned. "And send me a postcard."

Rock fidgeted. "Well, you see, that's just it—"

Tony braced himself. He knew Rock well enough by now to know that something was up. "Spill it, Rock."

"I don't have your ticket."

"Why not? You told me you took care of them."

"I did. I did take care of them. I mean, sort of." Rock was studying his hands. "I went to Milito's father like you said. He was real helpful. Like you said, he's a travel agent."

"Okay, I'm listening. What happened to our tickets?"

"Well, Antonio, that's his name, he said there was nothing he could do about the tickets. Absolutely nothing. I mean, without us paying a huge penalty to the airline."

"So why didn't you just do it?"

"Well," Rock squirmed on the charcoal grey leather seat, "Antonio had this other idea. He knew the guy in charge of entertainment on this cruise ship and they were desperate. Three musicians had jumped ship here, the drummer, the bass player and a rhythm guitarist. They'd replaced the drummer but they were still two men short. Us."

Tony groaned. If he'd been younger, Rock could have been the prototype for Jack of *Jack And The Beanstalk* fame. Never send Rock to sell your cow. "What exactly happened to our tickets?"

"I told Antonio to sell them for us. He said he'd wire us the proceeds, though we won't get what we paid for them—or actually, what Luis Angel paid for them."

Tony listened to his heart beating in his empty chest. Rock was looking at him with those big, expectant puppy dog eyes of his. "I hate boats."

"I know."

"Where's it going anyway?"

"Tahiti."

Tony looked at the cruise ship. He found the car door handle and pulled it open. He stepped out into the rain and began walking. It was cold. The air pungent.

"Hey, wait for me!" cried Rock.

Droplets of rain swirled around him, circling and ensnaring his unprotected face. A stiff breeze was forcing itself in from the sea carrying a million unknown smells. The King Leopold rose before him, swaying ever so slightly in the light chop, like a chariot to Heaven.

Tony kept his eyes fixed on the green light, shining like a beacon, visible atop the tall stack of the bridge.